The Summer *with* Ludmila

The Summer with *Ludmila*

Pat Benson

Matador
9 Priory Business Park,
Wistow Road, Kibworth Beauchamp,
Leicestershire. LE8 0RX
Tel: (+44) 116 279 2299
Fax: (+44) 116 279 2277
Email: books@troubador.co.uk
Web: www.troubador.co.uk/matador

ISBN 978 1784622 978

British Library Cataloguing in Publication Data.
A catalogue record for this book is available from the British Library.

Printed and bound by CPI Group (UK) Ltd, Croydon, CR0 4YY
Typeset in 11pt Aldine by Troubador Publishing Ltd, Leicester, UK

Matador is an imprint of Troubador Publishing Ltd

To Elizabeth, a very special lady.

Prologue

It was early autumn in 2008. At around 3am on a Saturday morning in a crowded nightclub in the City a young man slowly came round, having passed out earlier in the morning. His vision was somewhat blurred as he looked around. He could make out lots of people dancing and others drinking and chatting at the bar but he did not recognise anyone.

"Ouch."

"Sorry, mate." A man tapped him on the back of the head apologetically: he had inadvertently walked into him while carrying a couple of pints of beer from the bar.

With a big sigh the young man slowly got up. He looked around again and tried to recall the events of that evening. It had been another lads' night out for him and his work colleagues. The usual dare was that those of them who were single would try and pull the most attractive young female that they could find, and they would not know in advance where they would end up on the Saturday morning afterwards. Amusingly, one colleague had even gone as far as Exeter on one occasion. But, unsurprisingly, nothing much had happened that evening. The young man could not remember if he had actually spoken to any young ladies or had been warned off them.

Suddenly he clutched his head as the beat of the music became louder and seemed to explode in his ears. He felt his stomach heave. As he was desperate for some fresh air after all the beers he had drunk that evening, he forced his way slowly through the crowd to the entrance. The bouncers gave him a sympathetic nod as he staggered out of the nightclub.

In the street the young man soon found an unoccupied bench. At least the weather was still fairly warm and it was not raining. As there was no sign of any of his colleagues he would now have to hang around on his own until the Underground and the trains started running later that morning for him to get back home to Hampshire. As he slouched on the bench the young man noticed a group of four smartly dressed, attractive young ladies getting into a taxi. He looked at them quite longingly, particularly with their short skirts and their high heels, although he was fully aware that even if he had managed to get off with any one of them it would almost certainly not have led to anything serious. As the taxi departed the young man stared at the empty sky and then shook his head. It was going to be another dull weekend for him, made worse by the inevitable hangover – which was threatening to be quite a bad one. There surely had to be more to his life than this.

Far away in the tiny village of Crocmaz near the Black Sea, a young lady watched from a little window in the second floor passageway as the postman came along the street. He picked his way through the ruts and the puddles and went into the entrance of the block of apartments opposite. She gripped the window ledge as he came out again. He turned on up the road. Her heart sank. But then her big green eyes widened as she saw him stop. He looked at the letters in his hand and turned back. Her heart thumped against her ribs. He was coming across the street.

"Oh, please… please," she begged silently. "Let it be today." She tiptoed past the door of her mother's apartment and raced down two flights of stairs to the dingy entrance hall to find the postman.

"Hello, Rustam. Shall I take those for you?" she asked very politely but persuasively.

The postman frowned.

"I can't do that, Miss. It would be against the rules. Where's the caretaker?"

"Well, at least tell me: is there a letter for me?" She put on her sweetest face and blinked at him a couple of times. He puffed out his cheeks, hesitated – but then, overcome by her smile, he nodded.

"Here. A foreign one, it is."

She grabbed that letter, flashed the postman a grateful smile and rushed away before the caretaker arrived. Stuffing the letter down the front of her blouse, she hurried back upstairs. Her mother was shouting for her as usual, but today it didn't matter.

That letter had finally come. She had been dreaming about it for such a long time. Her world was surely about to change forever and she was certain that the streets of England would be paved with gold. There would also be so many wonderful opportunities in that far-off land, unlike in the inevitable future that lay ahead of her if she stayed in her own little village. She shuddered at the thought of that. But of course she would not show any relief or excitement at the village dance that evening and the letter would stay a secret until early the following week, when she would have to break the life-changing news to her family and inevitably face their wrath.

Chapter One

It was a grey September lunchtime. Ben Smith rubbed his stomach, still sore after the previous Friday's drinking session. He sighed as he looked out of his office window at the usual City scene during his lunch break. He saw people rushing around and darting in and out of the sandwich shops and coffee bars in the streets below, as well as the endless stream of traffic. It was a sight that had become all too familiar over the past few years. Now, in an instant, Ben realised that he could not endure it any longer. It was time to escape this routine or else his whole life was going to drift by in an endless pattern of grey days, relieved only by drunken episodes that were becoming just as boring and empty as the daily grind itself.

Ben took a sip of his coffee and lifted his gaze to the thick clouds which were threatening rain imminently.

Oh, yes: it was more than time for him to shake up his life, he thought. He grimaced. How had he managed to let all those years slip by? School, university, a second degree, and then living at home in Winchester with his parents. It was just supposed to have been while he settled into his accountancy job in the City. He had been so busy at first, anxious to do well in his job and glad of the comforts of home so that he had even ignored the occasional teasing at work about not living on his own. When Helen, his older sister, had married and gone to live in the Far East, Ben's parents had been even more eager for him to stay at home. And so here he was, thirty years of age, and so far he had not really managed to sow any wild oats. Ben set down the cold coffee and stared again at the window. Then, in a flash, he

1

nodded to himself and almost managed a faint smile, as if he had finally made that crucial decision about his future. It felt as though a huge weight had suddenly been lifted from his shoulders, and Ben breathed a big sigh of relief.

"What's up? Overdone it again last Friday night?" asked Peter, his closest friend at work, who was standing nearby with his hands in his pockets and looking disgustingly fresh-faced and cheerful.

With an effort, Ben straightened up and nodded.

"Something like that, I suppose." Ben frowned. "Well… you disappeared rather early in the proceedings, didn't you, then?"

Peter smiled and then shrugged his shoulders, but didn't offer any explanation. He shot a glance at Ben.

"You look as if there's something worse than a bad hangover troubling you."

Ben looked away. His gaze skimmed all the people at their desks, following their daily routine – as they had been doing since he had first started working there, and as they would be doing for the next who knew how many years. Slogging by day and drinking by night. Except that… one by one they all seemed to find the right girl at some point and then slip into a more settled life. Ben looked at Peter again. Probably Peter had found the girl he wanted to be in a permanent relationship with. There had been a different air about him recently. Although superficially still jovial and joining in the social activities after work, Peter had become a lot more guarded about his private life and would frequently leave those social events much earlier than he used to.

"It does look serious." Peter came and perched on the corner of Ben's desk. "Have you lost last week's figures or something?"

"Nope. Just feeling rough." Ben gestured to the coffee. "That's all the lunch I want today. Perhaps I'll get to the gym this evening."

With a laugh, his friend wandered off. It was far too soon for

Ben to say anything about his life-changing decision. He had always worked everything out before going into action. Ben had learned long ago that this was the only way to get what he wanted. The youngest in the family, he had always been expected to accept the advice his parents and his older sister kept giving him. And where had that got him? This was going to be a huge change, so he would have to prepare it all very carefully. No doubt he would discuss things with Peter, once he had set his new scheme in motion. But first of all, Ben had a lot of thinking to do.

So where would he go? Definitely away from Winchester: that was the first essential point. Having grown up there, Ben needed a complete change of scene. And definitely no more commuting into the City. Why, on some days it could even be as much a three-hour journey if the trains were running late or were cancelled and there were delays on the Underground as well – and he felt that he could certainly put that wasted time commuting to much better use. Ben brightened. It would be absolutely splendid to live and work in the same place. But that meant finding a town of a reasonable size which was not too close to nor too far away from his parents, so probably about a couple of hours' drive away would be OK.

That evening, Ben decided to give his gym session a miss. Instead, he sat down in his room at home and looked at the map of England and confirmed the radius for the accountancy firms that he would apply to. The limit would be Bristol to the west and Brighton to the east. However, the main thing for Ben was that it should be anywhere except Winchester or London.

Next, Ben googled potential firms of accountants within that radius on his laptop and made a list of the firms that he would apply to. He had figured that with it being a recession it would be better to apply to those accountancy firms directly rather than going through recruitment agencies, as not every firm used recruitment agencies to advertise jobs nor wanted to pay their fees. Ben had already mentally prepared a standard, speculative job application beforehand which he would email to all the firms of accountants he would be applying to, along with an updated copy of his CV. Within about a week he had sent off around fifty speculative job applications.

Never having searched for a job since his time at university, Ben was not sure what to expect. As the days passed without any response to his speculative job applications his spirits started to sink. He felt even more stifled by the atmosphere in his office and now found it hard to concentrate on work. Surely he would fit the requirements of at least one of the accountancy firms he had applied to given the status of his current firm? He tapped his fist against his desk, thinking about what further details he could have added in his job application emails. He then saw chatty little Tasha, one of the trainees, looking his way.

Not now, he thought, jumping up. He strode out of the office, looking so grim that Tasha stepped aside, and didn't even say "Hello."

Ben had to get out now. The thought of staying in the same job for his whole career shocked him. Why had he waited so long before realising that? Might it have been reaching thirty earlier that year that had finally jolted him? His father had worked for most of his career in the same profession. But times were different nowadays. Yet it was going to be extremely difficult to convince his parents that he was doing the right thing in giving up a well-paid job in the City. They were inevitably going to lecture him about the benefits of a steady and prestigious job as well as a comfortable pension, particularly with the current recession biting.

"Time to live a bit and then settle down with the right girl." he muttered to himself. But where and how was still unknown. How long would it actually take Ben to find another job? His mother would raise every obstacle she could to stop him from leaving home. It was also convenient for his parents to have him there, especially when they wanted to go away on holiday. Ben suddenly remembered that, as they were both retired now, they were planning to visit Helen and her family. They would expect him to mind the house for them during their trip to Dubai.

Ben stopped abruptly. Not that he particularly wanted to spend his holiday visiting Helen and her two small children in Dubai, but... His gaze lifted to the window and he stared, unseeing, at the rooftops on the other side of the street. Why didn't he take a year out and go travelling? He considered it, debating which countries he wanted to see most: Italy, Peru, New Zealand...

"You know, you have the loveliest smile, Ben. And those big brown eyes of yours are shining. Who is she?"

Ben came back to earth with a start. Amanda from his firm's HR department was watching him, her head on one side. For a second, he was half tempted to confide in her about his plans. She was a friendly soul, full of good advice. If only she had been ten years younger and single...

"Just thinking," he told her. "And not about girls, for once."

Amanda laughed and then walked away down the corridor, her heels clicking briskly. Ben followed her slowly, deciding that he didn't really fancy an extended holiday travelling the world alone. He made his way back to his office and, with a sigh, forced himself to concentrate on the thick files that were on his desk.

As he pushed his way onto the crowded train at Waterloo station that evening, Ben's mind returned to the intended forthcoming shake-up. His mother, who had been a primary school teacher, was so much in the habit of organising everyone that she had no doubt planned just what he would have to do while she and his father were visiting Helen, Paul and the two grandchildren. He frowned. Hadn't she told him to get some gifts for his nephew and niece?

Oh, well, he shrugged. He would give his mother some cash and ask her to choose their presents for him.

It was standing room only on the train that evening, as usual. Ben eased himself through the packed bodies to get close to the window, so that he had some illusion of space.

How soon would he get some replies to his further job applications? He couldn't wait to end this daily commute. At last the train pulled in at Winchester, and Ben shuffled off the train amid the throng of other passengers. Then when the crowd thinned outside the station, he decided to walk the mile or so to his home.

Not for much longer, he promised himself. *Surely there would have to be a job offer from one of those accountancy firms fairly soon?* Ben really wanted to get right away from home now, as well. It had become so urgent to turn the page in his life. His weekends were no fun any more. What with the after-effects of lads' nights out with his work colleagues and the weekly commute, he would often spend half his weekend sleeping to recover before it all started again the following Monday. In addition, by working away from home he had lost contact with pretty well everyone he used to know locally. They all seemed to work in nine-to-five jobs either in or very close to Winchester, and their social circle no longer included him. If ever Ben saw any of the people he had known at school they seemed to be pushing prams and trailing toddlers these days.

He might glimpse them on Sundays if he walked through the local park. He would nod or wave to some of them but they were all involved in their own happy family lives, playing with their small children or picnicking. They could only spare him a wave. This was in total contrast to the City life Ben had grown used to over the past few years. The City lifestyle usually consisted of large numbers of people hanging around in pubs and clubs into the early hours of the morning. Probably these happy young couples in the parks in Winchester had been through the local equivalent of pubbing and clubbing at some earlier stage in their lives but it had been a much shorter phase, and they had settled down sooner to family lives of their own. Ben wished that he could have somehow joined in this local and less intense social scene.

Further, Ben had not had a serious relationship for some time. There had been a couple of drunken one-night stands while working in the City but he had recently come to accept – particularly in noticing the change in his work colleagues once they had found their long-term partners – that it was far more important to be in a serious relationship, and that was what he now sought. Of course, Ben was well aware that there were no rules where relationships were concerned. Some of his friends and work colleagues had met their partners either at university, or at work or on holiday. Some of them had even met their partners in their teens. However, not too many of them had met their partners once they were past thirty years of age. Ben hunched his shoulders. He realised he was rapidly approaching the deadline. If he told any young lady who he was interested in getting to know better that he was still living at home with his parents it was a certain conversation killer, which would immediately end any interest that that young lady might have had in him.

Chapter Two

After a further nail-biting week with no news, Ben received the first replies to his speculative job applications:

Post already filled… We have decided to re-advertise… Only suitable for a newly qualified accountant… and so on. After another week he realised that a good number of the accountancy firms that he had applied to were not even going to reply at all. He crossed all these negative responses off his list. Late one evening, after a long and crowded train journey home, he sat down in his room to select some more accountancy firms that he would apply to.

Reminding himself of how serious the current recession was, Ben hesitated for a few minutes. Was there even any point in sending out any further speculative job applications? But he only had to remind himself of the commute and the City lifestyle.

No time to lose, he told himself. *I need to have my own place close to my work before I can join in local events and see if I can find my own Miss Right.*

With this thought he set to work again, hoping for the best. But now Ben was willing to look at places closer to home. After all… he would be keeping in regular contact with his parents, anyway. All he needed was his own space where he could invite friends – and especially all the girls he was (hopefully) looking forward to meet, once he really had become independent.

But, again, another week went past with no positive replies from any of his applications. Ben's confidence began to ebb. He felt even more dissatisfied with his current situation.

"What's up?" enquired Peter one morning when they had a

few minutes free. "You've got a face like a wet week, and you didn't join the usual night out last Friday."

"Nothing's wrong," shrugged Ben. "I'm just not very fond of getting up in the dark – especially when it's so wet and miserable," he added, glancing at the rain streaming down the windows.

"You should have taken a proper holiday this year," said Peter, "Rather that the odd couple of days here and there. That won't help to recharge your batteries."

"Perhaps next year," replied Ben, thinking that a holiday would not be a proper holiday if he couldn't share it with someone special.

What an irony, he thought, careful to keep his expression neutral. Peter had been to Kenya and enjoyed a splendid safari, together with his mystery girlfriend whom nobody had yet seen at work.

One day, Ben promised himself, *I'll go on an adventure holiday with my girlfriend.*

It took an effort but Ben made himself act normally at work. He kept up his usual routine, making himself respond politely to all the office gossip. He felt certain he was being his normal self and that nobody, apart from Peter, might have noticed any difference in him. He joined in that week's night out – and if he did drink rather less than he usually did, nobody commented about it.

By the following week Ben could see that he needed to try again. Near or far, what did it matter? There had to be an accountancy firm that would take him somewhere out there. He just had to find them. So that was going to take up the coming weekend.

"Third time lucky", he muttered, each time he sent off yet more speculative job application emails.

Then, mid morning on the Wednesday of that week, Ben was sipping his coffee when his mobile phone rang. He could hardly keep his voice from trembling when the caller introduced himself as Roger Hudson, the senior partner of Triangle Accountants in Oxford.

"Hello, Mr Smith. Thank you for your application. We have a vacancy coming up in November and from your CV, you might be suitable for this post. Can you come for an interview this Friday? Twelve o'clock? Good. I look forward to meeting you."

At last, something was happening. Ben really struggled to stay in his seat and appear calm, as he was shaking with excitement on the inside. He was still so anxious to escape from his current situation.

Oxford? Yes, that would be a very good place to live and work, he thought. He couldn't remember much about what he did and said at work for the rest of that day, but he did manage somehow to take the Friday off work as a holiday. That evening Ben hurried home from the station and set about researching Triangle Accountants in more detail. They were a small and traditional accountancy firm near Summertown in Oxford but they did have some important clients locally. If Ben could get this job then there would surely be many opportunities for him there. And his parents should consider Oxford a reasonable alternative to the City. But if they made any fuss, he could always point out that it was just a fairly short drive away, unlike where Helen lived on the other side of the world in Dubai.

On the Friday morning Ben was up very early, but his parents were both in the kitchen when he came downstairs. He took a deep breath. Time to explain.

"I… er… I'm not going into work today." He looked at their surprised faces. "Actually, I'm going to Oxford. I have a job interview there." His mother was speechless but Ben saw from his father's face that he understood and approved. Ben smiled at him. Mr Smith nodded.

"You've realised, haven't you? Time goes by. Well, good luck for the interview."

"Geoffrey," Mrs Smith found her voice again, "How can you be so casual? We don't know the first thing about this potential new job for Ben. And why on earth would you want to give up an excellent position in the City, anyway?" She scowled at Ben, who was trying to force down a mouthful of toast.

"Leave him alone, Caroline," said Mr Smith. "It's more than time for Ben to try something new and for him to spread his wings."

Ben shot him a grateful look, gulped his tea and went back upstairs to put on his best suit.

Oxford was well supplied with small cafes. At this time of year they were full of students as well as tourists. Ben made his way back to the same quaint old cafe he'd sat in while waiting before his interview. Now he felt in need of a cup of strong tea. He wanted to think over his impressions of Triangle Accountants and the people he had been introduced to there. It was certainly a far cry from a City firm of accountants.

The interview at Triangle Accountants had lasted well over an hour. Ben was interviewed by Mr Hudson and the other two partners, Mr Jonathan Brydell and Mr Colin Sykes, before they all went to a restaurant for lunch. Even though Ben had hardly had any breakfast, he still found it hard to swallow much of the nice meal provided. Mr Hudson had not stopped looking at Ben throughout the interview.

"Why do you want to work in Oxford?" asked Mr Brydell, quite abruptly. "And what would you do to integrate yourself locally if we were to take you on?"

"You have a very impressive CV," Mr Sykes said and smiled and nodded at Ben.

"It would be a lower salary and more of a hands-on role here than in your current job," said Mr Hudson, very seriously.

Ben thought he had answered the interview questions satisfactorily. He hoped he had impressed them sufficiently well to have a reasonable chance of getting the job. Mr Hudson had smiled at Ben as he said goodbye, adding that there were a couple of other candidates to interview but that they hoped to get back to Ben within a week.

As Ben continued to mull the interview over at a table in the corner of the cafe, three young ladies were laughing and chatting excitedly as they examined their latest purchases. Closer to him, two older women seated in comfortable chairs seemed to be about to nod off. Ben glanced at the large shopping bags around their feet and smiled. It was completely different from those cafes near his office in the City. They would all have sold out of food by now, after the frenzy of serving lunchtime sandwiches and snacks.

Ben liked Oxford. As he walked back towards the car park, he went past so many old and famous buildings. It was a busy town but he would be delighted to live there. The offices of Triangle Accountants were situated in a reasonably quiet street about ten minutes' walk from the top of the main Banbury Road. That would be an advantage. Ben would not have to contend with the hordes of tourists who made it hard to get through the centre of town quickly.

Over the next few days Ben came to realise how much more he wanted to move to Oxford, and he really hoped and prayed that he would get this job. Oxford would be perfect. It had such a variety of activities, clubs, theatres, the thriving student life – and it was a busy commercial town. In addition, he could not think of any other place that he had seen which was more picturesque.

At home Mrs Smith was continuing to be a total pain about the whole matter. She wanted Ben to carry on as he was. She kept dropping none-too-subtle hints about the benefits of living at home. In the end Ben lost his temper, and they were actually shouting at each other when his father came home.

"That's quite enough," said Mr Smith. "Ben, apologise to your mother at once."

Ben clenched his fists. He was trembling. After a long silence, he looked at his mother and saw her holding back tears.

"Mum… I am so sorry I shouted at you, but you must accept that I've made up my mind to leave home. I really do need to be independent now."

Mr Smith jerked his head for Ben to leave the room. As he strode out, Ben heard his mother sob. He was surprised to find that he did not feel any sympathy.

I've always given in, he thought. *But they really don't need me here any more.* It was one thing to want to leave home, but quite another to find the right opportunity to do so. Ben went upstairs to his room and googled possible accommodation in Oxford and did some calculations. He decided he could manage financially and, if things became tight, he could sell his car. But that would really have to be a last resort.

But the following week was going past and there had not been any reply from Triangle Accountants following Ben's interview. He guessed that they might only interview one candidate per day, if they were so thorough about it. In any case, he was not getting much response from his other speculative job applications, so he would have to wait and hope for some good news.

It really was difficult to summon up much enthusiasm for his work while he waited. Everyone there seemed more remote to Ben now, even the people who had been there since he arrived several years previously. Sometimes Ben caught one of them eyeing him and knew he had withdrawn from them as well as from the job itself. He could not resist checking his mobile phone more and more frequently. By the Thursday afternoon he felt convinced that he had not got the job at Triangle Accountants. With a sigh, he resigned himself to looking for more potential accountancy jobs over the coming weekend.

When Peter and a couple of the others asked if he was joining them at their usual lads' gathering, Ben nodded.

"Of course." He forced a smile. "The highlight of the week."

Peter narrowed his eyes.

"Well, at least look as if you hope to enjoy it. You look like you have a mouth full of lemons."

Ben tried to laugh.

"Just got bogged down in this file." He flicked it shut. "One of the most complicated I've had in ages." The others exchanged glances but left it at that.

"See you outside at 8pm, then," said Ben, pulling out his mobile phone again once the others had left his office. There was still no news of any job or interview, not even a rejection. Ben groaned and bent over his work once more. He didn't notice the looks and nods his workmates were exchanging as they glanced at him.

When Ben staggered home in the early hours, his head thumping, his feet aching – and cursing himself because he would have to get up in a few hours to set off for work again, he saw a thick envelope on the desk in his room. He shrugged, pulled off his clothes and made for his bed. Ben was about to turn off the light when his tired mind suddenly warned him that he should check that letter. He stood up unsteadily and went over to pick it up. The postmark was from Oxford.

Chapter Three

Ludmila gazed out through the windows of Chişinău International Airport. It was a mild October day with a blue sky. She had endured a bumpy and uncomfortable bus journey from Crocmaz to the capital city that morning which, on top of her not having slept well for the past few nights, had left Ludmila feeling totally exhausted. She had very carefully packed her clothes and belongings during the previous week, although she did not in fact have that much to take with her. She was also very conscious of not having money to spend in England, at least initially, and of needing to economise in every possible way. All she had with her in the departure lounge was her tiny rucksack, which was packed with a brochure and a pen and paper with the contact details for her host family in England.

The airport was relatively small. However, Ludmila didn't really notice that as she had never been to an airport before in her life. She half smiled while looking at the planes, realising that it would be an experience, too – flying for the first time, that is. Most flights from Chişinău were to Bucharest, so a flight to London Heathrow seemed to be a big deal as well.

Ludmila then looked at the landscape beyond the airport and had a moment of panic. It had finally dawned on her: here she was, waiting for the plane that would take her away from her home to a new land. Her stomach suddenly felt as if it was full of wildly fluttering butterflies. Although she had left home to go to university (which had unfortunately ended prematurely after a year, due to her father's illness) she had never previously been out of direct contact with her immediate family. Yet, on the other hand, Ludmila had fought so hard for this once-in-a-lifetime opportunity to go and live and work abroad that she could not possibly give up now – not when her family had all finally accepted that she was now determined to leave the farm and earn her living in England. Although secretly aware of her plans beforehand, Ludmila's family had – as expected – raised numerous objections to her going abroad, and she had had to endure several weeks of repeated refusals and then protests from them. Politely but firmly, Ludmila had stood her ground.

"I shall become fluent in the language and I promise I'll save up all my money to bring back home. I will never forget what you have all done for me and what a wonderful family you are," she said, when her older brother Nicolae had also that declared she could not abandon her family now that father was too disabled to work. Nicolae had left his job in local government to run the family farm and provide for them all.

Since having had to leave university Ludmila had come to find life in a small village completely unbearable.

This was now my only chance of a proper escape and a way of avoiding the inevitable future which awaited me at home, she reasoned, *as well as being a means of using my brains and improving my quality of life.*

In fact, I only have to think about the mud and the slow pace of life back home, all focused on work in the fields and feeding the animals. There is nobody now to share my interests, and only little Valeria to talk to about anything, Ludmila kept reminding herself as she battled the ever-increasing number of butterflies in her stomach.

However, the thought of her little sister made her gulp back a sob. Twelve-year-old Valeria had cried continuously for days when she realised that Ludmila would be going to a faraway country. She also felt a slight sadness, remembering playing in the fields of Crocmaz as a child holding her special little doll, watching the older boys as a teenager with her friends and reminding herself about the closeness of her family.

Turning her back to the window and having composed herself, Ludmila then walked over to the electronic departure board. She watched impatiently for the flight to London Heathrow to be announced as ready for boarding. She forced herself to think of the endless opportunities that she still believed lay ahead in such a rich country. But it was hard to keep her mind on such matters. The emotional goodbyes crowded into her mind. Mother holding back tears. Father just nodding, because he was unwell and afraid to show his true feelings. Valeria sobbing and clinging to her and refusing to let go. Ludmila had cried as well and, while gently stroking her little sister's plaits and gently rubbing her cheeks, had promised to write to Valeria every week.

Nicolae had lectured Ludmila many times, even after the family had finally given in and reluctantly accepted her plans. Just that very weekend, he had reminded her very firmly to save as much money as possible in England, to be polite and respectful towards her host family, not to get into any trouble – and, most importantly of all – not to bring any shame on her family back in Moldova. Now she stared again at the departure board. There was still about half an hour to go, so she forced herself to look round for a seat.

There were now more people in the departure lounge. Most of them were couples and families but she eventually noticed another girl, sitting quietly in a corner and reading a brochure. Ludmila nodded to herself. She recognised that brochure: it was the very same one that she had in her rucksack and which she had already read so many times that she now knew it by heart. She walked slowly over to the corner where the dark-haired girl was sitting.

"Excuse me. Hello. I am Ludmila. I saw you reading the same brochure. Are you going to England as an au pair too?" she asked politely.

The girl looked up and smiled back.

"Hello. My name is Yuliana. Yes, I am going to England. I had wanted to stay in London, but my job is in a town called Bath. What about you? Where are you going to stay in England?"

Ludmila sat down.

"Bournemouth. I had wanted to stay in London as well but now I think I'll like Bournemouth. It's a town by the sea on the south coast of England," she explained, as Yuliana had shaken her head in puzzlement.

"What will happen when you get to England?" asked Yuliana.

"My host family is coming to meet me at the airport. They'll then drive me down to Bournemouth this evening. I am going to be looking after two small children. I will do some housework for my host family and I will also attend an English course at a local college."

"Same here, except that I will only have one child to look after. Are you looking forward to it? What are your long-term plans?"

"Of course," said Ludmila. "I would like to stay in England as long as possible and… "

She suddenly broke off. She had only just met Yuliana and it was best to be discreet, particularly in relation to personal matters. Ludmila smiled and Yuliana smiled back, as if they both instinctively knew what they wanted to talk about but that it was better to keep that to themselves.

"How did your family react to you telling them that you would be going to England to be an au pair?" asked Ludmila, keen to change the subject.

"Oh, they were actually perfectly OK about it," replied Yuliana. "We are a big family and we live locally." Ludmila took the hint, although this was in stark contrast to how her family had reacted. "I even have a big list of requests for souvenirs and presents for when I come back for the Christmas holidays," continued Yuliana. "I will need to find time to go shopping in London a couple of times before then." Ludmila nodded. She doubted very much whether she would be able to afford to do the same but if she did find any nice things that she could send back to her family from England then, of course, she would do so without any hesitation.

At that moment, an announcement came over the loudspeaker to say that the flight to Heathrow was now boarding. Ludmila looked a bit confused and nervous.

"It's perfectly OK," said Yuliana, patting Ludmila on the arm. "Just follow me and the queue of people as we get on the plane." She had understood from Ludmila's demeanour that she had not been on a plane before, but she would certainly never have teased Ludmila about it.

As they went through passport control Ludmila and Yuliana looked at each other, smiled and raised their eyebrows.

"Here we go… " whispered Yuliana. "It'll be an experience for both of us. I'm sure."

Ludmila suddenly gasped. A whole new world would be waiting for her when she got off the plane.

Chapter Four

Ben woke up to find that he was still holding the precious letter. He was surprised he'd actually managed to sleep at all after having read it umpteen times. Perhaps it was a sign of better things to come. He raced downstairs to find his father already up and making a pot of tea.

"Here, Dad."

Ben thrust the letter at his father, and with trembling hands poured himself a mug of tea. He waited impatiently while his father fished out his glasses and read the letter through.

"All very correct," said Mr Smith. "But starting on 10 November only gives you a couple of weeks to find somewhere to live." He went through the letter again. "Six months probationary period... participate in business and networking events whether in or out of working hours... salary... hmm... " He looked over his spectacles at Ben.

"It's quite a bit less than you're getting now." He smiled as Ben started shaking his head. "Well... money isn't everything, but I'm sure your mother won't like it."

"I really do need a fresh start," Ben explained. "I'm feeling throttled in the City now. It's not really a life, Dad."

"I've been thinking for some time that you need to get away, son. It'll be good for you. Anyway, well done on getting a new job." He handed the letter back and patted Ben's shoulder. "But now you'll need to get a move on. First, catch your train and then start getting things sorted for your new job."

The journey to work for once did not seem quite so painful even though, as usual, it was standing room only on the train.

Almost over, he thought gleefully. Once he reached the office Ben went straight to see the senior partner to inform him about his job offer in Oxford. The senior partner appeared quite surprised and disappointed. Ben explained his reasons for wanting to leave the City but pointed out how grateful he had been for the experience that he had acquired and all the benefits he had received with this firm.

When that rather disagreeable meeting was over, Ben telephoned Triangle Accountants and spoke to Mr Hudson to accept the job offer. Ben said he would sort out references and accommodation so that he would, hopefully, be living in Oxford by the time his new job started. He tried to speak calmly but inside him the excitement was still building: it was indeed a mixture of relief and elation at achieving the first part of his plan.

But now Ben had to break the news to his colleagues. They were all surprised, and some of them even seemed quite sorry at the idea he was going to leave. At midday Ben went to lunch with Peter.

"So that explains the change in you over the last few months," said Peter, although he didn't realise that the same could have been said about him since he had met his mystery girlfriend.

"I was beginning to fear that I was going to prove Dr Johnson's saying to be true," answered Ben.

"But what would you actually expect from Oxford that you can't get here in the City?" asked Peter, quite abruptly.

"Well, I am very much drawn to the idea of living and working in the same place now. Commuting is certainly no fun, particularly when it can several hours to get to and from work on bad days – and I also feel as though I've been in the City long enough. I now really want to feel part of a local community." He pushed his plate away. "I know that many people love the City but the fact that I'm not living in London does seem to say it all. This job has given me many opportunities and a big salary, but now is the right time for me to move on."

Peter gave him a shrewd look. He had lived and worked in the City for quite a few years and really couldn't conceive of wanting to be anywhere else.

"Has it got something to do with you still being single? I wonder if the girls in Oxford look as good as they do in the City."

"Well, I'll soon find out."

They both laughed, but Peter had pretty much hit the nail on the head. Ben smiled wryly, thinking that everyone in his firm would probably guess that that was the main reason why he was leaving his job. It really was proving to be an exhausting day, since, in addition to all the excitement, Ben's current workload was proving to be very complex. He was glad when he had finally reached the end of that day. But now he had to face his mother.

As expected, Mrs Smith was violently opposed to Ben giving up a well-paid and secure job.

"And why on earth would you want to live in some poky little flat in Oxford?" she demanded, when he'd patiently answered all her objections about leaving his current post. "You won't have enough money to live anywhere like this."

"Well, maybe not." Ben gritted his teeth. "But it's no use, Mum. I've already handed in my notice at work. This is going to be an adventure. And please don't forget that Oxford isn't exactly on the other side of the world, you know." Mrs Smith frowned and went off into the living room. She certainly didn't appreciate Ben trying to score points over his older sister, nor reminding her that Helen lived in Dubai – and, particularly, not in these circumstances.

With kind permission at work, Ben was able to leave his job early. On his last day he was slightly late in as he went specially to buy some boxes of quality chocolates for his colleagues. He then had a leaving lunch followed by drinks in the pub after work. At the end, despite being a little tipsy, Ben made a brief farewell speech.

"I would very much like to thank you all for coming along this evening. It has been a fantastic few years here and I am eternally grateful for all the opportunities and benefits that this job has given me. However, I feel that the time has now come for me to move on and to live and work in the same place. I will miss every one of you and I wish you all the very best for the future."

Everyone clapped and Ben smiled appreciatively. He then suddenly fell silent for a few moments, realising that despite his life-changing plans he would indeed be leaving a great deal behind in the City.

After saying his goodbyes Ben walked slowly towards the nearest Tube station to go home. He still saw people rushing around in the streets even this late at night but he simply smiled to himself, relieved that it was now all over for him.

Now I can focus on my new life in Oxford, he thought as the Underground train rattled along towards Waterloo.

That weekend Ben spent most of his time looking at estate agents online and comparing the various prices for renting flats in Oxford. He was somewhat deflated by the cost of renting. Then it also became clear that finding a garage or a parking spot would be very difficult. But there was no way that Ben would be going to live and work in Oxford without his car, though. That was essential, especially if he was to get to clubs and activities as well as going to the networking events his new boss had mentioned. It took Ben the whole weekend, but by the following Monday he had made a list of three or four possible flats to rent in a suburb near the offices of Triangle Accountants.

On the Tuesday Ben went to view those properties and decided on the flat in Marston. It was within his budget. It also had a parking space for his car and, perhaps most importantly, it was within walking distance of the offices of Triangle

Accountants. The estate agent assured him that there was a regular bus service as well.

"Or, if all else fails," he added with a grin, "You can get in by punt from a local pub." Ben laughed and nodded at this. He then signed the tenancy agreement and paid the deposit for that flat.

Ben now began to feel like a new person. He was also enjoying being able to lie in and not having to get up at 6.30am and then commute into the City. By the following weekend he had organised all the things he would need to take with him to Oxford. Mrs Smith sniffed and shook her head and muttered about whether he would be eating properly away from home. But Ben made a determined effort this time not to get into any further arguments with his mother and simply smiled and ignored her provocative remarks.

That weekend Ben took his Sunday walk through a local park. But this time he stopped and then half smiled to himself when he saw the happy young parents playing with their small children. He even dared to hope that this might even be him one day in the not-too-distant future. As he was walking back Ben bumped into a former classmate from the same secondary school called Tom. Tom was out enjoying the nice weather with his wife and their two children.

"Hello, Tom," said Ben cheerfully.

"Is that Ben?" Tom took a moment to recognise Ben again. "It's been ages."

"I'll wait for you to catch us up in a moment," snapped Tom's wife. It was clear that she had no interest in being introduced to Ben nor did she like having her weekends interrupted, even if only very briefly. Tom simply shrugged his shoulders.

"Ah, the joys of married life," said Tom, and smiled sarcastically. "How are you getting on, anyway?"

"I've just left my job in the City and I am going to start a new role in Oxford very soon, " said Ben. Tom pulled a face.

"Sounds like madness to me. Who would want to give up a well-paid job in London to go and work in Oxford? Also, what's wrong with working locally?"

"I need to get away from home and start a new life for myself."

"I see. Like that, is it?"

"Tom," shouted his wife. Tom looked at her and nodded.

"Well, good to see you again, Ben. And the best of luck with everything."

"Bye, Tom." Ben watched as Tom obediently walked off promptly and then caught up with where his wife and children had got to in the park. That simply confirmed what Ben had feared about anyone who knew him and who was of a similar age. They were likely to be married or in long-term relationships, and other than a brief chat they would have no interest in socialising with Ben any more.

Taking further advantage of his free time, Ben also went to spend a couple of days in Oxford in order to start familiarising himself properly with the town. In particular, he looked for restaurants, pubs, cinemas, theatres and gyms as well as checking on where the local sports teams were. He smiled as he walked through the town centre while he looked at the impressive array of shops, restaurants and monuments. Ben was sure that he would enjoy life in Oxford.

It then got to the weekend before Ben's new job started. He wasn't unduly worried or nervous about his new job, but was a little anxious that everything should go well there so that he could then set about trying to find his Miss Right. On the Saturday Ben's parents drove up to Oxford as well. Ben wasn't overly keen about this but did appreciate his parents bringing some of his stuff, which was all too much to fit into his car. As well as his clothes Ben took his TV, laptop, music centre, CD collection and some basic exercise equipment. The flat that Ben was renting was quite well-furnished.

Ben went out for dinner with his parents in Oxford that

evening. They noticed that he was a little quieter than usual, but that was probably due to Ben reflecting on his plans. After a cup of tea in Ben's flat his parents left.

"Good luck, son." Mr Smith smiled and nodded at Ben.

"Thanks, Dad. I'm sure everything will work out fine here." He then turned to his mother.

"I'll come and see you in a couple of weekends' time, Mum." Mrs Smith smiled ruefully. She was sad to see her son go and was still not as understanding about Ben leaving the City as Mr Smith was. After his parents had gone Ben was lonely that evening. He had not felt like that for a long while as he had become so used to having his parents around, even though he accepted that his father was quite right to say that it was time for him to leave home.

On the Sunday, after going shopping for food in the morning, Ben walked round Oxford while doing plenty of window-shopping. He then walked down by the river in the afternoon. It was all very calm and appealing.

Ben sat down on a bench. He watched couples, some with small children – and younger people, including students, walking past. As the weather was now getting colder Ben walked back to his flat. He still felt confident that his job and his personal life would both work out fine for him in Oxford.

However, while watching television in the evening, Ben actually started feeling quite apprehensive about the following morning – although he didn't really know why. Of course, any concerns he had would hopefully all be over after the first day in his new job.

Just before going to bed Ben stood, opened the bedroom window and looked at the glow in the sky that was Oxford by night: it was an impressive sight as well as his new home. He then became aware of how chilly the night air was. With a smile Ben closed the window and waited for his new life to start in earnest the following day.

Chapter Five

By lunchtime on his first day in his new job Ben was already feeling shattered. The morning had been a whirl of new faces and information from the moment he had arrived at Triangle Accountants and had gone in to see Mr Hudson.

"Call me Roger", his new boss told him. "We accountants are all on first-name terms here. Now let's get the introductions done."

So Ben had met Karen, his shared secretary, followed by the rest of the staff at Triangle Accountants. It would probably take him a couple of days to remember all their names and faces. It did feel odd to be working in a small firm with fewer than twenty people, compared to the hundreds of people in his last firm in the City. Ben wanted to be sure that as well as knowing everyone's names he also knew what their roles were.

On the whole they seemed a fairly friendly bunch at Triangle Accountants. Most of the staff were older than Ben and his former colleagues in the City. After the introductions Ben had a long session with Roger in order to go through the workload he would now be taking over (and assisting Roger and the other partners with). He was very glad when they reached the end of the list of files. After a rather sleepless night Ben was not feeling at his sharpest. At 11.30am Ben was finally able to ask Karen where he could get a cup of coffee.

"I'll show you." She smiled and got up. She led the way along the corridor to a little kitchen area. "The milk is fresh each day," she said, and pointed to the fridge. "And tea and coffee are in that cupboard."

Ben took his coffee back to his desk and started sorting through the files. As he already knew, most of the clients of Triangle Accountants were local. This job was going to be much more hands-on than in his previous role in that Ben would have much more direct client contact, rather than working in a team for multinational clients but hardly ever speaking to them directly. Roger had told Ben that he would be joining a business group that met at lunchtime once a fortnight in central Oxford on Tuesdays. There he would be expected to promote Triangle Accountants and to make business contacts, which would hopefully lead to the firm obtaining some new clients. That was fair enough, and it would also be a chance to get out of the office and meet more new people and hopefully to get involved in some local business and social activities too.

Ben spent an hour or so on the files, then decided it was time for a lunch break. So far he had only spoken to Karen, and nobody else seemed to be moving. Ben's head was aching and so he went out for a short walk. About five minutes down the road he saw a pub.

No huge crowd milling round here, he thought with a wry smile. It seemed quite welcoming, so he went in. He sank down on the padded bench with a large Coke. For a few minutes he just sat there, staring at the table. But then why did he suddenly feel a little glum? This was a totally different world... and wasn't that exactly what he had wanted? Perhaps Ben felt a little isolated but he promptly reminded himself that despite the working hours and the commuting he had been rather spoilt in his last job, particularly with the number of colleagues and support staff assisting him. Ben sighed and then smiled briefly. Of course he would settle into Triangle Accountants very soon, and he would also get to know all the members of staff and everything would be fine. There were a couple of youngish-looking people, so maybe he could make friends of them. And Roger had also mentioned that he followed a local amateur rugby team that played its home matches on a Saturday afternoon. He said that Ben was also expected, if possible, to attend all the home matches that season along with some of his colleagues – and there would sometimes be business opportunities both before and after the matches. Ben understood perfectly well what Roger had meant by that.

Overall, the first week went well. Ben got to know Karen. She was an attractive lady with dark ginger hair: she was a little older than him and was married with two small children. There was also a young colleague called Mark who was of a similar age to Ben. He had recently got married and his wife was expecting their first child early in the new year. Nearly all of the secretaries and support staff were married as well. However, there was a very attractive young secretary called Sarah. She had light blonde hair, big blue eyes and was very slim. Ben would certainly have been happy to have got to know Sarah better, but he quickly learned that she was in a long-term relationship. She talked a lot about her forthcoming trip to Thailand for Christmas with her boyfriend Gary.

Ben chuckled to himself. It was a pity in one way, but Sarah did talk an awful lot. At least she was young and lively. Of course, he had not expected to find his Miss Right the minute he arrived at Triangle Accountants. Nonetheless, he still hoped that with some social events – or simply by joining in activities now that he lived locally – he would have opportunities to get to know some young ladies fairly soon.

Overall his workload was not too demanding, and the pressures were a great deal less than in the City. However, things were more formal at Triangle Accountants than they had been at his last firm. Ben laughed, as although it was fine for him to address the partners by their first names the support staff all had to address the partners as Mister. Now that was a novelty. There were also no large gatherings of secretaries and, as a consequence, there was considerably less office gossip. But, then again, it was a much smaller firm. Ben also noticed that the staff at Triangle Accountants did not hang around after work or go to the pub in groups either.

Ben's working hours varied. Some days he would leave work just after 5pm, whereas on other days he would be working late if there was an urgent matter or something that needed preparing for the following day. On the whole, the atmosphere was fairly family friendly and the accountants weren't expected to work long hours unnecessarily.

During his first week Ben tried out a couple of other pubs for lunch, with the idea that he would manage on a snack in the evening. He was not overly keen on cooking for himself, either. However, Ben did discover a local Greek restaurant near his flat and he made a sort of friend out of the waiter, Dimitris, who was helping his parents to run the restaurant. He was also studying business management part time. In addition, Ben registered with a library, found a DVD hire shop and joined a local gym as well.

On the Saturday after his first week at Triangle Accountants, having been food shopping – and, after a session at the gym – Ben went along to the rugby club as Roger had requested. He found Mark there and another colleague called Tony, who was an associate. Tony was in his mid forties: he was married with three children and was highly regarded by Triangle Accountants. It seemed that Tony was being groomed to be a partner at Triangle Accounts in the near future, with Colin Sykes looking to retire. Ben noticed that there was a fairly large crowd at the rugby match – and also that there were quite a lot of females at the match, including some young ladies – although they all seemed to be in groups, either with family or friends.

After the rugby match Ben, Tony and Mark went to the rugby club bar, where they met Roger. Tony did not stay for very long, as he said that his wife and children were waiting for him to go out for dinner that evening. Roger introduced Ben to a couple of his friends who were involved in the running of the rugby club, and he reiterated that he expected Ben to come to all the home matches that season.

By the Sunday Ben was glad to relax and think over his new life. He rang his parents and told them about his new job. In particular he mentioned how the working hours were shorter on the whole, that most of the staff were married, that they didn't hang round after work and that things generally were more formal than in the City. Ben assured his parents again that he was confident that everything would work out fine for him. He also mentioned that everyone was reasonably friendly and willing to give advice, particularly in relation to places to go to locally.

The following Tuesday Ben found his way to the venue for his first business group meeting where he would be representing Triangle Accountants. It was at a hotel in the centre of Oxford. He was introduced to the business group members. Robert was the president of the business group for that year. He had his own firm of architects in the town centre. The treasurer was called Phillip and he worked for an IT company locally. Bob was the secretary and he was a retired police officer who now worked as a consultant for a security firm near Witney. After lunch Robert introduced Ben formally to the business group and then asked him to say a few words. Ben stood up feeling somewhat nervous, but having half expected this.

"Thank you, Mr President. Good afternoon to everyone. I am delighted to be joining the group. I look forward to getting to know you all well and to hopefully making a long-term positive contribution to the group. As you know I have just started working for Triangle Accounts, having previously worked in London. I have also moved to Oxford and am enjoying it very much. Thank you all again for making me a member of the group."

Everyone clapped. Robert smiled, and then added how

fortunate Roger was to have such a young and impressive employee like Ben.

After the other announcements and, just as the meeting was ending, Ben was approached by Simon. He was a tall, good-looking young man with dark hair who was slightly older than Ben. It turned out that Simon was a very successful and wealthy independent business consultant. He had a fiancée called Natalie who lived in Banbury. Ben and Simon hit it off immediately and arranged to meet up on Thursday evenings – every fortnight, if possible.

"Let's make it a drinks and chat session to start with," suggested Simon. "We may have the energy to do some sports occasionally. But I'll tell you right away that I'm not usually around at weekends, unless there's some urgent work on the go. Natalie usually organises our weekends and she is to be obeyed," said Simon with a grin. Ben nodded, remembering that he would have to start looking in earnest for his own Natalie in the near future.

As promised, Ben went back to Winchester to see his parents on the following Sunday. They were so pleased to see him that he felt a sort of pinch in his heart for abandoning them. But he knew deep down that he had done the right thing. He spent most of the day explaining his new job to them in more detail, as well as about how he was settling into his new life.

"All in all it's really been a good start," he assured them. "I do think everything is going to be fine. And I really like Oxford." Ben's father nodded but his mother remained unconvinced.

"One thing I do find amusing, though… " said Ben, with a broad smile.

"What's that?" asked Mr Smith.

"It's OK for me and for the other accountants to address the partners by their first names. But all the support staff have to say 'Mister' to all three of the partners."

"And what is so bad about that?" asked Mrs Smith abruptly.

"I thought those days were long gone," replied Ben. Mrs Smith shook her head. Mr Smith didn't say anything. Perhaps this was due to him having worked in business too.

Even during lunch Mrs Smith was inspecting Ben closely.

"I hope you are eating properly, although I doubt it somehow," she said.

"Course I am," answered Ben thickly through a mouthful of roast beef and mustard. "But I don't get meals as good as this, Mum." He nodded eagerly as she offered him a second helping.

It was late afternoon when Ben drove back to Oxford. It was a slightly odd – but nice feeling, nonetheless – that after having lived in Winchester for all those years, Oxford had now become his new home in just a couple of weeks.

Chapter Six

As the weeks passed and Christmas drew near Ben still felt very pleased with how things were going at work, and he was also really happy with his new home. He enjoyed the various aspects of life in Oxford. There were no difficulties handling his own workload or in helping out the partners with their files when they asked him to do so. Mr Brydell was still a bit grumpy towards Ben, but Ben didn't pay too much attention to that. However, all in all, the partners did seem to be happy with Ben and the way he handled his workload.

Ben gladly joined in when his business group organised a couple of carol concerts at local schools. He became quite a hero afterwards when – having discovered a lost pupil crying – he escorted that child home, having checked the directions on his mobile phone.

"How nice to see such a caring young man," said the child's mother. "Where do you work?"

"I work as an accountant locally."

"Well, I never," she exclaimed and shook her head. "I can't possibly thank you enough," she continued, almost out of breath and with her hand on her heart.

Ben also found it rather amusing when he was asked to be an elf accompanying Father Christmas (who was seeing small children at a local garden centre for an afternoon). It reminded him of being taken to see Father Christmas himself as a very small child. However, Ben was more impressed by all the attractive young yummy mummies – particularly those who seemed to be dressed more for summer, despite the very cold weather. He found it harder to concentrate more on taking pictures of their children with Father Christmas than on them, though he was careful not to get caught out.

At work Ben did notice that Mark, while polite and reasonably friendly, did not seem to want to socialise with him. The only exception was when Mark came to the rugby club matches, which Ben had observed was not that often.

Thank goodness he had found a new friend in Simon. They carried on meeting up for drinks on Thursday evenings. It was a good opportunity to discuss their lives and to exchange news. Ben had just one regret, which was that these meetings were only for the two of them. It was not going to lead to any larger social events with the much-needed chance to meet any young ladies. Ben heaved a sigh but he knew Simon was preoccupied with Natalie. He had also observed that Simon did not appear too keen for Ben to meet Natalie either.

Ben then debated again how he could get to meet the sort of girl he dreamed of. In his mind he always thought of them as young ladies with a touch of class about them. It would not be easy to find them because they would have a career, and their social lives were no doubt bound up at least in part in events to do with their business lives. Ben had decided straight away when he moved to Oxford that he would not be hanging around on his own in pubs and clubs – nor in restaurants, on the off chance that there would be an attractive young lady there alone – but he accepted, nonetheless, that it was going to be difficult to meet any young ladies at all. Now that he was living alone (and his work colleagues all disappeared in the evenings) Ben felt the stark contrast with those occasions in the City when he and his work colleagues would go for rowdy nights out, usually on Friday evenings. But, reflecting on it now, that was one of the main reasons he had left the City. Being in Oxford was a new, more mature phase in his life.

Leave things until after Christmas, he told himself. *The hunt starts in earnest in the new year.*

A couple of weeks before the Christmas holidays Ben went to the theatre to see a Christmas show. When he went to book his ticket one day after work he was served by a young lady.

"Are there any tickets left for the Christmas show, please?" Ben enquired politely.

"So will that be for the two of you?" The young woman did not even look up from her screen. Ben felt a bit awkward.

"Err… no… just for me," said Ben.

"Oh… right." The young lady sounded surprised.

Ben sighed to himself afterwards, accepting that she wasn't to know anything about his personal circumstances, but it did show him that he was at an age when people generally expected him to be in a relationship. That really did rub salt in the wounds.

When he went to that Christmas show Ben felt very self-conscious about being there on his own. Most of the other people had come as couples or groups. Unintentionally he stared at a group of older women during the interval who seemed to be having a girls' night out. One of them noticed him looking, raised her glass to him in jest, said,

"Happy Christmas, handsome," and laughed with the other women. Ben smiled and then looked away. He guessed he should not have been so obvious.

The last working week before Christmas proved, surprisingly, to be rather busy. Ben was working on some company formations but he made sure that all his work was done and that all meetings and appointments for the early new year were arranged in good time. After going to his business group's Christmas lunch on the Tuesday he then went to another local business Christmas lunch along with Roger and Tony. Ben was delighted to find he was seated next to an attractive young lady from another local firm of accountants.

At last, he thought. *A social opportunity, and she is a very attractive young lady*. They chatted for a while, and she seemed interested in hearing about his career in the City. He asked her about her hobbies and pastimes, although she didn't give much away.

After the lunch Ben felt someone poke him in the back. He twisted round indignantly to find that it was Roger.

"A word of warning," murmured Roger. "Miss Williams is a member of O'Reilly and Ryan. I hope she hasn't been pumping you for information."

"It was just a polite chat," said Ben, somewhat surprised. His heart sank. So this young lady was totally out of bounds.

It's as bad as the Middle Ages, he grumbled under his breath, but kept away from her for the rest of the event. At that stage it was far more important to keep his boss happy than to chase after a possible girlfriend. He checked out all the other members of the group and shrugged. Miss Williams was one of very few young ladies there.

On the Friday Triangle Accountants officially closed its offices at 12.30pm and then everyone headed off to a large hotel in the centre of town for their Christmas party. Somehow they managed to find parking spaces and everyone trooped along to the hotel, laughing and chatting. Ben had never seen them all so cheerful. He was in the Christmas mood too and thoroughly enjoyed the party. They had drinks first, followed by another Christmas meal. They laughed and cracked jokes as they tucked into their food.

It was very pleasant, Ben thought, *to be part of a smaller firm and to know who everyone was. No wonder the atmosphere was so bright.*

After the meal Roger tapped his glass and then gave a brief speech.

"I would like to thank you all for your hard work and commitment to Triangle Accountants over the past year – which has been very challenging, due to the recession. I think we are all now in need of a well-earned break. The partners would like to wish you all a very Happy Christmas and New Year. Please join me in raising a toast to a more prosperous 2009."

Everyone raised their glasses and applauded Roger. Then it was time for the Secret Santa presents. Ben got a rugby shirt. There was a bit more chatter and people started to stand up, calling out Christmas greetings and saying their goodbyes. It was a pleasant surprise when Sarah gave Ben a hug and a kiss, although he tried not to let it show too much. In a very short time everyone had gone.

As he collected his coat Ben smiled at the contrast with Christmas parties in the City. Those events often went on into the early hours of the following morning and would also be characterised by major hangovers afterwards. He looked at his watch. It was barely 5pm. He had plenty of free time until he went home to his parents on the Sunday. That would be yet another Christmas dinner.

Ben decided to go to the gym that evening and again the following day. Otherwise he didn't think he would be able to eat another festive meal, and that would upset his mother. Meanwhile, he could do a bit of last-minute shopping for presents. He also found time to email his former colleagues in the City, sending them all good wishes for Christmas and the New Year. However, only Peter responded. Ben was a little disappointed but did accept that having voluntarily left his job in the City, his former colleagues, rightly or wrongly, would probably no longer be interested in hearing from him.

On the Saturday evening Ben was watching a DVD in his flat. He was relaxed, thoroughly enjoying being on holiday and just lazing around. When his mobile rang he frowned, half inclined to ignore it. He looked and saw the caller was Simon.

"Let's have one last meet-up," Simon said. "We can't leave without a Christmas drink. See you in half an hour."

Ben went willingly. After they had told each other about the various Christmas dinners and parties they had attended, Simon said,

"So… still no luck with the ladies, then?"

"Not so far," answered Ben.

"Never mind. Hopefully you'll find someone soon – but, remember, the world doesn't owe you a girlfriend – and you'll have to get yourself out there more and try much harder to meet some young ladies."

"I know," replied Ben, although rather annoyed by that comment – given that it was easy for Simon to say that, being in a long-term serious relationship himself at the moment.

"What are you doing over the Christmas break?" Ben asked, changing the subject.

Simon picked up his drink. "Oh, I'll be spending Christmas Day and Boxing Day with my parents." He drank and added, "Then I'm off to stay with Natalie at her parents' for the rest of the holiday. Nothing much planned, otherwise."

They chatted and got more drinks. At last they realised that the bar was almost empty.

"Looks like it's time to go home." Simon's speech was a little slower than usual. Ben nodded solemnly. He had drunk a lot as well. It seemed too hard to make the effort to go. Suddenly two very attractive ladies appeared in the bar and smiled simultaneously at Ben and at Simon. Simon winked at Ben.

"Need to go to the Gents." One of the ladies also disappeared. Ben stood up. The other lady was smiling at him so he moved across to her table.

"Hello," she said in a low, posh voice, "I'm Victoria. What's your name, and are you staying in this hotel?" She was very attractive and wearing a cocktail dress.

Ben shook his head, "Jus' w-waiting for my friend," he answered.

Victoria laughed at that.

"Would you like to come and see my room upstairs?"

Being a little the worse for drink Ben was half ready to accept her invitation, whereas normally he would have said "No" straight away. He blinked at her then looked around. Suddenly Ben noticed that some of the bar staff were watching him with grins on their faces. One of them said something and the others laughed. Ben then realised what was going on. He turned back to Victoria.

"E-excuse me... I just need to pay a visit. Back in a minute."

Ben got out of the bar and left the hotel immediately. Then it occurred to him that Simon was nowhere to be seen. He pulled up his coat collar, thrust his hands into his pockets and set out to walk home. That would certainly sober him up.

Ben was still reflecting on this incident next day as he drove to Winchester for his family Christmas. He had certainly not moved to Oxford for that kind of activity. Moreover, he absolutely had to avoid putting himself in any compromising situations – particularly with Triangle Accountants being local a local firm. Simon might well have considered it to be a joke but Ben would have to make it clear that he was not interested in joining him for such occasions. However, with a rush of seasonal goodwill, Ben decided that he would not mention that incident to Simon.

"Well, now we've heard all about your new life in Oxford," said Mr Smith as they were eating the last of their Christmas pudding, "It's clear you are happy with things there. No more commuting, eh?"

Ben pushed his dish away and reached for his wine glass.

"Some mornings I still wake up with that dread of missing the train or wondering if the Underground is running or not." He drank his wine. "I can't begin to say how much more pleasant it is to have an extra hour's sleep in the morning. And, particularly, being able to walk to work."

"That's wonderful, darling." Mrs Smith collected up the dishes and disappeared into the kitchen.

Mr Smith leaned forward, raising his eyebrows expectantly.

"So what about the social life, then? Have you got to know any young ladies in Oxford?"

"Not yet."

"And why not?"

"Well… it hasn't happened so far, and I've not really had many opportunities to meet and young ladies. And don't forget that I've only been in Oxford for about six weeks or so," said Ben, a little defensively.

Mr Smith frowned.

"That seems long enough to me to find clubs and activities. Is there really so much work to do?"

Oh dear. Along with Simon, his father was implying that he was slow off the mark with getting to know the girls. Ben thought again of the young lady from the rival firm of accountants at the Christmas lunch. She was a good-looking and impressive young lady and she had also been quite friendly to him. He wished he could have the chance to get to know her better, even if Roger didn't like it. Probably it was clutching at straws in even trying to focus on her as being his potential Miss Right, but he had to start somewhere.

As he lazed through the days at home Ben considered and rejected many plans for meeting suitable young ladies in Oxford when he returned in the new year. His clubbing days were now behind him – as they hopefully were, too, for any young ladies who would be potential girlfriends for him. He decided he would check out the events in town which might attract young ladies when he got back to Oxford early in the new year. In addition, perhaps some of his new colleagues had family or friends so that he could enlarge his social circle. Although quite proud, like most young men, Ben realised that he might have to swallow his pride to a certain extent and ask people directly for help if he was not able to meet any young ladies by conventional methods.

It was great that his sister Helen, her husband and his little nephew and niece had come back to England for the Christmas holidays. They came to his parents' house to stay for the new year. Ben enjoyed being an uncle. He played games with his nephew and niece, took them for walks, helped them build a snowman and also had playful snowball fights with them in the garden. But it did inevitably remind him that he still very much wanted to be a parent himself fairly soon.

On New Year's Eve Ben went out for a walk by himself. He was still feeling cheerful and positive. He had no regrets whatsoever about leaving the City and he considered that he was well on the way to achieving two of his three goals. When he toasted in the New Year with his family, he smiled to himself. He was quietly confident that 2009 would be his year and that he would find his Miss Right.

For the new year I'm sending you a book of photos of London, my dear Valeria. I've put an x on the pictures of places I saw when I visited London with my English group. One day maybe you and I can visit them together... '

Ludmila sniffed and put her pen down. She did miss her family. What else could she tell her little sister, knowing that the whole family would hear every word of that letter? She had described her host family, Mr and Mrs Foster, and little Emily and baby Jeremy enough times already. She propped her head on her hand and looked out of the window. She remembered Yuliana at Chişinău Airport and did wish to a certain extent that she could at least have spent Christmas and New Year's Eve with her family. However, Ludmila then smiled as she watched the snow falling in thick wet flakes. Here in her own upstairs room in her host family's house, she was warm and dry. It still felt so luxurious to have constant warmth and hot water and electricity whenever she needed them.

Ludmila also realised that she certainly could not write to her family about how free society was here or the fact that she had been persuaded by her friends on the English course to go clubbing a few times. She pulled a face, thinking of how Nicolae would fly into a rage if he knew that, or indeed if he had any idea of how the young men in England were so bold. It was nice to constantly receive admiring looks and attention but she was cautious. Coming from a stricter society, she could not accept a casual invitation from any boy. She would need to get to know a young man formally first of all before she could consider accepting to spend any time with him.

Soon after her arrival Mrs Foster had taken her to London for a day out. Ludmila had finally seen with her own eyes that the streets of London were not in fact paved with gold, and she had even heard some people speaking Moldovan there. However, Ludmila continued to dream of becoming a successful businesswoman one day. She really wanted to enrol on a business studies course here but first she would need to improve her English. Her standard was not yet good enough for her to read the textbooks and write essays competently, but she had decided that she would persevere until she could do so.

Chapter Seven

Ben returned to Oxford on the Sunday after New Year's Day, as Triangle Accountants was going to reopen the following day. He smiled to himself as he drove back to Oxford that evening. This was still so much better than the daily struggle in and out of the City. He was looking forward to resuming his new independent life. Even Mrs Smith had stopped making negative comments. She had sensed that Ben was much happier now. But… but now it was time to set about finding his way into events or groups where he could get to know some young ladies. Surely it wouldn't be impossible to meet the girl who would turn out to be his Miss Right fairly soon?

Back at work, he saw there was only one change in the personnel at Triangle Accountants after the Christmas holidays. That was Josh, the new junior clerk, who would be shadowing Walter (the senior clerk). This was in stark contrast to his job in the City, where there was a constant turnover of staff. Ben went round to speak to everyone on the first day back, asking them how their Christmas holidays had been and wishing them all a Happy New Year. He also made a point of welcoming Josh and pointing out that he was still quite new at Triangle Accountants himself, and that he was sure that Josh would fit in well too.

Sarah was showing the other secretaries her holiday photos from Thailand but, amid screams of laughter from all the girls, she hid them from Ben. He shrugged and grinned and walked past. Karen made Ben laugh by complaining how expensive Christmas had been for her and her husband with their small children. They had both demanded and had in fact received a lot of presents. Ben told her that his nephew and niece had been spoilt too, but mainly by his parents. By the end of the morning he had settled back into the usual routine. At the gym that evening Ben saw that all the people there were all the same as before. He had already made a discreet survey of all the fit young ladies at the gym but unsurprisingly, they were all with partners. Any girl working out alone seemed to have a boyfriend waiting for her in the reception area. Of course, when they had found the girl they wanted those men were going to warn any other blokes off them. So… still not much hope for Ben meeting any young ladies at the gym.

On the Thursday evening it was time to meet up for drinks as usual with Simon. They did not go to the same hotel that they had been to just before Christmas. Simon told Ben about how he had spent his holidays.

"All very sedate, really," he said, finishing his drink and getting up to fetch another.

When he returned Ben blurted out,

"Why did you suddenly disappear from that hotel bar at our last meeting?"

"Oh, well… I thought I'd leave you to it," said Simon, and winked.

"But you knew they were on the game. You knew that already, didn't you?'

"I was sure you could handle it, mate."

Ben breathed hard.

"That was not what I moved to Oxford for, Simon," he snapped.

"Oh, come on. Don't tell me that you've never been in these sorts of situations before. How many years did you actually spend in the City?"

Ben glared, but decided to let the matter drop. He swallowed some of his drink and then looked up to see Simon watching him with a mischievous grin on his face. Well, perhaps this was one person who would help him.

"The fact is," he began, a bit hesitantly, "I'm on a mission now to find my Miss Right. I would prefer it to happen naturally, but I just don't seem to know where to begin. No luck at the office – the only likely young lady I've met here so far works for a rival firm, and Roger more or less ordered me to keep away from her."

Simon nodded but made no comment. Ben waited hopefully, but Simon didn't offer any advice or help. Surely he or even his Natalie might have some single female friends locally?

"Good luck to you," said Simon, looking as if he found it amusing.

"I mean it. I've had enough of being single and I will do something about it but I don't know what yet," replied Ben, exasperated that Simon did not take what he had said seriously.

Ben reflected. So often family and friends – particularly female friends, ex-boyfriends and work colleagues – would do all they could to prevent any young lady from having a new boyfriend. However, Ben knew that every relationship had to start somewhere and that he was no exception. Now that he felt that he had settled into his job at Triangle Accountants and into living in Oxford as well, it was his chief priority. Surely he would find Miss Right, even if he needed a lot of perseverance and patience to achieve it.

January passed slowly. The weather was very cold, and Ben found himself busier at work and often doing longer hours. He went to his local Greek restaurant and was treated to a belated New Year's dinner by Dimitris and his family. Afterwards Dimitris' father patted Ben on the back, beaming at him.

"You are a good lad. My son, you see, he don't work hard enough and he chase girls. We must find him a wife from the island."

"No chance," laughed Dimitris.

Ben smiled. He himself didn't approve of arranged

marriages but was far too polite to say anything and knew that he could not interfere in such matters anyway, regardless of whether Dimitris' father was joking or not.

At the end of January the business group held an evening dinner, to which the spouses of the members were also invited. Ben did feel a little awkward going to this dinner party alone as it transpired that he was the only member there without a spouse. Simon wasn't there due to a very important business trip to the Cayman Islands. Over dinner the wives of a couple of the senior members of the business group asked Ben why he was single. Ben felt a little embarrassed. He really did not know what to say – particularly as most of the members appeared to have already been married by his age, and also some of the members of the business group had daughters in their twenties. Ben felt a bit aggrieved that there were no suggestions of any of those daughters being introduced to him. He had – of course – initially enquired politely about those daughters and what they were doing either university- or career-wise, but that was as far as it went.

"I'm single at the moment. I did have a girlfriend a while back. I'm enjoying bachelor life at present but I'm sure it will all work out fine for me soon," said Ben, rather awkwardly.

"Tut tut. Not good enough, young man. You should not be so lazy. You'll have to try a lot harder… "

Here we go again, Ben thought. He forced a smile but he felt that his evening had been spoiled now. Why would people assume that he was not trying to find a nice young lady? Nor did the members of the business group want to let him near their daughters. He didn't think of himself as being any sort of monster. Maybe Ben wasn't always the most cheerful of people but he was hopefully a reasonably likeable and professional young man who, on the whole, got on well with most people.

Valentine's Day then approached. It was not an occasion that Ben could enjoy if he didn't have a girlfriend. He could already sense the gloom descending on him a week or so beforehand. The local newspapers had some adverts for Valentine's Day parties for singles. He looked at the venues in the adverts yet, despite his plan, he decided against taking part. Ben didn't fancy meeting a girl just because they both had attended a singles party on Valentine's Day. He accepted that he was chickening out of it. At work only Sarah received a card and some flowers on the Friday for Valentine's Day, which did not surprise anyone. Otherwise, nobody else seemed to be particularly bothered about Valentine's Day.

Ben still felt a little down sitting in his flat on Valentine's Day in the evening which, unfortunately for him, was a Saturday.

This time next year, he promised himself, *I'll be sitting in front of a warm log fire with a lovely young lady and we'll be enjoying Valentine's Day drinking champagne together.*

A couple of weeks later Ben met up with Simon on a Thursday evening for drinks as usual. They had decided to try a new hotel. Ben had to listen to Simon's account of how he had taken Natalie out for an expensive dinner on Valentine's Day to a restaurant with a singer and a band. They had also bought each other quite lavish presents. Inevitably, hearing all this had hardly made Ben feel any better – but he knew it would be wrong for him to act like a wet blanket. He made appropriate comments and admired the new watch that Simon showed him.

"Any plans to get married?" Ben enquired politely.

"Not yet, but perhaps next year," answered Simon, and then changed the subject.

Strange, thought Ben. How touchy Simon seemed to be where Natalie was concerned. Every time he seemed to avoid any questions about her or their lives together.

In early March Mark's wife gave birth to a baby girl. Mark took a week off work and Triangle Accountants sent them a card with a present for the baby. Mark looked exhausted when he returned to work. Ben was quite keen to ask Mark about fatherhood but noticed that Mark was far more anxious to speak to the partners and the secretaries than he was to talk to him. When Ben finally managed to get a moment to speak to Mark he asked him how he was enjoying being a parent.

"It's ecstatic. I've never known such a wonderful feeling before," said Mark very candidly. "However, I don't anticipate getting much sleep for the next year or so."

They both laughed. Ben, however, felt his heart sink. He was of course delighted for Mark, but it was yet another reminder of the life Ben wanted but could not yet seem to find.

Later in March Ben travelled up to London for a training course. He chuckled to himself on the journey.

Oh, this was so different from the commuting to the City each day from Winchester, he thought. This time Ben actually managed to get a seat on the train. He even enjoyed the journey and watched the countryside for most of the way. A day out of the office, even though it was work-related, was quite a treat. London appeared much more busy and tense than even he remembered it. Ben felt the difference after being out of the rush for the past five months. Oxford was definitely much calmer and more relaxed. Ben still did not feel any sense of loss nor any desire to work in London again.

As soon as he entered the large hall where the course was taking place Ben saw that there were some very attractive young female accountants. He was pleased to be seated on the same table as a couple of them. They chatted politely but formally and Ben remembered from the incident at the Christmas lunch that he should not to say too much about either his job or his firm. One of the young ladies came from another top City firm of accountants and her mobile phone rang constantly throughout the day. Ben noticed she had huge dark shadows under her eyes and that she looked like a bag of nerves. He wondered if she had a boyfriend and guessed that she probably didn't. Perhaps she didn't even have time to clean her flat at weekends, let alone any time for a social life.

The other young lady was called Anna and her firm was based in Kent. She was quite friendly towards Ben, and they asked each other politely about their respective firms and about their particular specialisms. Ben warmed to Anna immediately. She was attractive, polite, focused on her job and – seemingly like him – had gone past the clubbing stage of her life. When she wasn't looking he glanced discreetly at her clothes. She was very smartly dressed, and altogether she looked immaculate.

She is certainly as well-dressed as any woman in a top City firm, he thought. At the end of the day he shook hands with her.

"It was very nice to meet you," he said, disappointed that they were leaving.

"You too," said Anna. "Here's my business card. Perhaps we might bump into each other again on another course."

"Thank you. Here's mine."

As he left the building Ben sighed. He guessed that he would probably not see Anna again. Had she been working closer to Oxford then he would definitely have tried to follow up on that day. However, it did seem ironic that the City – where Ben had hardly got to know any young ladies properly – had now given him a potential introduction to a young lady, albeit one from outside the City. Ben mulled this over on the train journey back to Oxford. He chuckled as he thought of the other young lady on his table during the course – who would no doubt be rushing back to her firm in the heart of the City and working until the early hours of the morning, whereas Ben's evening would consist of a DVD followed by a relaxing bath.

In April, as expected, Ben got through his probationary period at Triangle Accountants. Roger announced it to everyone and Ben would have very readily treated everyone at work to drinks that evening but, as he was well aware, it was not the sort of firm where the staff headed to the pub after work. Having telephoned his parents to tell them the good news, Ben went for a celebratory meal at the local Greek restaurant and treated Dimitris and his parents to a drink.

"Well done, Ben," said Dimitris' father, "You go a long way in that job." Ben grinned.

"I hope so."

"It's champagne on me," Ben told Simon when they met that Thursday evening.

Simon raised his dark brows, "Ah. Congratulations. So all's going well for you at work, then?"

"All's fine," replied Ben.

"Do you need any new client introductions?" asked Simon.

"No, but thank you. I'm very busy as it is," Ben grinned.

"OK. That's good for you. But let me know if you do." Ben nodded.

He also had a celebratory drink with Roger and Tony at the rugby club on the following Saturday.

"Well done," said Tony, raising his glass.

"Yes: well done, Ben," echoed Roger. "The other partners are very pleased for you too." He laughed. "You can take things a bit more easily now and perhaps try and be a little more relaxed and less formal at work."

Ben nodded. He knew what Roger meant, and he had understood that the transition from City life to life in the provinces would take a little while. He was delighted that his future with Triangle Accountants had taken its first significant step towards being secure.

Later on, after he had left the others, Ben smiled to himself. He had never been aware that he had come across as being particularly formal at work – although, ironically – he had considered things appeared to be more formal at Triangle Accountants than in the City, particularly as the partners still had to be addressed as Mister by the support staff. So how was he going to be less formal at work from now on?

By the following Sunday Ben realised that time was now passing since he had come to Oxford. He had achieved two goals, but had made absolutely no progress in relation to his third aim. He was no further advanced than on that fateful day the previous October when he had attended the job interview at Triangle Accountants. His attention had been focused elsewhere, even though it bothered him constantly that he was still single. So far he had not found any opportunities to meet any young ladies either at work or socially. Where were they all? He had not met any young ladies at the rugby club, either. So would he have to directly approach any young lady that he fancied in a pub, restaurant or wherever? It might, however, be a bit risky to try that.

The very end of April saw a minor heatwave. On the Sunday afternoon Ben went for a walk by the river. He strolled along, eating an ice cream. There were crowds of people in the fields by the river and on the paths, all enjoying the sunshine. Whereas in Winchester Ben had been preoccupied with the young couples with their small children during his walks in the parks, he now focused solely on the young ladies in Oxford. There were plenty of attractive girls out that afternoon, but they all appeared to have boyfriends in tow.

No young lady in need of a gallant knight to rescue her, he thought sadly. *And where were all these girls during the week?*

Suddenly it struck Ben hard: he had been so anxious to get away from the City... and while he was very much enjoying living and working in Oxford, being single outside the City was both a lot more difficult for him – and obvious to other people, as he had recently discovered. Further, with his thirty-first birthday rapidly approaching, had he somehow missed the boat where being in a serious relationship then looking to get engaged and then married was concerned? As he walked along the path by the river Ben's attention was drawn by a beautiful young girl with long fair hair and huge blue eyes, who was sitting on a park bench. Ben stared at this girl very intently. She could not have been more than a first-year student at the very most, and her boyfriend was sitting next to her. Ben smiled ruefully to himself. She was stunning but far too young for him, and he would not have been interested in having a student for a girlfriend anyway. But he was so taken with that young girl's beauty that he turned round to stare at her again after walking past, which was not something he normally did. He then shook his head.

Ben walked on, heavy-hearted. He really couldn't see any way of getting to meet young ladies by chance. It was time to swallow his pride and try out some singles events. He was certainly not the first person, male or female, to find themselves in this position. Admitting to a problem and then asking for help were the first steps towards dealing with it, and that included the problem of Ben not being able to meet any young ladies.

That evening Ben decided to let his mother organise his birthday celebrations. That would be the deadline. Straight afterwards, he would go to some singles events. And in preparation for that, perhaps he could do some shopping and get some more trendy clothes to try and brighten up his image. Just before going to bed he glanced through the last few pages of a local newspaper. He came across an article about a company that had recently gone into administration. It had been a well-established business but, according to the article, the company had not advertised itself properly to try and attract new clients.

Hmm, thought Ben. *That confirms my thinking in relation to meeting young ladies. Now I'll get straight on the right track*. He fell asleep with a smile on his face.

Chapter Eight

Ben celebrated his thirty-first birthday in early May. He was so busy at work that week that he was only able to take the Friday afternoon off to go and see his parents for the weekend. To mark his birthday Ben took cakes in to work for his colleagues. They were so surprised at this that he had to explain it was a work tradition. Not at Triangle Accountants, evidently. Ben would readily have treated everyone to a drink that evening but he didn't need reminding that the staff went straight home after work.

So much for being less formal, he thought, *and nobody – seemingly – wants to have any additional social interaction with their work colleagues.*

After his birthday visit to his parents Ben steeled himself to the idea of going to singles events. He considered his options. He didn't initially fancy responding to any lonely hearts-type adverts in the local newspapers. However, he was willing to try a speed dating event that would be taking place in a couple of weeks' time in Woodstock. It was a nice location, if nothing else. Perhaps some more new clothes would be a good idea, too. Ben even researched the internet for tips on the dos and don'ts for speed dating:

Do arrive on time; dress properly; be positive and relaxed.

Don't ask what car they drive; fish for compliments; get drunk; focus on the person on the next table; talk about your exes, your miserable love life or anything else that could embarrass or frighten the other person.

If it hadn't been for the fact that he was single Ben would have found most of these tips hilarious.

But... needs must, he shrugged. *I have to start somewhere.* Naturally, he didn't mention the speed dating event to anyone at all. He was actually looking forward to the event, albeit with some mild apprehension. The tips all seemed obvious, so there was nothing else to do to prepare. Ben reasoned that he could make all his mistakes the first time and would then know what to do if he did attend any further speed dating events. Some of his friends in the City had been to such evenings, but Ben had never himself ever paid any attention to speed dating before. Now he needed to try it. Ben realised that at least he would be seeing the females in person rather than running the risk of getting a misleading impression of them without a picture, as might be the case on a lonely hearts-type advert.

The speed dating event took place on a Thursday evening at 7.30pm in a pub in Woodstock. Ben was happy that he could go home, change and go out again by that time. That would almost always have been impossible when he worked in the City unless he had taken half a day's holiday, which he did not tend to do. Ben put on a light blue shirt and chinos.

The pub was a picturesque old building and full of character. When Ben walked into the event he saw there were about twenty people. The hall was laid out with tables and chairs. Most of the other people were clustered at the bar. Ben joined them and got a drink with the coupon he had been given on arriving. He chatted politely to some of the other participants, noticing that there were people of all ages. Some seemed to be barely in their twenties, whereas others appeared to be over sixty years of age. He smiled and nodded at a couple of elderly-looking gentlemen, acknowledging that they were quite brave to attend given how uncomfortable they looked. Ben didn't feel too concerned himself. Assuming that most (if not all) the people there were in the same position as him then it certainly was worth a try. He wouldn't be any worse off if he didn't manage to hit it off with any young ladies that evening.

Suddenly a whistle sounded and the event organisers explained the rules. The participants would all sit at tables, the men on one side and the women on the other side. They would have two minutes each to present themselves, and a whistle would blow halfway through and at the end. Afterwards the men would move along a seat and then speak to the next woman. There would be a break halfway though. Everyone would be given a sheet of paper and would write down the names of the people they would like to see again.

Ben started by speaking to a middle-aged lady called Linda. She was good-looking with dark hair and eyes and was wearing a black leather jacket. Ben was a little nervous, and just managed to politely say what he did and the things he liked to do in his spare time and the places he liked locally. Linda smiled and nodded. When it was her turn she said that she worked as a cleaner near Witney and was separated with a couple of children. Surprisingly, Linda then described a couple of recent relationships she had had. It was clear to Ben that Linda was not looking for a serious relationship. At the end Linda smiled and winked at him. She even gave him her mobile number on a piece of paper. Ben was too polite to refuse it but he guessed why she was doing that. He doubted that he would follow up on Linda's offer, somehow.

He then spoke to a lady who was slightly older than him. She was called Wendy and she was attractive with blonde hair and dark eyes. Ben explained how he enjoyed going to see a local rugby team. Wendy pulled a face at this, which annoyed him. There were plenty of females who attended the rugby team's matches, so why should this lady not like rugby? Even so, Ben found Wendy very appealing and did not mind her being slightly older than him. However, Wendy's comments made it clear that she was seeking someone to look after her and her children.

That did not appeal to Ben in the slightest. As the whistle blew, Wendy said,

"Sorry, but I don't think you're the right person for me. But it was nice to meet you, and good luck with meeting someone," she added with a smile.

After speaking to a couple of other females, including a student who Ben considered was far too young and immature for him, there was a break. Ben joined the crowd and got himself a drink at the bar. He spoke to a couple of the other men standing there. They all laughed and agreed that speed dating did take some effort as well as some getting used to.

"It feels like a public auction," grinned one man.

"Oh, it's not as bad as that," said Ben. "We do have to swallow our pride, but it's an opportunity to meet people we'd never otherwise see in our busy working lives."

"That's true," said another man. "But two minutes isn't much time to decide if you want to get to know a complete stranger."

"Well… it's an introduction, I suppose," said Ben, when they were all called back after the break.

The second part of the session went much better for Ben. The first girl he spoke to was called Emma. She was a primary schoolteacher in a school near Abingdon. She was in her late twenties. She was small and slightly tubby with brown hair and blue eyes. However, she came across as a nice and genuine person.

"So what do you do for a living?" she asked Ben.

"I'm an accountant in Oxford."

"Very impressive," Emma said, and looked at him keenly. "What hobbies and interests do you have?"

"I like cinema, theatre, travelling and sports. With my business group I get involved in local events, including some charitable ones."

"That's what I like to hear," Emma beamed.

Ben smiled. He laughed about it afterwards as he realised he was half consciously thinking that there were shades of his own mother in Emma – and that, just like his parents, a business man and a teacher could potentially be a good partnership… and that as a teacher, she might be a good homemaker too. Ben decided that he wanted to see Emma again.

Next he spoke to a businesswoman called Louise. She ran her own IT company and divided her time between Oxford and London. Louise came across as being rather too keen on her drink and even appeared to have had too much to drink already that evening. She then shocked Ben.

"You know my flatmate, Dave. He frequently tries to get me drunk. I'm sure it's so that he can try and have his wicked way with me," she said with a mischievous grin.

Ben nodded but did not respond. He remembered that that was another of the major don'ts for speed dating. Afterwards, he spoke to a young lady called Rebecca. She was very good-looking, with dark blonde hair and blue eyes.

"I'm training to become a doctor in Banbury. I am really looking forward to qualifying, as it has been my life's ambition."

"That's very impressive," said Ben, nodding his head in admiration.

That was ideal career-wise, he thought. She seemed quite interested in Ben too, and smiled when he told her he was an accountant.

"What are your long-term plans?" she asked next.

"I'm hoping to stay where I am for the rest of my career and become a partner."

"Wow. I'm very impressed. You'll be an important person."

Ben felt he could see himself quite easily becoming better acquainted with Rebecca. He was nonetheless surprised that someone in Rebecca's position – and with her good looks – would need to attend a speed dating event, but Ben was glad that he had spoken to her. It also ended any lingering doubts he might have had about participating in such events.

After speaking to a couple more students Ben then, finally, spoke to a young lady called Jess. She had black hair and green eyes and worked for the council. Ben liked Jess as she appeared to be friendly and down to earth, and also looked quite cute. But Jess didn't say much, nor did she drop any hints about whether or not she wanted to see Ben again.

The speed dating event then drew to a close and it was time to fill out the sheet of paper. Ben chose Emma, Rebecca and Jess as the three people he wanted to see again. Ben felt the need for a drink while he thought the evening through. He came away from the bar with his drink and noticed that Rebecca and Emma had already left, but he saw Jess talking to another young man. But the room soon cleared. As Ben drove home he thought about those young ladies and hoped they had all chosen to see him again too, although he was not too sure about Jess. If so, maybe something might come of it. If not, he had at least discovered how speed dating worked and he would be willing to try it again.

Otherwise, Ben's working life carried on as normal. His shared secretary Karen had now become more friendly and took a greater interest in him. Previously she had tended to be polite rather than friendly. Ben guessed that it was probably because he had got through his probationary period.

Early on during the following week, Ben received an email at his personal email address from the speed dating company. The email said that two people had indicated that they would like to see Ben again. One was Rebecca and the other one was Emma. Ben was very pleased. It really felt like a real achievement for him, particularly as it had been the first speed dating event that he had attended. He simply shrugged his shoulders in relation to Jess and decided to think no more about her. That email had given him both Rebecca's and Emma's personal email addresses. After work that day Ben wrote an email to each of them. He tried to remember what the other men at the speed dating event looked like and whether they had got in first.

However, surely he would meet both girls at least once. If it was a question of looks he would prefer Rebecca, but he was fair-minded and accepted that Emma had good qualities even if she was not as pretty as Rebecca.

Ben sent almost identical emails to both Rebecca and Emma:

From: Ben Smith
Subject: Hello Again
Date: Tuesday 26 May 2009 19.45
To: Rebecca

Hi Rebecca,

It was lovely to meet you at the speed dating event in Woodstock and I'm delighted that you would like to see me again. I would be very happy to meet up with you for a drink or a meal either after work or at a weekend.

Please let me know what would suit you.

Talk soon.

Kind regards,

Ben Smith.

Ben made sure he had changed their names and then sent the mails. He didn't expect an immediate reply but became increasingly disappointed when the whole weekend went past with no reply from either of them. But on the Monday evening there was an email from Emma:

From: Emma
Subject: Re: Hello Again
Date: Monday 1 June 2009 18.57
To: Ben Smith

Hi Ben,

Thank you for your email. It was good to hear from you.

I would like to meet up with you but I am tied up for this coming week, so perhaps if you could contact me again next week we can hopefully arrange something for the following weekend.

Talk soon.

Emma.

Ben was very pleased to get a positive response. His heart sank a little at the thought of having to wait nearly two weeks to see Emma. But he would have to be patient, as he felt she could be a suitable girl to have a relationship with. Meanwhile, he still hoped to receive a positive email from Rebecca too.

And then, on Wednesday evening, Ben did receive an email from Rebecca:

From: Rebecca
Subject: Re: Hello Again
Date: Wednesday 3 June 2009 20.03
To: Ben Smith

Hi Ben,

Thank you very much for your email. I was hoping to hear from you.

It would be great to meet up at the weekend. I am not sure about Friday evening yet but I am definitely free on Saturday afternoon. If you would like to meet up in Oxford town centre at 2pm then that would be great.

I look forward to hearing from you again soon.

Rebecca x

Of course, Ben was pleased and equally relieved to hear from Rebecca, although he did not know quite what to make of her email. It seemed a little bold for a suggestion for a first date. Or maybe life in Oxford had made him a bit prudish. Of course

Ben was going to accept. A date was a date and if he felt that Rebecca was not genuinely looking for a relationship, he would then focus on Emma. At this stage, he must not look too far ahead. It was an opportunity to have a couple of pleasant and, hopefully, constructive first dates. If things worked out, then he would have to decide which girl he wanted to know better and take things from there.

His conscience sorted, Ben sent a reply to Rebecca:

From: Ben Smith
Subject: Re: Hello Again
Date: Thursday 4 June 2009 19.21
To: Rebecca

Hi Rebecca,

Many thanks for your email. I was very pleased to hear back from you.

I would be delighted to see you on Saturday at 2pm. I look forward to seeing you again.

Kind regards,

Ben x

"You're very pensive tonight... " remarked Simon at their Thursday night meeting.

Ben roused from his thoughts.

"Am I? Sorry. Work's been a bit frantic these last two weeks." Simon raised an eyebrow but accepted the excuse. Ben made sure he kept his mind on their conversation for the rest of the evening.

On the Friday Ben went into Oxford town centre at lunchtime to choose a couple of polo shirts and a new pair of chinos. That evening he went to the gym. He had organised his time to get his food shopping and ironing done on Saturday morning. With luck he could clean the flat as well before getting ready to meet Rebecca at 2pm. On coming back from the gym Ben checked his emails. He frowned when he saw one from Rebecca, which had been sent a couple of hours earlier. Now what? Had she changed her mind about seeing him?

From: Rebecca
Subject: Re: Hello Again
Date: Friday 5 June 2009 18.57
To: Ben Smith

Hi Ben,

I'll be out in Oxford this evening. It would be great to see you if you are there. Otherwise I look forward to seeing you tomorrow afternoon.

Rebecca x

Part of Ben wished he had not gone to the gym so that he could have seen Rebecca that evening. However, the implications of a Friday night out were still not appealing given that he was no longer in the City. Ben was past that stage in his life. Suddenly Ben felt a little apprehensive about his date with Rebecca. He suspected she was not looking for the serious relationship that he wanted. But, if he was honest, he had to admit that he was still taken by her good looks. Maybe if she spent some time with him and got to know him, it was not impossible that they could hit it off. Ben couldn't get to sleep, so gave up trying and picked up a good book to pass the time.

Chapter Nine

Ben woke up on the Saturday morning at around 8am. He still felt slightly uneasy about his date with Rebecca that afternoon but he kept himself busy by doing his food shopping, ironing and housework in the morning. As they had agreed to meet up at 2pm he set off in good time, and was at the agreed meeting place near Oxford Town Hall by 1.50pm. There could be absolutely no question of him being late. Ben waited for around for about twenty minutes. He tried not to stare at the shoppers and tourists but (of course) he could not help but notice the pretty girls – especially those who were not wearing too much, even though the weather wasn't particularly warm that day. He was checking his mobile when Rebecca suddenly appeared. She kissed him on the cheek before he could even say "Hello." He noticed she was wearing a blue top which went quite well with his blue polo shirt.

"Nice boots," said Ben. He indicated Rebecca's pixie boots and grinned.

"So what have you been up to this morning?" Rebecca asked, casting a critical eye over his new shirt and trousers.

"Oh… the usual household chores," he said with a short laugh. "No time for food shopping and so on in the week. What about you?"

Rebecca didn't reply. He glanced down at her, wondering if she'd heard him, then he suddenly remembered her email from Friday evening. He said,

"I'm sorry I missed your email last night. I was actually working quite late. It doesn't happen that often, you know."

Rebecca stared at Ben for a moment and half frowned. Then she shrugged.

"Oh. It doesn't matter now."

They walked around the town centre a little, and Ben could see some of the men taking note of Rebecca's good looks. That made him to smile to himself.

"Shall we look for a cafe?" he asked.

She nodded.

"A drink would be good."

They soon found a suitable cafe. Ben ordered a coffee and Rebecca a J2O and they shared a slice of sponge cake.

"Tell me more about your training to be a doctor," Ben asked. "It does seem a very long course."

"Yes. It's intense and tiring," Rebecca agreed. "But it's been my lifelong ambition. I'm glad I stuck at it, as I've only another eighteen months to complete it all now."

Ben nodded.

"My training was quite intense as well. As I explained before I used to work in the City, but after a while you lose track of normal life. Now I've moved to Oxford there's time to enjoy so many more things." He wiped his fingers on the paper napkin and sat back. "Do you like Oxford?"

His eyes narrowed as he realised that Rebecca seemed to have lost interest.

Oh dear, he thought. Surely they could find some common ground? He mentioned his sister being married and living abroad and how he liked being an uncle, although he hardly saw his nephew and niece.

Rebecca said she had a younger brother called Steven. He had recently finished university and was hoping to become an engineer but was currently having a year out. She gave a saucy smile.

"You know, Steven went on holiday with a group of friends to Amsterdam last summer. He had thought that they were

65

avoiding the red-light areas – and one evening he and his friends were in a bar and he was chatting to a woman without realising that she was on the game, and his friends disappeared and left Steven with that woman and had a good laugh about it."

This immediately reminded Ben of what had happened with Simon just before Christmas. He smiled politely, thinking it was a rather odd thing to mention on a first date.

"What newspapers do you read?" he asked, to change the subject. "Do you think the recession will drag on for a long time? I mean," he added quickly as she stared at him, "Is it likely to have any impact on your training as a doctor?"

When Rebecca screwed up her face at this Ben realised he'd better try and find something of mutual interest quickly. So he asked Rebecca about holidays. Her response was markedly different. She talked at length about her past holidays – in particular, a fairly recent family holiday to Disney World – and she also mentioned how she was disappointed not to get the opportunity to go to Legoland in Norway. Ben politely pointed out that Legoland was actually in Denmark. That did not please Rebecca, either. Ben realised that it might have been better if he hadn't corrected Rebecca about Legoland.

She then began to talk about her ex-boyfriends. This was another don't for a first date. However, Rebecca did not mention how she had met these apparent ex-boyfriends, nor how long the relationships had lasted, nor even why or how they had ended. Ben assumed that Rebecca was trying to impress him and maybe show him that she could always get a boyfriend. As far as he was concerned, with her looks she could no doubt easily find a boyfriend.

Suddenly Rebecca finished her drink and asked if they could leave the cafe. Ben settled the bill and they left. He sensed they weren't making progress but Rebecca's good looks and his loneliness meant that he would keep trying to see if he could somehow make this date work out.

"Would you like to go for a walk by the river?" he suggested. Rebecca swished her hair and looked away up the street.

"Sorry, I have to leave now. I'm going to a party later."

Ben wasn't sure if he believed this or not. Was she annoyed because he hadn't answered her email the previous evening or was it quite simply that they hadn't been able to find any common ground? He stared down at her, desperately wanting her to stay longer.

"Well," said Rebecca, "I would consider you as more of a friend but I can see that you want to be a couple."

Rightly or wrongly, Ben couldn't answer. They said goodbye to each other without shaking hands or any smiles and Ben waited for Rebecca to go before walking back towards where his car was parked. He felt dismal and walked slowly with his head slightly down and his hands in his pockets. It could never feel nice to be rejected by a very attractive young lady even if the reasons for it were obvious.

Ben then reflected on his very brief date with Rebecca. He had liked Rebecca mainly for her good looks. The fact that she was slightly younger and training for a good career had made her more appealing to him as well. However, that was really as far as it went. It was clear that Rebecca wasn't interested in current affairs nor seemingly in anything cultural, which did surprise Ben. She hadn't wanted to talk about her work as a doctor in any great detail, even though she'd said it was her life's ambition. She seemed far more focused on her entertainment.

This failed date with Rebecca also suggested to Ben that there was a gap between life in the City and the life in the provinces. What would he need to do to fix this? Also... why had he not appealed to Rebecca in other ways? What was her real agenda? Ben spent the rest of the weekend mulling over those questions. Of course, his male ego had been damaged in that he had been unable to impress Rebecca. He shrugged. He had no choice other than to lick his wounds and carry on with his search for Miss Right.

Ben would certainly have felt a lot worse had there not been a further date coming up with Emma. Although Emma did not have Rebecca's good looks she was still reasonably attractive and, as a primary school teacher he hoped that she might possibly be a bit more mature than Rebecca. He desperately hoped that they could get on and that their date would work out positively. But, by the following Wednesday, Ben was starting to have a couple of butterflies.

After work he emailed Emma again:

From: Ben Smith
Subject: Re: Hello Again
Date: Wednesday 10 June 2009 19.41
To: Emma

Hi Emma,

I hope all's well for you and that you are having a good week at work.

Looking forward to seeing you again in Abingdon on Sunday morning at 11am.

Kind regards,

Ben.

Emma replied on the Thursday evening:

From: Emma
Subject: Re: Hello Again
Date: Thursday 11 June 2009 18.13
To: Ben Smith

Hi Ben,

Thank you for your email.

I'm fine, thanks, and I hope you are too.
I look forward to seeing you too.
Regards,
Emma.

It was a fairly quiet week at work, which allowed Ben more time to focus on the fast-approaching date. On the Friday afternoon Ben was seated at his desk, shuffling papers and half daydreaming about the perfect date. For him it would still be walking along a seafront hand in hand with a very attractive young lady.

Ben did his usual chores quickly on the Saturday morning. He telephoned his parents to say that he would be coming to see them the following weekend and managed a visit to the gym. He also found a couple of hours in the late afternoon to buy a smart dark blue shirt that he thought would go well with his chinos, which he ironed to within an inch of their life. The evening passed quietly. He hoped he could get on better with Emma.

On the Sunday morning, as he ate his breakfast and got ready, Ben reminded himself that even if the first date with Emma turned out to be positive he would still have to take things slowly with her and that he should try not to think too far ahead at this stage.

Ben got to Abingdon in good time but, surprisingly, Emma did not turn up for nearly half an hour. She was dressed in a grey top and jeans and was not wearing any make-up, and paid little attention to what Ben was wearing. She gave him a rather formal handshake and a very faint smile as a greeting. Ben was immediately conscious of a sinking heart. It was evident that Emma was not particularly bothered about their date. Even so, he hoped that something good would come out of their meeting, so he kept a smile on his face.

"Well, shall we go for a coffee?" said Emma. "There's a nice cafe just up the street."

After they had got their coffees Ben asked,

"So how have you got on this week?"

"No different from any other week," Emma responded sharply. "I have to prepare for a parents' evening next week."

"So a lot of extra work for you to do, then?" said Ben.

Emma nodded and took a sip of coffee.

"I have some meetings with potential clients lined up in the next few weeks," Ben said. He was keen to explain a little more to Emma about his job. However, Emma showed no interest and simply looked outside and remarked on the weather.

Ben asked whether it was difficult to teach young children, particularly nowadays. Emma said that she had to be very careful, both in the classroom and away from the school as well. As an example, she wouldn't want to be seen getting drunk in pubs by the parents of the schoolchildren she taught – not that she was much of a drinker, anyway. She also watched certain television programmes in order to understand what her pupils were talking about at school. In relation to her career plans, Emma said she was looking to become a deputy head teacher in the next few years.

Ben asked Emma about her family. Emma said that she had an older sister who was married and living in Cornwall. Emma then suddenly let it slip that she was looking to move to Cornwall in the near future. Ben mentioned the speed dating event that they had met at. Emma didn't answer. She suddenly looked at her mobile phone and said she had to leave. Ben checked his mobile phone and was very shocked to see that they had barely spent twenty minutes together. This was turning out to be even worse than it had been with Rebecca.

"Is something wrong?" Ben asked with some concern.

"I need to do some work for next week," Emma replied tersely.

"Have I upset you or something?" Ben stared at her, anxious to find out why this date had not worked out, either.

She gave a little shrug and stood up.

"Well, you are just not the sort of person I'm looking to meet. But if you don't mind, I do need to go now."

Ben felt desperately awkward. He followed Emma out of the cafe. Emma suddenly asked Ben where he was parked. He pointed to the nearby car park. Then, to his great shock and disbelief, Emma pointed him towards the car park and followed him. Ben suddenly realised that she seemed to have become paranoid and obviously needed to see him leave. Had she had some very bad experiences with other young men in the past to make her behave like this? Ben hurried on, stopped for a few seconds, considering that he should not be forced into doing this – but decided that there was no point in trying to argue with someone behaving so irrationally. He got into his car and, having checked that the car park was clear, drove off promptly without looking to see where Emma was.

Ben drove home, feeling totally rotten nonetheless. He changed his clothes, tried to eat a roll and then decided to go out. Perhaps a walk would help him to calm down and get over the sensation of rejection. He tried to console himself by Emma's comment that she was looking to move to Cornwall, although possibly she had simply said that to put him off. Ben tried to work out what had gone wrong – and also what else might have happened to both Emma and Rebecca on other dates or in past relationships to have made them both react so negatively towards him, having both chosen to see him again at that speed dating event.

During his time in the City Ben had never come across such reactions as that from any of the young ladies he'd met or had been introduced to by friends and colleagues. Of course, none of them had ever been introduced to him as potential girlfriends – and maybe the fact that other people had been present meant that those young ladies had been more civil to him than they might have otherwise been.

Ben only had that one comment from Emma to go on:

"You are just not the sort of person I am looking to meet." That evening it still felt very demoralising for Ben to have had two young ladies react in exactly the same negative way to him, particularly as they had both given him the initial impression of being potential girlfriends for him. Ben still liked to think of himself as being a genuine and a reasonably good-looking young man. It did upset him that Rebecca and Emma had both treated him as if he was some sort of monster. Eventually Ben forced himself to put the problem to the back of his mind. He would have been more than happy previously to have got to know either of them better with a possible view to a serious, long-term relationship in due course. However, they had shown him straight away that they were not interested in him. Although it would have been pointless for them to have pretended otherwise, Ben's male ego was nonetheless still very hurt.

Chapter Ten

At work Ben carried on with his job as normal. It was now mid-June. He went out on a couple of potential client meetings. One was successful, while the other one wasn't. It was an unpleasant surprise for Ben when he found that Roger was more concerned about the unsuccessful meeting. He even called Ben into his office to speak to him about it.

"I am very disappointed, young man," said Roger. "I really wanted Mr Duxbury and his firm as clients. I don't know what happened during your meeting but I expect an improvement from you in future. Do you understand?" Ben nodded firmly to show he had understood what Roger meant. He still felt annoyed that Roger had not acknowledged the new client that Ben had got for Triangle Accountants.

Through a notice at his gym Ben entered a local charity fun run. He managed to get quite a lot of sponsors from both Triangle Accountants and from the business group. It was hard going on the day, but Ben found he made better time because of the competition. He was nonetheless glad to have a quiet Sunday afterwards.

When he met up with Simon for drinks on the Thursday evening meeting with Simon, Ben did not say anything about his two unsuccessful dates. It was obvious that Simon was in a very good mood.

"Go on... tell me," said Ben. "I can see it's something important. Have you won the lottery or something?"

"I wish," said Simon. He raised his eyebrows and grinned. "Natalie and I are going on a long holiday to Mauritius next month."

"Oh," said Ben, then added hastily, before he could sound jealous, "That's great for you both."

"Yeah, it's a dream of a place. The photos in the brochures are so enchanting."

They sat in silence for a while. Simon grinned. Ben made a determined effort not to show that this news had hit a raw nerve. He realised that Simon was speaking.

"… Sorry, I missed that."

"I was asking what you've planned for your holiday."

"I haven't thought about it yet. Work is still quite busy so I'll probably only get a short break, maybe at the end of August or even in September."

"You do need a holiday, Ben." Ben nodded.

The following weekend Ben considered other ways to try and meet young ladies. He didn't want to try speed dating again just yet. Despite his earlier reservations, he made up his mind to try the lonely hearts-type adverts in the newspapers. On the Sunday morning he purchased several newspapers and checked the local female adverts. One did appeal to him:

Oxfordshire. Attractive professional female, thirties, dark hair and blue eyes, seeks local professional male for possible relationship.

He gritted his teeth and called the relevant number. He left a message saying:

Hi. My name's Ben. I'm thirty-one years old and I live and work in Oxford as an accountant. My hobbies include travelling, eating out, theatre, cinema and sports. I follow a local rugby team. I am about five foot ten, medium build with light brown hair and brown eyes. My friends would describe me as a genuine, open-minded and tolerant person. It would be great to hear from you soon.

If speed dating had not worked for him so far, even after having seen the young ladies in person beforehand, then it was very possible that lonely hearts-type adverts might well not work for him either. He just had to hope that there were some genuine people advertising that way. Anyhow, it seemed worth giving it a try.

On the following Tuesday evening Ben got home late. He had been to the gym straight from work. He was pleased to find a text message from the lonely hearts advert that he had responded to. It read:

Selina Tue 23 Jun 20.06
• *Hello Ben. Thank u v much 4 yr nice msg. How about meeting up 4 a drink Thurs even in Kidlington? Regards, Selina.*

Ben clasped his hands as if in prayer and looked upwards and said,

"Thank you." He realised that he should not really have to be so grateful in an ideal world, yet he appreciated a further opportunity to meet a young lady. Surely this date could not be any worse than the last two dates he had just had?

As it was late now, Ben decided that it would be more polite to respond to Selina's text the following morning. He got to work promptly at 8.50am and watched the clock for the next ten minutes. Karen walked past Ben's office and smiled as if she had half guessed that Ben's preoccupation related to some young lady. At 9am Ben sent Selina a text:

Ben Smith Wed 24 Jun 09.00
• *Hi Selina. Many thanx 4 yr txt. I can get 2 Kidlington 4 7.30pm-8pm if that's OK with u. Look 4wrd 2 meeting u. Kind regards, Ben.*

Ben was fidgety for the rest of the day at work. He kept glancing at his mobile phone in anticipation of receiving a further text from Selina. Karen kept smiling but did not say anything. That evening he was preparing to go out to the cinema when there was a further text from Selina:

Selina Wed 24 Jun 19.47
• *Hi again. That's great. C u there @ 8pm 2moro eve.*

So this is going to go ahead, Ben thought, and felt pleased. It was another date, and maybe it might actually work out this time. Anyhow, he could now go out now and enjoy the cinema and then focus on meeting Selina on the following evening.

On the Thursday work was going as usual. Ben felt slightly anxious, as a client meeting which had started quite early did not finish until 5pm. Roger then asked Ben to prepare a note of that meeting but said that it could be finished the following day. Ben could have performed somersaults on hearing that. He raced home, shaved, jumped in the shower and then put on the same clothes that he had worn when he had gone to meet Emma. He could not help feeling a little tense. Inevitably, the two failed dates had served to damage his confidence. He hoped that Selina would be an attractive, slightly older lady who would be more mature than Rebecca and Emma. He really prayed that she would not react to him in the same negative and unpleasant way that they both had done.

Ben drove to Kidlington, got there in fairly good time and parked his car. He looked around and waited for Selina to arrive. He did not expect her to be early and resigned himself to a wait. At about 8.15pm his mobile phone rang. Selina had just arrived. Ben looked round and saw her and waved. She was quite tall, in fact taller than Ben. Ben noticed that she had a pretty face with her dark brown hair and blue eyes, although she had not put any make-up on and she was only wearing jeans and trainers. This was not what Ben had expected from her personal advert.

They greeted each other. Selina smiled thinly.

"Hi. There's a wine bar along the road. Shall we go there?"

"OK," said Ben, thinking that she could look a lot prettier with make-up on. "How's your day been?" He pushed open the door of the wine bar but Selina looked as if she didn't appreciate that polite gesture. She went in and sat at a table near the window.

"My day… " she repeated, picking up the wine list. "Well, I feel quite tired, actually. I'm looking forward to the weekend." She flashed him a look as she said that. The waiter came and took their order. Selina asked for red wine. Ben chose white. He waited for her to ask a question but realised that it was up to him to keep the conversation going.

"I've only just moved to Oxford," he told her. "My family live in Winchester. I do like it here, although the work is a bit intense at the moment. What about you? Do you live in the town?"

Selina nodded.

"Do you work here?"

She shrugged and sipped at her drink before answering.

"I'm self-employed. I work as a web designer."

She wasn't giving much away. Ben persevered.

"I'm glad you came to meet me. It's hard getting to know anyone outside work and everyone there disappears as soon as the office closes. I've got past thirty now and I really want to meet a nice young lady and settle down. Eventually… " he added, seeing Selina frown at this. He hurried on, talking about some of his interests, although he was aware that it was traditionally considered to be impolite to spend too much time talking about them. When he mentioned the local rugby team, Selina immediately interrupted.

"Huh. I can't stand rugby."

"Oh?" snapped Ben, then checked himself. It would be silly to argue. He continued, "I wasn't that much into rugby myself in the past but I've learned to take an interest in it and now I like it better, as I understand the game. I also noticed that there were plenty of young ladies who attended the home matches."

"Perhaps they were there for other reasons," Selina laughed sarcastically.

There was a silence while Ben swallowed down his desire to retort. He forced a smile and asked Selina about what her hobbies and interests were. She struggled to say anything more than that she liked to hang out with friends in pubs and wine bars. She then added,

"I have a friend called Rob. I visit him quite a lot at weekends. He has a yacht but sometimes I stay at his place."

That was a surprise. It even made Ben wonder why Selina had actually needed to do a personal advert.

"Do you like foreign travel?" Ben wondered if this would interest her. "I would like to visit Machu Picchu and the Great Wall of China one day."

Selina pulled her mouth down.

"I'm not fussed about going abroad. I've got most of what I want locally."

"Oh. Well... er... what sort of books do you like? What are you reading at the moment?"

Selina snarled, "What sort of question is that to ask?"

That was it. Ben had had quite enough.

"Could you please tell me what the problem is?" he said sharply. "I contacted you in good faith, genuinely hoping that we might be able to get on. I have only tried to be polite and take an interest in you. In return you just seem to have spat fire at me." Selina puffed her cheeks out but didn't say anything. Ben continued. "I didn't expect this sort of reaction, given what you put in your personal advert."

"Look, you're a nice bloke," said Selina not reacting to Ben's annoyance, "However, you're not at all what I'm looking for and I think you really do need to wake up to the real world." She got up to leave. Ben stared at her for a second and then looked away. They did not say goodbye to each other and it was a slight relief for Ben that Selina didn't seem anxious about him leaving or following her. Not that she needed to flatter herself about that. Ben wondered whether she might even have a heavy waiting for her outside. He sat for a moment and then checked his mobile phone. It was barely 8.30pm.

Suddenly, Ben was furious. Of course he had grasped that Selina seemed to have no proper interests and was only really concerned about her immediate group of friends. If the story about her friend Rob with his yacht was true then the hint was obviously that any man looking to woo her would need to have a considerable amount of money to start with, and also would have to contend with an immediate rival. Nonetheless, Ben did feel bad.

So now three young ladies had all rejected him in turn. He still had no idea what the real problem was, although two of them had said that he was not the sort of man they were looking for and Selina had also told him that she thought he needed to wake up to the real world. What did she actually mean by that?

Ben then felt total despair. What could he do? Why did he get this awful reaction when he was simply trying to show a genuine interest in those young ladies? Was this the way they were all going to behave towards him? Should he perhaps have stayed in the City and tried to get to know some young ladies properly there? They were definitely a different breed from these three he had just met.

His dismay was compounded by the fact that he was well aware that this was not how any young lady would react to any man she did like and wanted to get to know better. Had he suddenly become Quasimodo's twin brother in the eyes of young ladies? Ben tried to laugh to himself about it just being a bad set of circumstances, although when he thought about these three dates his laughter almost turned to despair. He picked up his wine glass, looked at it and put it down again. He'd better go home. There was no point in him hanging round the wine bar on his own.

Feeling very desolate back in his flat, Ben decided to telephone Simon. Without giving too many details or repeating everything that those young ladies had said, Ben explained to Simon what had happened on those dates.

"You know, I did all this in good faith and genuinely hoped that these were young ladies that I could get to know better – and, hopefully, with a view to a serious relationship in due course. I tried to be polite to all of them. I didn't ask them improper or personal questions: rather, I tried to take a genuine interest in them… and their response was simply to shun me and to walk off rudely and abruptly."

Simon laughed and said,

"Ben, I think you might have been too earnest and keen for those women. I don't think they were looking for their Mr Right on their dates with you, somehow. Did you consider that they might not even have been single, and were just looking for a night out and nothing else?'

Ben gulped. He had not thought of this. He remembered a couple of successful rowdy nights out in the City a couple of years earlier, but had not considered that anyone might be using speed dating and personal adverts in newspapers for such purposes. Then Ben realised that perhaps Selina's comment had some truth in it after all.

Simon continued.

"I probably shouldn't mention it but I was having a laugh at a family friend who was moaning that his son's girlfriend spends all her time at their house.' Ben really gnashed his teeth on hearing that.

Simon then changed the subject to say that he and Natalie would be leaving for their holiday to Mauritius for a month that following weekend and, due to their preparations, Simon would not be able to meet up with Ben for their usual fortnightly drinks that Thursday. That hardly made Ben feel any better. He nonetheless wished them both a fantastic holiday and looked forward to seeing Simon again with all his holiday snaps when he came back. Simon said that he did not know if he could help but that he would ask his and Natalie's circle of friends to see if they could introduce Ben to any young ladies. Ben somehow did not feel inspired by this now, fearing some further very short blind dates – which would more than likely result in the young ladies seeing red for whatever reason, being unpleasant to him and then storming off. This was certainly not what Ben had envisaged would happen when he had first moved to Oxford.

Chapter Eleven

Ludmila walked back home, her steps slowing as she reached the end of the road. It was going to be another evening of putting the children to bed and then watching television or perhaps some reading. The routine was not difficult, but it was beginning to become rather boring. Some of her friends from her English group were going clubbing that evening to celebrate the end of the course as well as passing their exams. However, Mr and Mrs Foster were going to an important dinner party and were depending on her to be at home to look after Emily and Jeremy.

Ludmila sighed. Well… at least she had passed her exam and could now enrol on the next English course, which would be an intensive one. This time it would be a real challenge to reach the standard in written and spoken English, but she would still work hard and succeed. Her determination was even stronger now. She still very much wanted to be able to enrol on a business studies course at a university in the near future. That evening she would write to Valeria and tell her the good news about passing her exam. She hoped that Nicolae would be reassured and consider that she was working and was also behaving well.

Given the choice of spending her evenings at home with the children or of being back on the farm in Crocmaz, Ludmila smiled to herself. Life was so much more interesting here. If only…

Inevitably, Ben spent an uneasy Saturday. He kept himself busy all day with chores: housework and ironing, followed by a visit to the gym in the early afternoon. He then decided to treat himself to a nice dinner at Dimitris'parents' restaurant. Dimitris looked tired. He had just finished his exams and was worried about whether he had passed them. Ben told Dimitris that he was sure that he had done well and to try and take his mind off the exams. Of course, Ben himself found it almost impossible not to think about the failed dates he had recently had.

"Is everything OK?" said Dimitris'father, looking keenly at Ben.

"Fine, thank you," replied Ben politely. He certainly wasn't going to discuss what was bothering him, although he did find it rather difficult not to look glum. The old man shook his head and raised his shoulders in a shrug as he looked from one young man to the other.

On the Sunday Ben read his newspaper very slowly to pass the morning. He decided to go to the Ashmolean Museum in the afternoon. He was particularly fascinated by the oriental collections. Seeing them would help, if only very slightly, to take his mind off his failed dates for a little while.

Quite by chance, as he was walking to the Ashmolean Museum, Ben saw Jess from the speed dating event he had attended. He noticed that she was on her own and was carrying a couple of bags of shopping. Ben hadn't forgotten that Jess had not chosen him as one of the people that wanted to see again but nonetheless Ben decided that he would say hello to her again and be polite.

"Hello, Jess. Do you remember me from the speed dating event back in May in Woodstock?" Jess looked around her quite nervously and then said,

"Shush. You don't know who might be listening. And what do you want?' Ben was a bit taken aback by this.

"I just happened to see you again. Anyway, how are you and how did you get on at that event?"

"Well, it's got nothing to do with you," Jess replied very abruptly. Ben was starting to feel somewhat offended now but thought it was worth one attempt to try and break the ice.

"If you are not seeing anyone at the moment then I would be happy to go out with you sometime, if you like," said Ben. Jess looked at Ben very intently for a moment before responding,

"But I don't know if I could trust you. You might even be seeing some other girls for all I know."

That really was the last straw for Ben. However, rather than say anything about Jess's rudeness or her seemingly bad experiences with other young men either, he calmed himself and then said,

"OK. I'm sorry I bothered you. Goodbye, then." Ben walked off quickly. That really was a nasty shock: to be accused of seeing other young women, when the reality was that no young woman seemed to have any interest in getting to know Ben at all. He calmed down afterwards by reminding himself that Jess hadn't wanted to see him after that speed dating event – which might have explained, at least in part, why she had been so hostile to him just now. But those types of accusations were totally uncalled-for.

Ben enjoyed going round the Ashmolean Museum again and it helped to take his mind off Jess and his failed dates. However, much to his great shock, just as he was looking through the ancient Chinese collection he saw Rebecca walking past arm in arm with a young man. She did not see Ben but he certainly noticed her, and that she was perfectly happy with her young man and was actually taking an interest in the museum. Ben could simply not believe his eyes. What was this? *Jekyll and Hyde*? Rebecca had given Ben the impression that she had no interest in anything cultural, yet here she was in the Ashmolean Museum with another young man on a Sunday afternoon.

Ben felt both angry and offended. So Rebecca's negative

reaction to him had been personal after all – as he had feared, deep down, and it also suggested that young ladies would make an effort and even take an interest in things they did not particularly like when they found a young man they fancied.

So, anyone but me, he thought. And where would he go from here? Ben gnashed his teeth and then, as he continued to wander round the museum, felt even grumpier than he had done after bumping into Jess.

In the early evening Ben was sitting out on the porch of his flat watching the sun setting. He was brooding on Simon's words about those young ladies not having been genuinely looking for long-term relationships. Well, surely that was just not true. He only had to think of Rebecca going round the Ashmolean Museum with a young man, and that made him feel worse than ever. Why could he not make contact in such a way, to attract young ladies?

Ben frowned over the problem for a while. Then he suddenly remembered Linda from the speed dating event. He still had her mobile number. So why not give her a call? It would surely be better than what had already happened to him. He pulled out his phone and keyed in the number.

"Hello?"

"Hello, Linda. It's Ben. Do you remember me from the speed dating event in Woodstock?"

"Hello, young man. Yes, I remember you. How you doing?"

"I'm fine, thanks. Sorry I didn't get back to you sooner. Do you fancy meeting up?"

"Of course. Why don't you come over to Ducklington in about an hour?"

"Great. See you there."

Ben didn't bother showering or shaving. He jumped straight into his car and drove off to Ducklington. He went straight to the pub. To his surprise Linda was already there, and she beckoned him over to a quiet table in a corner of the pub. Ben smiled and was pleasantly surprised as Linda kissed him. He noticed that she was wearing the same black jacket that she had worn to the speed dating event but he was impressed by her short skirt and her high heels. Ben went and got their drinks.

Linda seemed quite at ease. She took a mouthful of wine and sat back. She smiled at Ben and started chatting about recent events.

"My last bloke, he took me and my kids to Malta on holiday. We had a great time snorkelling but when we got back a couple of weeks ago, he suddenly said he wanted to go back to his ex." Linda shrugged her shoulders and pinched Ben's cheek. "What about you, then? I'm sure you've had some girlfriends since that speed dating event." Ben was taken aback but, equally, he didn't need any reminding about his failed dates with Rebecca or Emma.

"Err... no. Not so far," he replied rather awkwardly.

"But what about that pretty young doctor girl? Bet you fancied her, right?"

That really stung Ben but he did his best not to let it show and didn't answer.

"Like that, was it?" laughed Linda.

Ben then noticed Linda letting one of her shoes flop and he was impressed by her black toenails. Linda then moved slightly closer to him.

"So, any plans for holidays soon?"

Suddenly he felt Linda's hand on his knee. Then it slid up, up... until it was at the top of his leg. Her fingers pressed into his flesh. Her mouth was smiling but her eyes were sharp. He swallowed hard.

"Actually, I haven't got round to it yet. Perhaps I'll have a couple of day's holiday in August or September."

Linda suddenly moved away. Ben thought he saw her press her mobile phone but nonetheless it rang and Linda stood up and answered it.

"Hello. Oh, no. That's terrible. OK, Max," she said, "I'll be there very shortly, love." She put her phone away and looked up, "I'm sorry, Ben. My son's unwell and he needs me now."

"Of course," said Ben, staring at her. Linda picked up her bag and left with just a "Bye".

Ben frowned. He didn't recall Linda having a son called Max. He realised straight away what had happened. He felt ashamed of himself, even though Linda was probably only after a man for another holiday for her and her family. Nonetheless, Ben had behaved as badly if not worse than Rebecca, Emma, Selina and Jess had all behaved towards him. He had only been to see Linda for a cheap evening out. Jess's comment might even have been justified by his behaviour that evening if she had been there to see it, although she had perhaps contributed in part to him deciding to go and see Linda in the first place.

Ben knew perfectly well that Linda was not the right woman for him. But why had he then gone to see her? Being single was still really getting to him. He didn't bother checking his watch. He'd probably beaten the record for his shortest date, but this time he was more taken up by his feeling of shame. He didn't linger, and drove home. His head was down for the rest of that evening. Ben promised himself that he would not behave like that again. It had simply compounded his agony. Ben shook his head as he went to bed. He really wanted to dream again about walking along a seafront hand in hand with his Miss Right, although he felt as though he actually had more chance of winning the lottery jackpot at that particular moment.

Chapter Twelve

Ben's despair turned to real anger the following week, even though he still felt very bad about how he had behaved in going to see Linda. He knew he was being too quiet at work, but when he felt so moody and withdrawn he couldn't manage anything better. He did try not to take his frustrations out on anyone unintentionally, but it just kept overwhelming him.

How dare those young ladies behave like that towards him? he thought. He still wondered if he had grown a second head or something since living in Oxford, and what the real reason was for all that unnecessary hostility towards him.

On the Tuesday evening Ben represented his firm at the business group's annual dinner. The current president, Robert, would be handing over to the incoming president, Mike, for the forthcoming business year. Ben had never experienced anything similar in the City and he enjoyed the pomp and ceremony of the event.

At 7.30pm he arrived at the venue wearing black tie. Of course he felt disappointed that Simon was not there, as he was now on holiday with Natalie. Looking round, however, Ben saw plenty of acquaintances from the business group and he chatted quite happily with them during the pre-dinner drinks. Then as the group were sitting down for dinner, one of the senior members told his wife that she would be sitting next to this *handsome young man.* There was a general laugh and Ben laughed with them, wishing inside that there was a pretty young lady sitting next to him.

The wife was a charming lady and she and Ben chatted

comfortably throughout the meal. They had reached the coffee stage when she asked Ben his age and whether he had a wife or girlfriend. Ben shrugged his shoulders.

"I'm single," he said, rather abruptly, and changed the subject.

After that the lady turned to the person on her other side.

Oh dear, Ben thought. He had been impolite. She wasn't to know she had hit a raw nerve. In fact he felt annoyed that all anyone seemed to want to know was whether or not he was married. Ben fumed for the remainder of the evening. He understood that he absolutely had to keep his anguish and annoyance about being single to himself. It was imperative not to let it show either professionally or socially, as it did cause offence to other people. They would find it hard to believe what had happened to him on those recent dates. All right, he accepted what Simon had said at Christmas: that the world did not owe him a wife. Yet Ben felt very bitter. Again he asked himself how and why he managed to put off all the young ladies he met. He knew he was exaggerating but it did seem that by his age everyone else – at least locally – was in a steady relationship, if not already married.

For a while Ben wondered if he would be happy now if he had stayed in his last serious relationship. At university he and Alison had been a couple. That had not pleased his parents, as they had felt he should have been concentrating more on his finals. In the event that relationship fizzled out within a year. And then about three years ago he had become very close to Jennifer, who was a fellow trainee accountant. It had been fine for a time, but when Jennifer had accepted a better-paid job in Newcastle they agreed that neither of them could sustain a long-distance relationship. Ben had been sad at the time but he had assumed he would find another girlfriend fairly soon afterwards. Now he wished he had not taken that for granted.

Ben also suddenly realised something very fundamental.

Whilst he had frequently been baffled by other peoples' relationships, he saw that there needed to be some sort of connection between people to begin and to sustain any kind of relationship. Much as the media had always seemed to suggest that chance meetings could lead to long-term relationships, as far as Ben was aware those chance meetings rarely happened. The other important thing was that although Ben didn't really suffer from any pseudo-macho pretentions, he now accepted that he might need to ask for help where appropriate (and in the right way) in trying to meeting young ladies. So, changing his mind, Ben now decided that he would ask Simon for – hopefully – an introduction or two to some other young ladies locally when Simon came back from his holiday, and that he would wait until then.

The next day at work Ben apologised to his Karen for the way he had behaved recently. She asked if everything was all right and suddenly he blurted out how upset he felt about his recent failed dates.

Karen frowned and shook her head.

"That was very nasty of them," she said. "They may well have changed their minds beforehand or, quite simply, they were never that bothered in the first place." She hesitated for a moment and then added, "Actually… my brother was in his thirties before he met his wife, and I frequently heard similar stories from him before he met her. Anyway, he's now settled and happy."

Ben realised she was trying to offer him some comfort. He nodded and tried to smile.

"I did notice that you have been a bit out of sorts these last couple of weeks," Karen went on. She tapped a finger to her lips. "Just a minute. I've remembered something. I might actually be able to help." Somewhat surprised, Ben looked at her intently.

"A friend of mine lives in Bournemouth. Her neighbours have a young lady from Moldova staying with them. She is their au pair and is having English classes too. I think she is looking to make some friends here. If you are interested I can perhaps get her contact details for you."

Ben froze for a second.

Moldova? Where was that, and what would she be like? he thought. But then he suddenly nodded. This might actually be a good way to get an introduction to a young lady.

"OK," he said. "I really appreciate that. May I think about it first before you do anything?"

"Of course," said Karen.

During his lunch break Ben thought it over. Like most other young men, he had noticed the Eastern European girls with their pretty faces as he went about his daily business in the City. A lot of them had come to England in the past few years but he'd never got to know any of them personally. However, it had not been a surprise when their boyfriends, husbands and children had come over a couple of years later. Anyhow, could a Moldovan girl actually be the right girl for him? Would she herself have any sort of agenda in this country, and would she be here alone? His parents had always been quite open-minded as far as other countries and cultures were concerned and had taken him and Helen on a few foreign holidays when they were growing up, and had also encouraged them both to try and understand different cultures. Ben knew that it was imperative to try and understand a foreign person according to the customs and traditions of the country where they had grown up, rather than expecting them to immediately adapt to a new way of life here.

He researched Moldova on the internet on his mobile phone. He was taken aback to see that it was Europe's poorest country and it raised his concerns again, as to what this young lady might want from him. Furthermore, he still clung to the romantic vision of his Miss Right as a beautiful, slim young lady walking hand in hand with him along the seashore. He had never thought of her as being from a foreign country. But after his experience with Rebecca, Emma, Selina – and, to a lesser extent, with Jess – why was he so attached to the idea of automatically finding an English girl? And he was getting ahead of himself anyway.

One step at a time. Don't be too earnest. Hadn't Simon warned him about that? If things didn't work out with this young lady he would not be any worse off than he already was.

Without any further hesitation, Ben jumped up and went to find Karen. She was just opening a packet of mints and she offered him one. He took it with a nod of thanks.

"Karen, I would really like to meet this young lady. Please pass on my contact details and let her know that she is welcome to contact me directly."

"OK. I'll give my friend a call and let you know," said Karen.

Ben felt relieved that he had done that. Maybe that young lady might not want to meet him. She could have reservations as well about getting involved with a foreigner.

Wait and see, he thought. Meanwhile, in another speedy decision, Ben decided to look for a short summer holiday that he could take in the next month or so. He'd get his chores done quickly and go to a couple of travel agents to get some ideas for holiday places as well as doing some research on the internet.

So that's my weekend sorted, he thought on Friday morning.

Later that morning, Karen came into Ben's office.

"I spoke to my friend and she called me back last night. The young lady is called Ludmila. This is her mobile number." Karen handed Ben a piece of paper with Ludmila's mobile number on it. "She's happy for you to call her."

"Oh, err… thank you, Karen." Ben nodded and Karen gave him a kindly smile as she went back out. Ben looked at the bit of paper. Ludmila.

What will she be like? he thought again, with his concerns resurfacing. He'd better wait until he got home to phone her.

Fortunately, work was quiet and Ben was able to leave the office shortly after 5pm. That was quite unusual, but on that day he was glad of it.

At about 6.30pm Ben pulled out that bit of paper. He was not sure if it was appropriate to try and call Ludmila on a Friday evening – but then, there seemed no particular reason to wait. He took a deep breath and dialled Ludmila's mobile number.

"Hello?" The voice was quite deep and Ben could hear the sharp vowel sound.

"Hello. Is that Ludmila? This is Ben. How are you?"

"Hello, Ben. I'm good. How are you?"

"Very well, thank you. Is this a good time to call?"

"Oh, yes. Is fine. In the day I am busy. I work as au pair. I also have English course."

"That's very interesting. I am an accountant in Oxford. How do you like England so far?"

"So so. I want better job here one day."

"I understand. Err… if you don't mind me asking… "

"Don't be shy, Ben." Ludmila chuckled.

"Would you like to meet up sometime?"

"Of course. Why don't you come to Bournemouth on Sunday?"

Ben blinked. Well, Ludmila certainly had a very direct manner.

"Fine," he said, with a bit of an effort.

There was a noise in the background and he could hear someone calling "Ludmila."

"OK. I have dinner with family now. I see you about midday at train station. Vot you look like?"

"Very handsome," joked Ben.

"I decide," Ludmila laughed.

"Seriously… light brown hair and brown eyes; five foot ten and medium build."

"OK. So you call me when you arrive."

"Thank you. I look forward to meeting you. Goodbye."

Ben raised his eyebrows. He laughed to himself about Ludmila's direct manner. This time he was going to treat it as a day out. This was hardly what he had had in mind when he had decided to leave the City the previous year: a girl from Moldova. Whoever could have foreseen that? Would she actually turn up at the station? Ben didn't know Bournemouth at all, as his family had always been to Poole as their seaside town. But it might actually turn out to be a bit of an adventure. Tomorrow he'd look for a new shirt; something suitable for a day at the seaside.

Better get a map of Bournemouth as well, he decided, picking up his novel to while away the rest of Friday evening. He was not overly worried about Sunday as he did not expect anything much to happen, even if he did actually meet Ludmila.

Chapter Thirteen

Ben was up promptly at 7am on the Sunday morning. While he drank his coffee and prepared for his day out he kept his apprehension at bay, but as he set off in his car he had to admit that he did feel a little worried. The previous rejections had still badly dented his confidence. Even the fact that this young lady wanted to meet up at the train station was puzzling him. It seemed an ideal place for an ambush or perhaps a quick brush-off. But he reminded himself that she was staying with an English family and that he had been put in touch with her via a colleague. He shrugged.

OK, maybe it was a rather odd place to meet up for a first date – but whatever, he thought.

It was a ninety-odd mile drive from Oxford to Bournemouth. He reached the town just after 10.30am. Knowing that it was a popular seaside town, he was surprised at how quiet the roads were. Well, at least that was a bonus. The streets were wide and gave a peaceful impression. He soon found a multi-storey car park in the town centre. It was a pay-on-departure car park. Ben gave a sardonic smile, remembering how his previous dates had all run off so fast that he would hardly have needed a ticket for more than half an hour. As he had a good hour to kill before meeting Ludmila he decided to have a quick look round to see what interesting shops and activities were available. And he needed to find where the train station was, and maybe he would have time for a coffee.

Just before 12pm Ben walked to the station. He was now feeling quite nervous. He had no idea what Ludmila would look like and he realised that he had not even asked her. Would she be short, overweight and unattractive? Hopefully not. Ben still felt a little uncomfortable too at the thought of meeting her at the train station, and whether she would actually be there alone. Promptly at midday he called her number but there was no answer. He tightened his lips. A text message, then:

Ben Smith Sun 5 Jul 12.02
- *Hi Ludmila. I'm @ train station. Look 4wrd 2 meeting u shortly. Regards, Ben*

Still there was no response. Ben looked around and saw a couple of trains arrive and all the people coming and going. Of course he noticed the pretty girls, especially those wearing short skirts and high heels. He wondered how Ludmila would be dressed if indeed she was still coming to meet him. After about twenty minutes Ben was hesitating as to whether he had been stood up. He would call her once more before giving up. He pulled out his phone and was pressing the keys when a voice behind him said,

"Hello. Ben?"

Ben whisked round in surprise and he gasped with amazement when he saw a beautiful young lady with dark blonde hair and big green eyes and a very slim figure. Wow!

"Y... e... s. Ludmila? Err... delighted to meet you." His voice sounded strange: not surprising when his heart was pounding so hard he could scarcely breathe. She was stunning. And she was smiling at him.

They shook hands quite formally and then Ludmila did something which Ben found highly amusing. She stared directly at both of his trouser pockets as if she was inspecting them. Ben had his wallet, mobile phone, credit cards and car keys as well as a couple of tissues in them. Ludmila then nodded. Meanwhile, Ben had been examining her. She was wearing a light blue sports top, jeans and trainers. This was hardly summer attire but Ben assumed that she might have had a more conservative dress sense, perhaps due to the way in which she had been brought up.

Ludmila indicated a road leading towards the beach.

"Shall we walk towards park? Is very nice. Then we can have game of crazy golf. Yes?"

"Oh, err... yes, of course." Ben was still dazzled. As they walked along at a fairly brisk pace he did notice lots of men staring at Ludmila. Then he saw how their eyes switched to him. He enjoyed this attention and smiled to himself. But now Ludmila was talking again.

"I come from Crocmaz, in Ştefan Vodă in Moldova."

"Who?" asked Ben.

"No, not person. Region," she laughed. "Now I tell you about me. I am twenty-four. I have older brother and lovely little sister. I miss her very much." She swallowed hard. "My father was a farmer but he cannot work any more. He is ill. My brother runs farm. He is married with baby son. He give up his job to run farm. Me, I study at university for one year. It was business studies course. But when my father was ill, I had to stop and go back home." She sighed. "There, I talk enough. Now you."

Ben was still digesting all this. She was just so different from English girls, and he liked her direct manner.

"Right," he said. "My turn, then. I have one sister older than me, and she is married with two children. My parents live in Winchester... "

"Close to here," commented Ludmila. "But you... ?"

"I live and work in Oxford now. I'm an accountant. I hope to become a partner one day and stay with my firm for the rest of my career. How about you?"

"I don't mind being au pair. But one day, I want to work in marketing." Ben raised his eyebrows at this, but the conversation ended as they had reached the park.

Unsurprisingly, Ludmila won the game of crazy golf easily. Ben had not played the game for some years and he assumed that Ludmila might have played on this particular crazy golf course quite recently. Afterwards they went on an open bus and had a long trip around Bournemouth. Ludmila pointed out one or two places she had visited in the town.

Then she did something that really touched Ben. She showed him some photographs of herself and some female friends during a recent visit to London.

Ben jokingly pointed at one of the pictures of Ludmila.

"Who's that?" he said. She stared at him with a question in her eyes.

"Vot you mean? I can't recognise my own picture?" Ben smiled and then Ludmila grinned. "Oh… you joke, huh?"

"They're very nice pictures," said Ben reassuringly. He noticed that Ludmila did not show him any pictures of any young men in her visit to London. Perhaps that was deliberate or maybe she had conservative views in such matters as well.

Ben smiled to himself. So far he was thoroughly enjoying the company of this beautiful young lady. He was still noticing how different Ludmila was from any of the young ladies he had met recently, and even from the girls he had met earlier in his life. He was still also appreciating the attention he was getting, with people assuming that he was her boyfriend. But most of all, so far, Ludmila – despite having a firm and slightly abrupt manner – had shown none of the unpleasantness that the other young ladies had shown him during his recent dates, and did not seem to feel any need to do so. Ben wondered if this might have been due in part to the business world not yet having negatively impacted on her. Whatever the reasons, he very much appreciated it.

Any lingering thoughts about Rebecca, Emma, Selina and even Jess soon disappeared. Here was a beautiful young lady who could easily have knocked them all for six. Ben wanted to hold hands with Ludmila, hug her and kiss her – and perhaps do more – but he had only just met her and he knew that none of that could ever happen unless or until Ludmila wanted it to and that he would, of course, carry on being gentlemanly towards her.

After the bus ride Ludmila said that she wanted to eat, so they headed towards a restaurant that she knew. They passed a cafe when suddenly a young waiter came out, said "Hello" to Ludmila and kissed her on both cheeks. She said,

"Hello, Pierre." He nodded at Ben but did not speak to him. Pierre then asked her how she was and said that there would be a party the following weekend. Ludmila smiled and Pierre realised that there were customers waiting for him and then went off to serve them. Ben and Ludmila walked on. After a short silence, Ben managed to ask,

"Who was that?"

"That is Pierre. He is student and has English course with me." It was clear that Ludmila was not intending to say anything further about Pierre. Ben did not mind him greeting her like that but he thought it was an attempt to show Ben that he was also interested in Ludmila. Mentioning the party in front of him was a definite challenge. Ben shot another glance at this lovely girl, walking along so quietly by his side. But why was he surprised? Obviously Pierre was smitten by her good looks, like everyone else. In another moment Ben guessed that if Ludmila had wanted Pierre as her boyfriend then she could quite easily have done something about it before now.

They had an early dinner in a quiet but smart restaurant.

"My host family bring me here sometimes," Ludmila explained. "You like it?" When Ben said yes, she added, "Yes. Is nice here." It was noticeable too that the waiter serving them liked her. He came to check that they were enjoying their meal more times than was necessary. Ben was starting to feel a little exasperated but noticed that the waiter was smiling at him as if to say that he had grasped that it was Ben's first date with this lovely girl, so Ben smiled and nodded back at the waiter.

While they ate, Ludmila talked a little more about Moldova.

"Is a very poor and small country. We need a lot of foreign help." Ben nodded but was far too considerate to say anything less than polite so he simply responded,

"I hope things improve there very soon."

Then, much to Ben's surprise, Ludmila suddenly asked,

"Vot you think about European Union? Vot will be future?" Wow! Ben almost choked. It would have been unthinkable that any of his previous dates would have wanted to discuss such a topic. This was indeed a challenge, but a good one. They discussed the matter throughout the rest of their meal.

After dinner Ben checked his mobile phone. It was 7pm. The day had flown past. Ben laughed at the thought of how much the car park would cost now. He would never have believed that any first date could have lasted so long. He was nonetheless still so happy to be in the company of this beautiful and fascinating young lady and he really did not want the day to end, but knew that inevitably it would have to fairly shortly.

As they left the restaurant Ludmila said that she would like to go to the cinema. Ben was surprised but nonetheless delighted and asked her to lead the way. He bought the tickets for the film she wanted to see and got popcorn and drinks as well. It was fairly busy in the cinema. Ben's mind was on pleasing Ludmila – who was, hopefully, pleased with all the treats of that day. He would not himself have chosen to see that particular film, but it hardly mattered. He gave her the popcorn and a drink. Ludmila settled down in her seat, smiling and eager to watch the film.

Ben noticed that Ludmila was not trying to lean into him or to hold hands with him. Nor did she make any attempt for their hands to touch by chance, either, so Ben did not bother to try any of those tricks. However, he cheekily decided to blow discreet kisses towards her from the side of his face. He smiled to himself when he saw that every time he did this Ludmila seemed to lean towards him but, unfortunately for him, she did not blow any kisses back.

The film finished at about 10pm. They came out of the cinema and walked along the main road outside.

"What's your week going to be like?" Ben asked.

"Oh, I work as au pair and I have my English classes as usual."

"Now, are you OK to get home from here? It's getting a bit late."

Ludmila nodded.

"You come with me. I show you." Ben walked with her as far as she wanted. At a certain point she stopped. He judged that she didn't want him to see where she lived. Despite still feeling elated about that day Ben felt very nervous, as he would now either have to ask Ludmila the inevitable question or at least drop a major hint along those lines.

"It's been a lovely day, Ludmila. I've really enjoyed meeting you and spending time with you. You are a very nice person. I hope I will see you again and get to know you better."

She looked steadily at him for a few moments and then finally nodded and said,

"I think I understand you."

They shook hands and, to Ben's surprise, her handshake lasted a long time and she smiled warmly at him. Remembering Pierre's greeting earlier that day Ben decided to make his mark on Ludmila as well, so he leaned forward a little nervously and kissed her on the cheek. She smiled at him but moved away. She raised her hand in a little wave, turned the corner and disappeared.

After watching her go Ben made his way back towards the multistorey car park in the town centre. The cost of his ticket was of absolutely no importance. He would gladly have paid double for it. It had been an amazing day. He checked his watch again.

How was it possible that a first date could ever have lasted so long? he thought. Yes, Ludmila was different, but she was beautiful and lively. Just as importantly, she had made Ben feel good about himself. That would almost certainly have seemed impossible that morning before meeting her. Ben's self-esteem was recovering.

It was after midnight when Ben arrived back at his flat in Oxford. He laughed to himself about the time and simply wanted to sing along to 'Perfect Day'. He knew that he would be groggy the following morning, but that was irrelevant. He now felt like a new person, and even dared to think it could be possible that he had just met a young lady who might just turn out to be his Miss Right one day. Although not wanting to disturb the neighbours Ben was too elated to sleep, so he sang and danced for a while in the living room.

Chapter Fourteen

Ben woke up in a very good mood on the Monday morning. He was still singing some of his favourite pop songs as he skipped along to work. Even wondering what Ludmila had meant by her parting phrase, "I think I understand you," could not dampen his mood.

He called out very cheery "Good mornings" to his colleagues, who all smiled and gave him speculative glances. As soon as Karen arrived at work, Ben went to see her.

"I met Ludmila at the weekend," he told her, smiling. "I had such a great time. She was beautiful and also a very nice person. Thank you so much for giving me the opportunity to meet her."

"That's perfectly all right," replied Karen. "Are you going to see her again?"

Ben stopped short for a moment.

"Well… I really hope so." He smiled again briefly but then went straight to his office to start work for the day. Karen's question had suddenly cast a shadow over his pleasurable state of mind. The memory and effect of that almost perfect blind date could not last forever. He so much wanted to get to know Ludmila better. Well… she was very direct, so surely she would send him a message if she wanted to see him again.

The day dragged past. Ben checked his mobile phone incessantly but there was no text message from Ludmila. By the following morning Ben was starting to feel rather down. He was doing some work for a client called Martin, who ran his own printing business near Didcot. As Martin was about to move to Devon, he had invited both Roger and Ben for drinks on the following Saturday. Roger said that he had a prior engagement but that Ben would attend. Ben had to bite back a protest. What would he do if Ludmila suggested meeting up again that weekend?

Unable to bear the suspense any longer, Ben decided that he would have to contact Ludmila first. That evening Ben texted Ludmila. He rewrote the message several times before finally managing to send it:

Ben Smith Tue 7 Jul 19.28

• *Hi Ludmila, I hope u r well & that u r having a pleasant week. I wanted 2 tell u again how much I enjoyed meeting u & the day we spent together in Bournemouth on Sun. I find u a very nice & interesting person & I wld really like 2 c u again & get 2 know u better. I hope u enjoyed Sun 2 & that u wld like 2 c me again. Speak soon. Ben.*

He breathed out a long sigh.

That should get a reply, he thought. *But will it be positive?* He squeezed his eyes shut. He really hoped and prayed that she wanted to see him again. He didn't know if he could cope if she did not.

But the suspense continued at work the next day as there was no response from Ludmila. He went out briefly after work with Tony for a drink. Of course Ben said nothing about Ludmila, nor did he check his mobile phone. Tony talked a lot about his children and how his family were all looking forward to their summer holiday.

"We're going to Barbados. Julie and the kids can barely wait. What about you?"

"I haven't sorted out a holiday yet," replied Ben, shuffling his glass around on the table.

"Well, you should probably get on with it. I assume you're still single?"

Ben nodded but did not answer. He accepted that Tony

would not have realised that he might easily be rubbing salt in the wounds for one lonely young man.

The following day Ben attended a training course in Birmingham. Like all the other attendees there, he had to switch his mobile phone off. It proved very hard to concentrate on the course with his thoughts firmly fixed on Ludmila and his hoping that she would respond to him positively. The funny thing was that there were quite a few attractive young ladies on the course, but Ben did not really give any of them a second look. Ludmila had become that special to him so quickly. Ben did check his mobile during the breaks and at lunchtime but still there was still nothing from Ludmila. When the course was over Ben found it hard to go home. He was not keen to sit at home alone that evening with just the one inevitable thought on his mind. There was no room in his head for music or reading at present.

The Friday did not pass much better. Ben still found it extremely hard to concentrate at work. He spent his lunch break deep in thought as he wandered around. He returned to work a little late and Roger berated him. Ben explained that it was unintentional, but his boss was in a bad mood. Ben was too disheartened to push the matter any further, although he thought Roger might remember that Ben was giving up his Saturday evening anyway.

After work Ben decided to get to the gym to shake off his miserable feelings.

Supermarket, washing, cleaning. What an exciting weekend, he thought, as he shoved his towel into his rucksack and picked up his keys. Then his mobile phone flashed to show that a text message had just arrived. Anxiously, Ben checked. The message was from Ludmila:

Ludmila Fri 10 Jul 19.21
• *Hi Ben. Thank u 4 yr txt. I am good, thanx & I hope u r 2. I enjoyed Sun 2. I liked yr personality even though I saw u only once &*

I did not spend much time with u. I let u know if I can c u again. Have a nice wkend. Ludmila

Ben lost a couple of heartbeats while reading Ludmila's text message several times. He was not sure quite how he should react to it. It was an enormous relief to see that she had not said that she did not like him or that she did not want to see him again. On the other hand, her reply was rather evasive. With an exclamation, Ben suddenly remembered Pierre telling Ludmila about a party that weekend. Was that the reason she was not too interested in him? Pierre had been trying to warn him off, he could see that. With much reluctance, Ben accepted that he could not work out what Ludmila's text message meant. He then set off for the gym, still in a bad mood.

Ben met up with Martin in Didcot on Saturday evening. Martin explained why he was moving down to Devon but said that he was sad to be leaving Oxfordshire. He talked warmly about the help he had received from Triangle Accountants. Ben wished Martin all the best and said he would miss working with him. Then on the Sunday Ben went to Winchester to see his parents on Sunday for lunch. He knew he was a bit moody and quiet but he was too down to make an effort.

"Everything OK?" asked Mr Smith.

"Yes. Fine," said Ben. He then explained about going for drinks with a client the previous evening.

"Are you seeing anyone at the moment?" asked Mrs Smith.

Ben thought for a moment before answering,

"Nobody in particular."

Ben's parents looked at each other meaningfully. Then Mrs Smith rushed into speech, telling him the latest news from his sister Helen. Afterwards, Ben told his parents about going for drinks with Martin on Saturday evening.

"That's very good," said Mr Smith, "I'm sure your boss will be very pleased with you doing that, particularly at the weekend."

Ben smiled and nodded. He enjoyed being praised by his father, who of course understood the extra requirements of Ben's job.

The afternoon slipped away and Ben then drove back to Oxford. Back in his flat – and having had a cup of tea before going to bed, Ben pondered again on the dilemma with Ludmila. He decided that he would only respond to her text message in a couple of days' time. He knew better than to keep hinting at a second date unless or until Ludmila was ready for him to do so. He could not possibly forget his blind date with her and what a wonderful day it had been. However, it could not last forever and he needed to know where he stood with her and – most importantly – whether she wanted to see him again, and then whether they had any sort of future together. Ben's mood that Sunday evening was the opposite of what he had felt driving home on the previous Sunday. He eventually got to sleep, still feeling very restless.

Chapter Fifteen

The following week started slowly and quietly for Ben. Work was fairly relaxed as a lot of the clients of Triangle Accountants were on holiday, as were some of the firm's staff. Barely half the members of the business group were present at the following meeting on the Tuesday lunchtime. People were even being allowed to leave work early. Ben was still feeling very tense, wondering whether or not Ludmila wanted to see him again. He didn't want to seem too eager, but decided he should call Ludmila. That way he would solve this growing problem. But by the evening he decided against it. Her comment about letting him know if she could see him again was self-explanatory. Ludmila was not jumping up and down to see him again and the waiting game was now really starting to get to Ben.

To make matters worse Simon was still away on his long holiday, so there was no meeting for their usual chat. How was he going to get through the lonely week? He recalled that he had enjoyed the pub in Didcot where he had gone for drinks with Martin the previous Saturday. In fact, now he thought about it, he had noticed some quite nice pubs with gardens on the route. In addition, they all seemed to have quite a lot of young people there. It was time to go out a bit more and find a few nice places, whether with or without Ludmila.

During his Friday lunch break Ben started to plan his weekend. He took a look at some of the pubs on his mobile phone and chose a couple to try.

Time to think about a holiday as well, he thought. *I really do need a break.* He put the phone down while he considered where he would like to go when suddenly his mobile phone flashed. It was a text message from Ludmila:

Ludmila Fri 17 Jul 13.45
• *Hi Ben. I hope u r OK. I am free on Sun & can come 2 Oxford if you like. Ludmila.*

Ben drew in a very deep breath. He wanted to shout and jump up in the air. He reread the message slowly. Yes, Ludmila wanted to see him again. Could his dream now be a reality again? He could now freely admit to himself that he liked her so very much that he felt quite giddy with delight. Despite not being a particularly religious person Ben held his hands up above his head as if in prayer. Never mind the long, lonely week he had just spent: he now felt that he could have a very special Sunday ahead of him.

Not wanting to seem too keen, Ben waited an hour before sending a reply. If he left it any longer she might make other arrangements for that day.

Ben Smith Fri 17 Jul 14.46
• *Hi Ludmila. Many thanx 4 yr txt. I'm fine & I hope u r 2. I look 4ward 2 cing u again on Sun. Pls let me know what time u r coming. Ben x*

As he sent the message Ben laughed. With all his usual chores to do he was now going to have a busy Saturday. He must also get to the gym, so that Sunday could be entirely free for Ludmila. Of course, this second date would be very much make or break with her. Either they would be on their way to starting what Ben hoped would be a serious and long-term relationship or that would be it. He felt he would shrivel up if it were the latter.

On the Saturday afternoon Ben sent Ludmila a further text message:

Ben Smith Sat 18 Jul 16.04

• *Hi Ludmila. I hope u r having a nice day. What time r u coming 2 Oxford 2moro & what places wld u like 2 c? I'm really looking 4ward 2 cing u again. Ben x*

Ludmila responded quite quickly:

Ludmila Sat 18 Jul 16.49

• *Hi Ben. I come by train & hope to arrive in Oxford 11am. U show me Oxford. C u 2moro. Ludmila*

Ben was pleased that Ludmila would be arriving at 11am as that would hopefully give them an extra hour together compared to the day in Bournemouth (if she stayed all day). He couldn't help smiling at Ludmila's direct manner. While she was leaving it to Ben to decide what places to show her, it was also clear that in a way it was an order. Ludmila wanted to see Oxford. Well… that was natural enough, and he looked forward to seeing how she would enjoy it.

Ben planned to show her the main sights and possible places to stop for a drink or a rest as they went round. Then he wondered if he should get Ludmila a present or a flower. Reluctantly he decided that she would probably not want a present from him yet and that it would probably be an inconvenience for her to carry a flower around all day, anyway. Ben hoped that there might be a bit of romance, but only if it happened naturally. He didn't need to remind himself that she was from a stricter culture.

Promptly at 8am on the Sunday morning Ben was up and eating his breakfast. The extra hour's sleep had been welcome, and now he was full of energy and hoping that all would go well throughout the day. He glanced out at the sky. It was a bit dull but hopefully it would brighten up later. Ludmila had been quite casually dressed in Bournemouth but Ben decided to dress smartly. He pulled a dark blue polo shirt and chinos out of the wardrobe. As he gulped down his coffee he went through the list of places he would show Ludmila. If he planned the day well they could spend a long time together. Of course, he would allow for Ludmila to get back to Bournemouth at a fairly sensible time if she wanted to.

At the station he checked and saw that the Bournemouth train was on time. He decided not to text her but simply to wait for her in the station as near to the platform as he could get without having to buy a ticket. Looking eagerly for Ludmila, Ben watched all the passengers getting off. Finally he saw her. He drew in a long, deep breath. Ludmila was wearing a white dress and matching white sandals. Ben was very impressed and had some difficulty in controlling his male excitement. He even wondered if Ludmila had managed the journey without any men trying to chat her up. Her outfit was in stark contrast to the clothes she was wearing when they first met two weeks earlier.

Ludmila walked towards him, smiling.

"Hello, Ben," she said.

"Hello, Ludmila." Ben kissed her on both cheeks. He could barely conceal his delight at seeing her again.

"Did you have a good journey?" Ludmila took a step back.

"It was OK, but hot weather," she answered, walking out of the station with him. "Vot we do now?" she enquired, looking round eagerly.

"Oh… " Ben paused. He was still overwhelmed by Ludmila's appearance. "We'll have a walk around the shopping centre and then we'll go to the famous Ashmolean Museum."

Ludmila nodded.

"Good."

While Ben noticed all the attention Ludmila was getting – and the attention he was getting, as well – she seemed just as keen to look at all the shops as she was to talk to him. Ben was still turned on by her dress even if he was slightly disappointed that she hadn't painted her toenails, something he had always admired in attractive ladies. He thought to himself that he had to be a bit bolder, so he put his hand through her arm. Ludmila did not seem to mind, and Ben felt that he had made a little bit of progress. Of course. Why was she dressed so smartly, if not to impress him?

Ben asked about her week but certainly did not ask about Pierre or whether she had been to the party that Pierre had mentioned. He noticed that Ludmila did not say what she had done the previous weekend. Ben simply said that he had had a night out with friends the previous Saturday.

In the Ashmolean Museum Ludmila was very impressed by the Middle Eastern and the Far Eastern collections and Ben tried to explain a little bit about them. Afterwards they had a drink in the Eagle and Child pub, and Ben told her about the famous writers who had used to frequent that pub. She nodded and said,

"I like Oxford. It has good shops and interesting museum and is big town."

"It's always full of students," said Ben.

"That is me too," laughed Ludmila.

They then went to the Botanic Garden. Ben still had his hand through her arm, which she didn't mind, but he did notice that she made no effort to hold his arm or his hand. He told himself that he just had to be patient and not force the (hopeful) blossoming relationship. He did not need any reminding of how special and important it was for him to be spending time with a young lady and how lucky he was that Ludmila was beautiful, as well as being lively and bright.

As they walked along he asked about her plans over the summer.

"My friends and I, we go to Italy for two weeks in August," said Ludmila. Ben's heart sank completely on hearing that. He was not concerned about her friends but the thought of Ludmila going away bothered him. He felt as though he was missing her already.

"Where are you going?" Ben asked politely.

"We visit Rome, Florence and Milan."

"Are you going with other au pair girls?"

"Yes. Why?"

Ben did not answer. They walked on a little way. He did not need reminding of the irony of him wanting to visit Italy.

"And you?" asked Ludmila.

"I haven't planned a holiday yet due to work commitments." That was true. However, since he had met Ludmila, Ben had put his holiday plans on hold. Of course she had arranged her holiday before she had met him, but she was hardly going to change any holidays for Ben at this stage. He would not have expected her to, either.

Ludmila shook her head.

"That's not good. You should have holiday."

Ben realised that she was right. He did need a holiday, and he should get on and arrange a short break for himself. Now that he was aware of when she would be away he could perhaps have a week's holiday then – or perhaps, better still – have a holiday with her later in the year if their relationship had developed that far by then. The thought of a holiday with Ludmila made him smile.

"Vot?" said Ludmila, again unintentionally emphasising her Eastern European accent.

"Nothing," said Ben, trying not to smile too much. He then added, "Yes, I will try and book myself a holiday soon."

"Good," said Ludmila.

They then walked past several of the colleges in Oxford and the Sheldonian Theatre and The Bridge of Sighs. Ludmila had a look in the bookshops too. She was impressed by the size of the shops and the variety of books. She shook her head, saying,

"I like to read but I don't have time to read just for pleasure. I must study, you know."

"Oh, yes, I remember those days," said Ben. "Are you

hungry?" She nodded eagerly, so he took her along to Dimitris' parents' restaurant. The family were all very surprised to see Ben accompanied by a beautiful young lady. They all greeted them both very warmly. Dimitris smiled at Ben the whole time he was there, and his father nodded approvingly at Ben too.

Ludmila chose the lamb koftas and a bean salad. She seemed very pleased and told Ben that the food reminded her of Moldovan cooking. She rejected the offer of wine, asking for a fruit juice instead. During the meal she talked a bit more about her life in Bournemouth.

"My host family is very nice. Children are sweet. I am happy there. English course is difficult but I make progress."

"That's very good," said Ben. "Everything's fine with my job. I used to work in London but am much happier now. I still want to stay in Oxford with my current firm for the rest of my career."

They chatted more but Ludmila did not ask where Ben lived in Oxford, nor did she express any wish to see his flat. In any case, it would not be appropriate to invite her to go there. Also, while she was very open and seemed to be pleased with the way the day was going she made no comment about any further meetings. He decided not to jeopardise the day by trying to push for that.

When Ludmila made a brief trip to the washroom, Dimitris whispered to Ben,

"Well done, mate. She suits you."

"Fingers crossed it works out," replied Ben. Dimitris' father winked at him as well.

They left the restaurant and went for a walk. The weather was now very warm. They eventually came to the same park that Ben had walked through back in April on his own. He recalled how distressed he had felt at that time, doubting whether he would ever find his Miss Right – and, equally, feeling aggrieved by seeing young people barely half his age in relationships. Now he could have jumped up and down with happiness. For the first time since he had been living and working in Oxford he was accompanied by a beautiful young lady, and he felt so complete.

They stopped and sat on a park bench for a little while. Ben noticed that Ludmila sat slightly away from him on the bench and he felt a little disappointed. He would not try and embrace her, but half in jest he rested his head on her shoulder. She turned her head slightly away but did not seem to mind otherwise. Ben really wanted to laugh, as so many people passed them while walking through the park – and particularly the teenage girls appeared to look at them both somewhat enviously. This was the complete opposite to what Ben had experienced a few months earlier when he had thought that those pretty young girls could attract any man they wanted effortlessly. Ben concluded that other people were evidently just as affected by displays of affection as he was.

After a couple of minutes Ludmila gently pushed Ben's head off her shoulders. He knew that enough was enough. He sat up and asked,

"Are you OK? Are you enjoying the day?"

"Yes. Is nice."

It was now time to ask the obvious question. With his heart beating ridiculously fast, Ben said very nervously,

"Ludmila, you know that I like you a lot and I would really like to carry on seeing you and to get to know you better."

"I know. Slowly. We see," she replied. But she did not appear to be surprised by Ben's words.

Ben was not sure that he understood quite what Ludmila meant but at least it was not a *No, I don't want to see you again* sort of response.

They carried on walking. Ben held Ludmila's arm, as he had done for most of the day. Impulsively he then tried to hold Ludmila's hand. Ludmila allowed him to hold her hand only very briefly before she held his arm instead. Ben smiled to himself, accepting that this seemed a fair compromise. They still got a lot of stares from people out walking. Barely a couple of weeks earlier this would have seemed totally impossible. He thought about how much he wanted to thank Karen. If he had never mentioned his personal circumstances to her he would no doubt have been spending that day sitting in his flat brooding once again.

Not meeting Ludmila did not bear thinking about. There he was, Benjamin Robert Smith aged thirty-one, having spent about nine months in Oxford and planning to be a top accountant and a partner one day but still a bachelor… possibly having met his Miss Right, a beautiful young lady from Moldova. Whoever could have foreseen that?

It was now getting towards 9pm. Ludmila said that she needed to go home. Of course Ben would have been overjoyed if she had wanted to see his flat and spend the night with him but it was not going to happen unless or until she wanted it to, and certainly not that day.

"Take me to train station now, please," said Ludmila politely.

"Of course not," he replied, looking quite serious.

She stared at him, looking very concerned.

"It's getting late and I've kept you far too long in Oxford. Please allow me to drive you home," Ben continued.

"I'm not sure… and, err… and is long journey," she stammered.

He stared at her, looking forlorn quite intentionally.

"You know how much I like you and care about you. I'll drive you home safely, I promise."

Ludmila's embarrassed expression slowly melted into a very faint smile.

"OK."

They then walked towards Ben's flat. Ben made a point of not telling Ludmila which was his flat, and he went and got his car. He did find this a little odd: surely, knowing which was his flat would not have been an issue for a young lady here. While driving to Bournemouth Ben smiled as he saw Ludmila nod off. He was pleased that she felt she could trust him. About halfway there Ben realised that the car needed petrol, so he stopped at the next petrol station to fill up. She was still asleep. After he had paid for the petrol Ben cleaned the windscreen, which had become covered with insects. Ludmila suddenly woke up and looked a little awkward.

"Don't be embarrassed. I can see you're tired," Ben smiled at her.

She smiled back.

"But is rude of me."

"Well, now you're awake, tell me about your week ahead."

"Is the same as usual. Now I really look forward to my holiday in Italy next month."

Ben felt his heart sinking again. She was not making any mention of if and when she wanted to see him again. He felt sad, and wondered what exactly she might want from him. He told her briefly about his coming week. Once they reached Bournemouth, Ludmila directed Ben to where her host family's house was. Ben stopped on the opposite side of the road.

"It's been a lovely day, Ludmila," he said, smiling at her. Ludmila nodded. Ben leaned forward and kissed her on both cheeks. She was about to get out of the car when Ben impulsively moved his cheek towards her. Ludmila stared at him. Ben's eyes were saying 'Kiss me'.

After a moment's hesitation she kissed him on both cheeks. Ben could have soared through the roof of the car! He didn't move for a couple of seconds. Without thinking he kissed her cheek and then her hand as well. Ludmila laughed to herself and then got out of the car very promptly. She was feeling a little uncomfortable.

Having calmed down Ben got out of the car slowly, hanging his head slightly and putting his arms behind his back. He smiled a little awkwardly.

"Goodnight, Ludmila. Have a nice week. I really hope to see you again soon."

"Goodnight, Ben," said Ludmila. She hurried into her host family's house without turning round to wave to him or to see him off. Ben sighed. That was Ludmila's manner. Anyhow, he was on cloud nine now she had finally kissed him. Her kisses already felt priceless. He drove back to Oxford beaming all the way. It was by far the most important thing that had happened to him in a very long time. While Ben was still a little nervous about what exactly Ludmila's intentions towards him might be, he felt that he could almost laugh now about his previous dates. He went to sleep that night smiling at the thought that he might be making progress, albeit very slowly, with his potential Miss Right.

Chapter Sixteen

Inevitably Ben woke up tired the following morning. He was nonetheless still elated about Ludmila having kissed him. However, their supposed relationship was progressing at an agonisingly slow pace and he did wonder in what direction it might be going. However, this time Ben had no hesitation about contacting Ludmila again. He texted her during his lunch hour, while eating a sandwich in the pub:

Ben Smith Mon 20 Jul 13.09
• *Hi Ludmila, I hope u r well. It was great 2 c u again yesterday & I hoped u enjoyed the day & visiting Oxford 2. I am looking 4ward 2 having a half day on Thurs 2 go 2 the opera in the afternoon. I hope u r having a nice day & 2 c u again soon. Ben x*

Ben felt a flutter as he sent that text message. He knew he was wearing his heart on his sleeve but he could not deny for a second that he was totally smitten by Ludmila and her great beauty. His recent bad experiences with his previous dates had made him wary of hoping for too much. Yet Ludmila was so different in her ways, but she did at least want to spend time with him. No wonder Ben felt bemused as he finished his sandwich.

That afternoon passed slowly. It was hard to concentrate on his work, and he couldn't help checking his mobile phone frequently to see if Ludmila had responded to his text message. He stuck to his usual routine, going to the gym and then to his local pub for a drink that evening.

Still nothing from Ludmila. Shortly before going to bed Ben did begin to worry.

Had he upset Ludmila somehow? Did she actually want to see him again? Had she perhaps found somebody else? Those thoughts kept going round and round in his head. He did not sleep well that night. He woke up a couple of times and when he finally got to sleep he had a nightmare that he was in Bournemouth on the pier, looking for Ludmila… but she was nowhere to be found.

The next day proved to be more difficult for Ben. At work he was dealing with some more tax returns. He had made his mind up that he would concentrate all his efforts on trying to form a long-term relationship with Ludmila, if that was what she actually wanted. He had no interest whatsoever in meeting any other young ladies now.

After work Mark, who was going on holiday shortly, invited Ben out for a drink. Mark explained that he would be taking a week's holiday.

"How are you getting on with your baby daughter?" asked Ben.

"She's great but as you can imagine, Dawn and I are hardly getting any sleep. I think it will be quite an experience for us going on holiday with her."

"I can imagine," smiled Ben.

"Have you sorted out a holiday for this year yet, Ben?" asked Mark.

"Not yet," answered Ben. "But I must try and book a short holiday very soon, though."

"Well, you'll have to be fairly quick if you want a summer holiday this year," Mark went on. He raised his eyebrows. "Are you still a single man?"

Ben set his glass down carefully before replying, "Well, I have just started seeing someone. But it's nothing too serious at the moment."

"I see. I hope it works out for you." Mark nodded, and took a long swallow of his drink. Ben wondered why Mark had enquired. The conversation then turned to the rugby club and the forthcoming season. Mark said he hoped to attend more home matches but that would probably depend on his parental responsibilities at weekends.

Afterwards Ben was walking home when he suddenly saw his mobile phone flash. There was a text message from Ludmila. Feeling very nervous, he nonetheless read it straight away:

Ludmila Tue 21 Jul 18.51
• *Hi Ben. Thank u 4 yr msg. I enjoyed Sun 2 but please be careful about yr feelings 2wards me. Talk soon. Ludmila.*

This was confusing. Surely Ben hadn't done anything wrong on Sunday. He thought he had behaved like a complete gentleman towards Ludmila. He had treated her with courtesy and respect and he had certainly not tried it on with her. He might have been a little too passionate for Ludmila's liking after she had kissed him in the car, but surely that hadn't harmed her in any way. He read the message again. There was no mention of her wanting to see him again but Ben was slowly and reluctantly becoming used to Ludmila's different manner, so he read into her text that the *Talk soon* might suggest that they could possibly be seeing each other again that weekend. But then again it might not.

The more Ben thought about those words the less sure he became of Ludmila's intentions. He had to give it to her: she certainly knew how to keep him guessing. On the Wednesday Ben had started to feel very agitated by Ludmila's text message. While he did not agree with what she had said he accepted that he should perhaps be a little less obvious with his intentions towards Ludmila and not try to insist on the next date in every message. But he was going to keep texting her. When he had a few minutes free that afternoon he quickly keyed another message to Ludmila:

Ben Smith Wed 22 Jul 15.12

• *Hi Ludmila. I hope u r well & having a nice week. I am looking 4ward 2 going 2 the opera 2moro afternoon. Speak soon. Ben x*

This time he made no reference to hoping to see her again. In fact he genuinely was looking forward to going to the opera but he deliberately exaggerated it in order to show Ludmila that, just like her, he also had other interests. Reluctantly he accepted that he wasn't likely to see her the following weekend, so he promised himself he would go to a few travel agents to try and sort out a holiday for himself before the summer was over.

On the Thursday Ben was a little calmer, if still unsure about the next steps he should take with Ludmila. Anyhow, he was genuinely looking forward to going to the opera that afternoon. Mid morning, totally unexpectedly, there was a text message from Ludmila:

Ludmila Thur 23 Jul 10.33

• *Hi Ben. I hope u r good. How do I get ticket 4 opera, please? Ludmila.*

Ben was flabbergasted. This was certainly the last thing he would have expected from her. He was in the middle of assisting Jonathan with a company formation. Ben excused himself for a moment, although Jonathan groaned. He telephoned the theatre and, very fortunately indeed, there were a few tickets left for the performance that afternoon. Unsurprisingly Ben had to purchase two new tickets for seats next to each other, as there could be absolutely no question of Ludmila sitting away from him. He then checked the train times on his mobile phone and called Ludmila. He grinned as he heard her accent when she answered her mobile.

"Hello, Ludmila."

"Oh," she exclaimed. "… Ben?"

"Yes, it's me. I have a surprise for you. I've got you a ticket for the opera this afternoon."

There was a gasp before she said,

"Oh… Thank you… thank you very much."

"You need to catch the 1.45pm train and I will meet you at the train station at 3.30pm."

"Yes. Thank you so much. See you later."

Ben grinned. He had decided to go cool on their relationship. His clever plan had worked, although he wasn't sure he was her number one priority in this. Nevertheless, he told himself with satisfaction, she trusted him enough to go to the opera with him. And he was just delighted to be seeing her again so soon after their last date.

Afterwards Jonathan rebuked Ben a little, saying that Ben should keep his private life away from work as much as possible and concentrate on his work fully. Ben apologised and explained that all this had been totally unexpected. Jonathan still shook his head and sighed.

Ben's afternoon plans had now changed. He had hoped to have a snooze but he raced home, having stayed until 2pm to try and appease Jonathan. He showered again, had a bite to eat and put on some smart clothes for the opera. He drove to the station for 3.30pm to collect Ludmila. He decided to buy her a box of chocolates as a present.

Her train arrived on time. As usual, Ben saw Ludmila first. She was wearing a nice blue dress with tights, although not necessarily a formal dress for the opera. Ben raced up and kissed her on the cheek and smiled at her.

"Hello, Ludmila. It's great to see you again. You are looking lovely."

"Hello, Ben. Thank you."

They walked towards Ben's car. Ben held Ludmila's arm. He had remembered her text message about being careful about his feelings towards her but he was still going to hold her arm, regardless. Ben explained that he was keen on *Carmina Burana*. Ludmila said she liked it too and was really looking forward to finally seeing it live. They drove to the theatre. Ludmila wanted some ice crea, which Ben bought for her. She then noticed the programmes and asked what they were. Ben explained. Ludmila said,

"I want programme, please."

They queued up for a programme. When it was Ben's turn the older gentleman selling programmes commented,

"Hello, young man. You're looking very smart. You're no doubt looking forward to the performance."

Ben felt a little awkward and then wanted to laugh, but managed not to.

"Do you live locally?" the gentleman continued.

Ben was muttering "Hurry up," under his breath, and noticing that the queue behind him seemed to be getting exasperated too. Ludmila was smiling broadly. At last the gentleman sold Ben a programme, which he handed to Ludmila straight away. Ben said,

"What was up with him?"

"Nothing. What makes you think that?" Ludmila looked quite puzzled.

Ben smiled and Ludmila nodded. They then took their seats and the performance began. Ben noticed that Ludmila again made no attempt to hold hands with him, so he did not try to hold or catch Ludmila's hands either. Of course Ben did look at Ludmila as often as he could, and smiled broadly at her whenever she looked his way.

During the interval they both had soft drinks. Ludmila inspected the audience.

"In Moldova many young people go to opera. Why not here?"

Ben shook his head.

"Usually it is older people who go to the opera in England," he said awkwardly.

"But you go," Ludmila pointed out.

Ben jokingly pretended to look a little offended. Ludmila laughed. When the performance was over she thanked Ben again and said how much she had enjoyed it. With a little laugh she then said she was hungry and asked if they could eat. Ben suggested that they should have a walk outside and find a restaurant. Ludmila smiled. They came out into the street. Ludmila held his hand.

Ben was delighted. He had by now got somewhat used to the attention he got from other people when he was with Ludmila, but to be holding hands with her now made him feel ecstatic as well as that much closer to her. She held his hand quite tightly and made no attempt to let go.

After walking round for a few minutes Ben and Ludmila came to an Italian restaurant and decided to have dinner there. They both had a ricotta and spinach ravioli and mineral water to drink. They were still holding hands at the table and Ben was trying very hard not to get carried away, but he impulsively started rubbing Ludmila's hand. She smiled for a moment and then stopped and said,

"Vot does it mean?" Ben then said,

"*Frumoasa*." He had checked online earlier and understood that it meant beautiful in Moldovan. Ludmila looked very surprised but said nothing. Their dinner arrived at that moment so he let go of her hand.

Ludmila talked about there being a concert in London the following week that she and her friends wanted to see. Ben responded immediately that he would look into it and would try and go if he could. Ludmila then asked,

"How is your work now?"

"Fine. As I said before, I am still really enjoying my job and living in Oxford. I hope to stay here for the rest of my career and to be a partner in my firm one day."

"Good," smiled Ludmila. She ate another mouthful, then

announced, "You know I want to work in business too. Is my dream. I am very interested in marketing."

Ben suddenly had a brainwave.

"Why don't you give me your CV and I will see what I can do?" He could circulate copies of Ludmila's CV at the business group and see if anyone knew of any suitable job opportunities for her. Of course the idea would be to try and find her a job in Oxford and then, he hoped, she would come to live with him as well.

"Vot is CV?" asked Ludmila.

"It's a résumé or brief summary of your work experience to date that you give to a prospective employer when you want a new job," Ben explained.

"Oh, I understand. Is curriculum vitae. You say 'CV'?" She nodded, committing it to memory. "OK. I prepare my CV and give it to you." Her smile was dazzling.

They finished dinner and Ludmila asked to go home. Ben did not ask but had assumed that Ludmila might have not bought a return train ticket. Of course he would drive her home anyway. He could have even laughed as he had not driven his car that much up to now (since he had started living in Oxford). He felt a bit sad that Ludmila did not talk about their blossoming relationship. Well, he would not broach that subject either. She had still not suggested seeing his flat, either. Ben was sure that if he was seeing any other girl then by the third date they would probably be spending the night together, but he didn't need to remind himself that Ludmila was different. He respected her wishes, and he was perfectly aware that he would never force himself on her or upset her in any way.

Softly, softly, he cautioned himself. The thought of never seeing her again was too distressing to even think about.

Ludmila again fell asleep in the car on the journey home. Ben was disappointed, but it was obvious she was tired. He did, however, think that she would need a bit more stamina if she was going to work in business successfully. Ludmila slept until Ben had almost arrived at her host family's home. He pulled up and turned the engine off. Only then did he remember the chocolates he had bought earlier that day, so he went opened the boot of the car. As he straightened up he saw that Ludmila had already got out of the car.

"I got these for you." He held them out. "I hope you like them."

Ludmila stared at the box, then at his face. At last she took the chocolates.

"Thank you, Ben." She sounded pleased. The next moment she leaned forward and kissed him hard on the cheek. Ben could have jumped for joy but, suddenly remembering last time, did not try and do anything.

"You're very welcome," he managed to say, rather gruffly. He was having difficulty not to put his arms round her and kiss her properly.

"Goodnight, Ben. I see you again soon." Ludmila went into her host family's house but did turn and wave goodbye on the doorstep before going inside.

Ben was on cloud nine again. True, it would have seemed bizarre to anyone else here that it was taking him so long to woo Ludmila. However, he found her rather stricter behaviour appealing and now he really was making progress. And, of course, he needed no reminding that Ludmila's kisses were worth their weight in gold. It was not entirely impossible that Ludmila might be working in Oxford and also living with Ben in the not-too-distant future. He drove home carefully, completely oblivious to the time. He sang along to 'Can't Take My Eyes Off You'. His life just felt so much better now.

Chapter Seventeen

Ben went to work very happy on the Friday. He had really enjoyed the previous afternoon and evening and felt a lot more relaxed, and had now started to believe that his relationship with Ludmila genuinely had the potential to become serious and long-term. While he felt a little sad at the prospect of not seeing Ludmila again that weekend he accepted that it was inevitable at the moment. He would send her a text message after work for the weekend.

Ben was looking forward to Simon coming back from holiday so that he could catch up with him. As well as hearing about how wonderful Simon's holiday would surely have been, Ben could tell him a little bit about Ludmila and show Simon, in a pleasant way of course, that he had met a beautiful young lady who might turn out to be his Miss Right.

In the afternoon – and before he had texted Ludmila – Ben's mobile phone flashed, and there was a text message from Ludmila. Very eagerly, Ben read it:

Ludmila Fri 24 Jul 15.08
• *Hi Ben. Thank u 4 lovely eve. I prepare my CV now. Have a nice wkend. Ludmila.*

Ben raised his eyebrows. That was typical Ludmila: polite but showing very little affection or emotion, and again making no mention of their relationship or the next steps. Ben felt agitated. Although he had accepted that his relationship with Ludmila was advancing one step at a time, he had thought that they were making better progress. It now felt as if he was drifting back to square one and he found himself at a complete loss in trying to work her out. Unsurprisingly, he struggled to concentrate on his work while he debated what she meant. The mystery was too much. About an hour later, Ben called her. There was the usual brief "Hello."

"Hello, Ludmila. It's Ben."

"Hello, Ben."

"How are you?"

"I'm good. Looking after children now."

"I'm pleased you enjoyed last night and the opera."

"Yes. Of course."

"Are you preparing your CV?"

"I do it later. Vot you do at weekend?"

Ben lost a heartbeat. Was it actually possible that he might see her again that weekend? Would she come and see his flat and, dare he even think it, would she even spend the night with him? He drew in a breath and stuttered,

"I'll do my food shopping, iron, clean my flat, go to the gym and have a quiet and relaxing Sunday. Oh, I might go and buy some new clothes as well."

He heard her laugh.

"What about you?" Ben held his breath.

"Oh, I am busy," she replied abruptly.

In the background Ben could hear the voice of a little child crying. He sensed that Ludmila was needed.

"OK. Have a great weekend. Speak to you again soon. Goodbye."

"Goodbye, Ben."

Ben felt very deflated. Yes, it was as though he had just deliberately banged his head against a brick wall, but he had hoped that calling her might have encouraged a more positive response. Was this how Ludmila had been brought up? Were all Moldovan girls like that? Certainly she was still an expert in not showing her feelings. Ben wondered why that was. Might Ludmila have had bad experiences with other young men in the past? Perhaps her family might not even have allowed her to have boyfriends, so maybe she had had to see them discreetly. Anyhow, he would just have to accept that Ludmila was not going to jump up and down about him at the moment – and certainly not in the way he would have liked her to.

On the Saturday Ben did all his jobs, just as he had told Ludmila. At the gym on Saturday afternoon he did a longer session than ususal, to try and work off all his frustrations. On the Sunday he went to see his parents. During lunch Ben decided to tell his parents about Ludmila.

"I should mention that I have started seeing a young lady," Ben said, a little nervously.

"Oh, well done." Mr Smith looked somewhat relieved.

"About time," exclaimed Mrs Smith.

"What does she look like?" His father winked at him.

"Typical," said Mrs Smith, casting her eyes up.

"She's beautiful. Dark blonde hair, green eyes and slim," said Ben.

"What's her name?" His mother was smiling happily.

"She's called Ludmila. She comes from Moldova."

"Right," said Mrs Smith. The silence that followed this stretched out uneasily.

Mr Smith set down his knife and fork with a clatter.

"And what exactly does she want from you?"

Ben glared as a surge of rage swept through him. But even as he sought for words to protest, he suddenly felt uncomfortable. Could his father be right in suspecting that Ludmila might have her own agenda? Of course Ben certainly did not want to hear anyone say anything against Ludmila. He kept silent for a moment then burst out angrily,

"I'm very surprised at both of you. You always taught me to be tolerant and open-minded towards other peoples and their cultures. Why do you suddenly change your tune now?"

The uneasy silence started up again. Ben's parents looked at each other and Ben avoided their stares. Eventually Mrs Smith pushed her chair back to go for more vegetables. She came back and said, as she put the serving dish down,

"As long as you're happy with her… anyway, I hope your job is still going well." They then talked about Ben's job and did not mention Ludmila again.

Ben drove back to Oxford in the late afternoon. Despite his parents not being keen on the idea of him seeing a girl from Moldova, might they change their minds if they met her? Also, how would they react if they thought that she was his potential Miss Right? He felt the irony of this as he needed some sort of sign from Ludmila that she intended their relationship to continue and deepen. He drew a shaky breath. He desperately hoped she did.

That night Ben did not sleep easily. He certainly didn't want to fall out with his parents but, equally, he wanted to see Ludmila again soon. At about 3am Ben heard a noise outside. It looked like a couple of teenagers, although he couldn't tell where they came from. Ben was shocked to see that the boy, although as some sort of joke, kept slapping the girl's bottom quite hard – and even though the girl didn't like it she was tolerating it. Worse still, the boy was trying to set some dry grass alight. They were there for a little while until some other people walked along and they then disappeared, fortunately without having started any fires.

Ben started the following week feeling somewhat perplexed. He was still totally smitten by Ludmila. In his mind they had been through the first stage of their relationship – which was blind love, at least for him – to the second stage, which consisted of anger and resentment. Then he hoped they would reach stage three, which would be tolerance and commitment. With a heavy heart Ben knew he had to try his best not to show

Ludmila how much he adored her. He had to make her understand, too, that he could live without her in the same way as she seemed to be living without him. So he would wait a few days before contacting her. He sighed more than once. Nonetheless, those few days stretched out like an eternity.

On the Tuesday Ben went to his business group as usual. They had planned to hold a charitable event the following week on the Wednesday evening, with a lecture and a raffle. It was an event for spouses as well. Ben almost laughed to himself, but with a strong element of disappointment.

On the Wednesday Ben was just going out to the gym after work and was also looking forward to meeting up with Simon again on the Thursday evening. There would now be a bit more for them to discuss. Suddenly Ben's mobile phone flashed. There was a text message from Ludmila:

Ludmila Wed 29 Jul 19.58
• *Hi Ben. I hope u r good. I prepare CV and is nearly finished. Speak soon. Ludmila.*

Ben shrugged his shoulders. Of course he was always happy to hear from Ludmila, even though it was now the usual sort of text message from her. There was nothing to say how much Ludmila missed him and could not wait to see him again. With some difficulty Ben hardened his heart. He set off for the gym. He was not going to respond immediately.

Ben was delighted to catch up with Simon again. On Thursday evening Simon showed Ben his holiday snaps, of which there were plenty. Ben noticed that while there were lots of pictures of Simon and Natalie together there were none of Natalie on the beach or in her swimwear. Simon confirmed that he and Natalie were planning to wed the following year. Ben mentioned the charity evening at their business group the following week. Simon said that he unfortunately couldn't attend as he would be visiting a new client in Manchester that day.

Eventually the conversation got round to Ben and his seemingly endless search for Miss Right. Ben remembered that Simon had said before he went on holiday that he would try and help if he could. Hopefully now, thanks to Ludmila, Simon's assistance would no longer be necessary. Ben was a little nervous about explaining about her but he was grateful to finally be able to tell someone properly, particularly as his parents had been so negative about it.

"I have met a young lady," Ben said slowly. Simon raised his eyebrows. "She's beautiful and slim and works as an au pair and studies part time," Ben continued.

"Well, well. Miracles do happen," Simon laughed. "When did all this happen?"

"While you were away," Ben answered.

"Really?" said Simon a little sarcastically, "OK. Well… tell me about her, and show me some pictures of her too."

Ben paused for a moment. Of course. He needed to take some pictures of Ludmila. Why hadn't he thought of that before?

"Her name is Ludmila. She comes from Moldova. She is dark blonde with green eyes. She lives in Bournemouth. I have seen her a couple of times already."

"No pictures, hey? Doesn't sound like a very serious relationship to me. Where are you with her now? Are you seeing her this weekend?"

"I don't know yet," said Ben. He was taken aback by Simon's comments but realised that just like with his father, there was an unfortunate element of truth in what Simon had just said.

"I'll say no more," said Simon. "It's clear already how much care about this young lady – but I'd guess that she has not been to your flat nor spent the night with you, so be careful with her for your own sake."

Ben looked away. He was not a violent person, but if anyone else had said that to him he might not have shown as much restraint as he did at that point with Simon.

"I'm still happy to try and help you find a serious girlfriend if you like," said Simon. "I'll be going for drinks with some friends on Sunday evening and you are welcome to come along."

"Thank you," said Ben. Of course there could be no question of him still being interested in any young lady other than Ludmila. However, he could do with a night out and – assuming that he was not going to see Ludmila that weekend – then he would gladly go out with Simon for drinks on the Sunday evening.

That weekend passed slowly for Ben. There was this constant sense of unease about knowing when he would see Ludmila again. No doubt he would see her again at some point but he had to accept that she was obviously not madly in love with him, however crazy he was about her. The longing to be with her and the pain of not knowing exactly where he stood with her was becoming immense.

It was Saturday evening before he responded to Ludmila's latest text message:

Ben Smith Sat 1 Aug 19.08
• *Hi Ludmila. I hope u r well & having a nice wkend. Pls let me know when yr CV is ready. I'm going out with friends Sun eve & looking 4ward 2 my biz grp's charity dinner next Wed. Talk soon. Ben x*

Ben thought he would keep the tiny sign of affection at the end of his text messages to Ludmila. He did frequently dream of kissing Ludmila properly and her kissing him, but it obviously wasn't going to happen any time soon. He would still never force himself on Ludmila nor try and make her to do anything she did not want him to do.

On the Sunday evening he arrived at the pub and found Simon at the bar ordering drinks. Simon then introduced Ben to his friends Jason and Pete. Jason worked as an engineer and Pete was an estate agent. Jason was celebrating a recent engagement. Ben felt a little awkward on hearing this, as it made him think even more about Ludmila. When the conversation got round to Ben he quickly said that although he was single he had just started seeing someone, but that it was not serious at the moment. Simon did not say anything. Jason and Pete looked at Ben and jokingly said that he needed to sort himself out soon. Ben noticed that Jason and Pete were drinking a lot, but they were fortunately not driving home that evening.

There were some ladies sitting at the next table. Eventually Jason and Pete went over to that table and started chatting to those ladies. They looked at Ben and Simon and smiled. Simon smiled in return and Ben nodded politely. After a while they all came back over to the table. One of the ladies sat between Ben and Simon. It was clear that she too had already had too much to drink. She started chatting to both of them although her speech was a little slow and slurred.

"What's your name?" she asked Ben.

"Ben. And you?"

"Shirley."

"Pleased to meet you, Shirley," said Ben politely.

"And what do you for a living, young man?" asked Shirley.

"I work as an accountant in Oxford," answered Ben.

"Oh," said Shirley.

"What about you?" asked Ben.

"I'm a nurse. Enough questions." Shirley then turned to Simon and had a similar conversation with him. Ben saw the other lady behaving in a similar way with Jason and Pete. Suddenly Shirley turned back to Ben and smiled a little saucily at him. She ruffled his hair and Ben started to feel a little embarrassed. He had not had a night out like this for about a year and didn't remember too much about them anyway, as he had usually been far too drunk at the time.

"Come on, handsome. Liven up," said Shirley. Ben felt himself going somewhat red. Surely he should not be embarrassed. Why, had his experiences with speed dating and blind dating damaged his confidence? Of course they had, but then what about Ludmila? Ben was impressed by Shirley's slim figure and by her miniskirt. Totally unexpectedly, Shirley moved herself over and sat on Ben's lap. Admittedly Ben couldn't pretend that he did not enjoy an attractive female sitting on his lap, and it was rather difficult for him not to get aroused. It did, however, make him realise how much he needed a female – and equally, what was missing in his relationship with Ludmila so far. Simon was winking and smiling at him and Ben also saw that other people in the pub were amused by Shirley sitting on his lap. Shirley eventually got off him, smiled, and blew Ben a kiss.

By the end of that evening Shirley and the other lady had disappeared. Ben had had a good time. He was of course able to take Shirley's antics in jest. But it reminded him of what he was missing – and indeed, what he would like to be happening with Ludmila. As he got home he smiled, wondering what Ludmila would have made of Shirley's antics. Would she have laughed? Cried? Perhaps she might have hit Ben and stormed off. Would she ever behave like Shirley had with other young men? He realised that there was no point speculating, and that the evening had simply made him realise how much he was missing Ludmila.

Chapter Eighteen

At work on the Monday morning Ben was busy preparing some management accounts when he saw his mobile phone flash. There was a text message from Ludmila:

Ludmila Mon 3 Aug 10.48
• *Hi Ben. I hope u r good. I wld like 2 come 2 charity dinner. Is possible? Ludmila.*

Ben was so surprised that he had to read it several times. Then his heart leapt with delight. He would be seeing Ludmila again soon. It would also surely enhance his status at the business group for the other members to see him accompanied and by such a beautiful young lady. But immediately he had a moment of panic, wondering whether there were any tickets left for the event. He grabbed his mobile to speak to Derek, a local surveyor, who was one of the senior members of the business group and who was in charge of organising the charity dinner.

"Hello, Derek. It's Ben. How are you? I'm just ringing to check whether there are any spare tickets for the charity dinner."

"Hello, Ben. Yes, there are a couple of tickets left."

"That's great. I have a female friend who would like to come to the dinner with me."

"Fine. I'll make sure you're seated together. Look forward to seeing you both on Wednesday evening."

It was an hour before Ben could stop grinning as he carried on with his work.

It was a pity that Simon would not be at the dinner, Ben thought, but he nonetheless looked forward to showing off Ludmila and didn't doubt for a second that her looks would be a great hit among the male members of the business group. Ben texted Ludmila back during his lunch break:

Ben Smith Mon 3 Aug 13.17
• *Hi Ludmila. I got u a ticket 4 charity dinner on Wed eve. Pls get 2 Oxford by 6pm & I will meet u @ train station. Pls rem 2 bring yr CV. Look 4ward 2 cing u again. Ben x*

As Ben carried on with his work through the afternoon his mind was turning over the problem that was Ludmila. He was still delighted at the thought of seeing her again but he could not help but still feel a little exasperated by how slowly their relationship was progressing. Every time he saw Ludmila it seemed as though it was a continuation of their first date. But Ben knew how he felt about Ludmila and that nobody mattered more to him than her now. He would have to wait for however long it took for her to become his Miss Right.

After a snack evening meal Ben was going off to the gym. Just as he was leaving his flat there was a reply text from Ludmila:

Ludmila Mon 3 Aug 19.23
• *Hi Ben. Thank u. I look 4ward 2 Wed eve & I bring my CV. Ludmila.*

Ben smiled, but a little ruefully. That was another standard Ludmila response. He could not help feeling a slight doubt about her motives as well. Was she interested in seeing him or was he simply the means by which she hoped to get a better job in Oxford? And if that was so, what would happen afterwards?

Well, at least she was going to be his date for the business group's charity dinner. Then he exclaimed as he remembered that it was a black tie event, and for the ladies that meant black cocktail dresses. While Ben did not doubt that Ludmila would try and dress smartly, it occurred to him that he might have to help her get some suitable clothes. But if he was only meeting her at 6pm just before the charity dinner started, what would he be able to do about it?

On the Tuesday Ben was still feeling concerned about how Ludmila would be dressed for the charity dinner. So there could be only one possible solution. He would have to take the Wednesday afternoon off work and try and get Ludmila to come earlier to Oxford and take her clothes shopping. Ben had been spared this chore since he parted company with his last girlfriend but this was a good opportunity to spend a little more time with Ludmila. Surely it could only serve to improve their relationship. In his lunch hour he called her.

"Hello, Ludmila. I'm calling about the charity dinner tomorrow evening."

"Ye... es?"

"There is a dress code for the event."

"Vot you mean by 'dress code'?"

"You must wear a black cocktail dress."

"Vot is that? You being rude?" Ludmila snapped.

Ben rocked his head back slightly. He felt awkward, but he plodded on. This was now his opportunity.

"If you can come tomorrow early afternoon, then I can take you to the clothes shops in Oxford."

There was a long pause. Then, in a much friendlier tone, Ludmila said,

"OK. I am working in morning. I come to Oxford about 3pm."

Ben tried not to laugh. That seemed to be a prime example of cupboard love.

"Fine. I look forward to seeing you then. Bye."

It was only at this point that Ben realised that he had not

actually booked the Wednesday afternoon off work. He should have checked with Roger first. He hurried straight to his boss. Roger frowned and hesitated until Ben explained that he had suddenly realised he needed to get some new clothes for the business group's charity dinner. Then Roger nodded and agreed. Ben was surprised. Why was Roger so reluctant to give him a little time off work? It was August, and things were still fairly quiet in the office.

The Wednesday morning passed quite slowly. Ben felt slightly uneasy given Roger's reaction the previous day, but he worked hard and completed all his current tasks for that day. This took until 1.30pm – so he then rushed home and got ready, keeping a constant eye on the time. Ben had not intentionally planned it, but Ludmila would obviously need to come to his flat to change. He resolved to be just as gentlemanly towards her in his flat as he had been everywhere else.

At about 2.45pm Ben went to the train station. He waited a little anxiously but fortunately Ludmila's train was only a couple of minutes late. He couldn't help smiling with pleasure when he saw Ludmila get off the train. She waved at him. He went towards her and kissed her on both cheeks. Ludmila smiled at him.

"How are you? Was it a good journey?"

"I am good, thank you. Journey OK."

"We will go clothes shopping now."

They went to the city centre. Ben was pleased that Ludmila was holding his arm. Of course he would have preferred to have been holding hands with her. He was so happy to see her again he didn't want the time he spent with her to go quickly. When he asked about her English course she said she was fairly pleased with the progress she was making with it, although it was still a demanding course.

Taking her to a department store, Ben explained that she would need a black cocktail dress and matching shoes. Ludmila nodded and they made towards the Ladies department. Ben did his best to take a proper interest in the clothes that Ludmila needed, although he kept a discreet eye on the time. She tried a couple of dresses but they weren't suitable. They then hurried to another department store. Here Ludmila found a very smart outfit and tried it on. She came out to show Ben.

"Wow. You look fantastic in that," he said, trying to control his voice. At that moment he felt as though he had just fallen in love.

"Is good?" asked Ludmila, turning from side to side as she examined her reflection in the mirror.

"It's perfect," said Ben, totally enchanted by the outfit. With an effort he raised his eyes from the lovely figure in the smart dress to Ludmila's face and saw that she was looking at him very longingly. He shrugged his shoulders and smiled, fully understanding what that look meant.

Ludmila grinned. Ben knew perfectly well that he would have to pay for that outfit. He'd known it all along, but it didn't hurt for her not to take it for granted straight away. They took the dress to the cash desk and Ben paid for it. Ludmila then gave Ben a big kiss on the cheek. Ben stopped for a second and smiled. It had been worth it.

"We still need to get shoes," he said. Ludmila was now holding hands with him as they walked along. They tried a couple of shoe shops. Ben light-heartedly pointed out various pairs of high-heeled shoes. After a little while Ludmila did find a smart pair of high heels and Ben, almost without realising it, was ready to slip the high heels on to Ludmila's feet. Ludmila looked a bit surprised but then laughed.

"You like my feet?" she said. Ben winked at her. He thought to himself that he would have liked them even more if Ludmila had painted her toenails, but that would still have to wait for another occasion. She tried the shoes on and they fitted her. Ben didn't wait for the longing look from her this time and simply nodded and went to pay for the shoes. Outside the shop Ludmila still held Ben's hand. She thanked him several times for buying her the outfit and the shoes. They then went for a coffee and a slice of cake. Ben was delighted that Ludmila was still holding his hand as they sat in the cafe. He smiled happily at her.

"You know… your name, Ludmila, is a very nice name… but do you have a nickname or something?"

She set down her cup and smiled a little shyly at him.

"In Moldova my family and friends… they call me Ludy." Ben smiled broadly. He thought it was so sweet.

"Vot? Vot?" asked Ludmila. She was half smiling too, but seemed doubtful if she should be.

"That's a very nice name," said Ben. He made doe eyes at her. "May I call you Ludy too?"

"Yes. Of course." answered Ludmila.

Ben smiled and impulsively kissed Ludmila's hand. She smiled back. The time was passing and they would need to go to his flat to get changed for the charity dinner. Ben tried to deal with this potentially difficult topic as carefully as he could.

"You know, Ludy, we will have to go to my flat to get changed for the charity dinner."

Ludmila paused. She suddenly stopped holding Ben's hand. Ben's heart sank.

"OK," she said, looking a little concerned. They left the cafe and drove to Ben's flat. Ludmila was quiet and distant. Ben could have laughed to himself. Finally, after almost a year of living on his own in Oxford, he would be showing a beautiful young lady the flat where he was staying. But he could not fail to notice how reluctantly she was walking alongside him. Once they had got to the flat, he saw her examining everything inside. The bedroom with its double bed was first on the left. Ludmila walked quickly past it into the lounge area.

"Is nice," she commented, nodding her head.

"Thank you, Ludy," said Ben, "Would you like anything to eat or drink?"

"Fruit juice, please." Ben duly obliged and they both sat down on the sofa a little way apart. Ben was conscious that Ludmila was not at ease and that it was up to him to show her that she had nothing to be afraid of. He went and got himself a glass of water, smiled at Ludmila and then asked,

"Would you like to have a quick shower before we go to the charity dinner?"

"OK. Thank you." Ben went and got a couple of towels and gave them to Ludmila. He showed her the bedroom and put out the hairdryer. Sensing that Ludmila was still feeling a little apprehensive, Ben showed her the door to the lounge area and made a point of closing it. Ludmila nodded as if she understood what Ben meant. Ben noticed that Ludmila took a rather long time to have her shower and was becoming a little concerned that they would not have long before they needed to go out.

Suddenly Ludmila appeared in the outfit and shoes Ben had bought her. His jaw dropped.

"You look amazing," said Ben. He could feel his face heating up.

"You go get ready now," said Ludmila firmly.

Ben nodded. He had become used to Ludmila's abrupt manner. He left the television on and a newspaper out for Ludmila to occupy herself with while he got changed.

At 7pm they left the flat and drove to the charity dinner, which was being held at a large hotel near Blenheim Palace. Ludmila talked incessantly about her CV, which Ben said he would circulate at the next business group meeting. They arrived at the charity dinner in good time. As Ben had predicted, it was literally smiles all round when he appeared with Ludmila, particularly given that they had got used to the idea of only ever seeing Ben on his own. Ludmila's looks and slim figure got a lot of attention too. Unsurprisingly, most of the male members of the group pressed around to greet Ben and to be introduced to Ludmila. As soon as he could Ben took her to see the president of the business group.

"Hello, Mike. May I introduce you to Ludmila?"

Mike nodded but scarcely glanced at Ben.

"Hello, Ludmila, and welcome. Where do you come from?"

"Hello. Thank you for your invitation. I come from Moldova."

"Oh. That's very interesting. I hope you enjoy the evening."

Ben and Ludmila then took their seats at their table. They had a very nice dinner and chatted freely with the other members and their spouses. Ben did observe that Ludmila was quite happy to talk to the men on her table but did not talk much to the ladies – although there were no young ladies of a similar age at the event, anyway.

When the meal was over the president gave a short speech thanking everyone for attending, and then turned to the particular charity that the event was sponsoring before introducing the guest speaker. They then sat through a very interesting talk about South America, with a slide show. Both Ben and Ludmila and everyone else gasped at the beauty of the scenery and Ben noticed that Ludmila looked at him a few times and then smiled, and he smiled back. Might she have been hinting that she would like to have a holiday in South America and with Ben? He certainly hoped so. She then whispered in Ben's ear,

"The talk is good but I am tired. I wish it could be earlier in day." Ben smiled and nodded at her. He remembered about her going to sleep in the car on the journeys back to Bournemouth, and it reminded him that if Ludmila was going to work in business successfully then it would inevitably mean working long hours and attending events like this one out of hours. But now was hardly the time to tell her that.

After the talk there was a raffle. Ben had bought himself and

Ludmila some raffle tickets. He explained how the raffle worked and Ludmila looked very interestedly at the prizes, which included bottles of champagne, a sponge cake and a top prize of a £50 gift voucher. Everyone listened carefully as the winning numbers were drawn. Although Ludmila smiled politely and clapped for each prize winner, Ben sensed a slight disappointment in her. Suddenly, one of Ben's tickets was drawn: he had won an oil painting set. They all clapped as Ben collected his prize.

"You are very lucky," said Ludmila.

"I deserve it," laughed Ben. Ludmila then laughed too.

As the event came to a close the president came to speak to Ben and Ludmila again.

"Ben, how long have you known Ludmila?"

Ben paused for a moment.

"Err... a couple of months now."

"You look after her. You're a very lucky young man. She's beautiful."

Ben and Ludmila looked at each other and smiled. Ben especially felt a sense of satisfaction. The new president had only stated the obvious. Ben would of course have felt a lot better if he and Ludmila had been a proper couple, but it was very encouraging indeed that at least other people had that impression of them. They walked back to Ben's car. Ludmila was holding Ben's arm.

"Ben, do you think I have chance to get job in Oxford?" asked Ludmila.

"I'll see what I can do for you, Ludy."

Ben was hoping that Ludmila might want to go back to his flat but he was not really surprised when she said,

"I want to go home, Ben. I am very tired now."

"Of course, Ludy," he answered, swallowing his disappointment. It seemed appropriate now to take their relationship to the next stage, but Ludmila obviously did not want that. He knew he needed to question her about this but he couldn't bring himself to do so. He felt weary while driving Ludmila back to Bournemouth but he was becoming used to it and accepted that it was part of his relationship with her at the moment. She again fell asleep in the car but did wake up intermittently and smile at Ben, who smiled straight back at her. He woke her up as they reached her host family's house.

Ben now really wanted to kiss Ludmila properly. It seemed ridiculous that he had known her for almost two months and they had not even shared a proper kiss. As he stopped his car outside Ludmila's host family's house he plucked up his courage.

"Ludy, may I?" he said, leaning towards her. Ludmila had already got out of his car. He wondered if she had seen or perhaps had even anticipated Ben's gesture towards her. He jumped out of his car and walked up to her.

"Ludy, I really enjoyed this evening. I hope you did too."

"It was lovely evening, Ben. Thank you very much."

"You are very welcome," replied Ben. He suddenly remembered that the prize he had won during the raffle was in the boot. He went straight and got the oil painting set and then walked straight back up to her.

"This is for you," he said.

"Oh, Ben. You are so nice."

Ludmila then did what Ben had wanted her to do for so long. She kissed him properly. Ben could have seen the stars jump over the moon and out of the sky. It had already occurred to him that the prize would be a nice present for her anyway. He was overjoyed with the effect of giving Ludmila the prize. He smiled to himself, seeing again what the key to Ludmila's heart was.

"Ludy, that was beautiful. You are just so amazing."

"Thank you, Ben." She smiled but then blushed slightly.

"When will I see you again?" he asked, smiling helplessly at her.

"Oh, you forgot? I have holiday at weekend in Italy for two weeks."

"Oh. I see." Ben suddenly remembered. He helplessly rubbed his hand over his eyes to hide the sudden tears. "I remember. I hope you have a great time. I will miss you so much." Although he felt embarrassed by his emotional outburst, he was glad that Ludmila had seen it and that it was a genuine reaction of someone who, if not already, then certainly was almost in love with her.

Ludmila, although always firm and sometimes abrupt in her behaviour, seemed to mellow on seeing Ben's reaction. She wiped Ben's tears away and then held both of his hands.

"Ben, I understand. But we still take things slowly." She then kissed Ben on both cheeks and walked towards her host family's front door and then turned back and waved at Ben. He stood glued to the spot. He was laughing and weeping inside at the same time. He suddenly realised that he could not stand there all night so he waved and smiled back as best he could. He drove off, still not knowing whether to laugh or cry. He had enjoyed a special evening with Ludmila but the thought of not seeing her again for over two weeks, and where their relationship would be when she came back, was quite simply unbearable. This caused him to shed some more tears on the drive back to Oxford.

Chapter Nineteen

Ben got home in the early hours of the morning. He was shattered, but his mind was so busy wondering how to take Ludmila's comments that he just could not sleep. 'Ain't No Sense in Love' was playing over and over in his head. He made himself lie down, but the problem kept his mind speeding along. Yes, he was aware that Ludmila might not necessarily be the ideal young lady he was looking for when he had decided to leave the City almost a year earlier but he adored her nonetheless. She was just so beautiful and enchanting.

However, despite their outings and the time they had spent together nothing had really happened between them apart from one proper kiss. But Ludmila was different from young ladies here. It was worth being patient in the hope that things would develop between them.

It's called wooing, he reminded himself with a faint smile. The bleak prospect of not seeing her over the next two weeks fretted his mind. Those two weeks would seem like an eternity. He gritted his teeth, thinking that he would need to find as much to occupy him as possible in an attempt to make the time pass as quickly as possible.

When he did finally manage to get to sleep he dreamed that he and Ludmila were walking along by the seaside holding hands, embracing and laughing. He then turned to her and said, *I love you, Ludy*. But Ludmila had suddenly disappeared and, despite his frantic cries, she was nowhere to be found. Ben woke up with a sigh of relief, which turned to shock and horror when he saw the time. It was nearly 10am.

Roger was waiting for Ben when he got in. The inevitable earbashing concluded,

"Young man, I don't know what's happened to you recently, but you seemed to have lost focus on your work. I suggest that you think hard about things and get back to how you were when you first joined us."

Ben nodded somewhat nervously.

"I'm really sorry for oversleeping. It won't happen again." Roger frowned but then made an effort at a smile and told Ben that he expected him to come along to the friendly rugby match on Saturday. Ben smiled in return and said that he would be looking forward to it. It was something at least, if only for a couple of hours, to take his thoughts away from Ludmila – as impossible as that would be.

As Simon was away that week Ben decided to go to the gym on the Thursday evening. He sent Ludmila a text message just before going out.

Ben Smith Thur 6 Aug 19.49

• *Hi Ludy. I hope u r well. I really enjoyed Wed with u. It was so special. I hope u enjoyed the eve 2 & the oil painting set. I will c if any1 @ biz grp can help u get a job in Oxford. I hope u have a great hol. I will miss u loads & can't wait 2 see u again when u come back. Ben xx*

Ben wasn't so concerned now about getting an immediate text reply from Ludmila. Her replies were formal and polite but now there was the question of her CV and, hopefully, the possibility of her getting her a job in Oxford. So Ben guessed he would get a reply when she was ready. He did check his mobile phone several times but was not surprised to see that she had not sent any message yet. That evening Ben went to bed in good time. He was at least as anxious not to oversleep as he was to hear back from Ludmila.

149

The Friday went past slowly and quietly. By the end of the day Ben was feeling tired and had inevitably become slightly miserable, as Ludmila had still not sent any reply. He spent a quiet evening with a glass of wine and reading a book. There was still no text message by the end of the evening so Ben now felt sad and ill at ease. Surely Ludmila had enjoyed Wednesday too? He went to sleep eventually and spent another restless night searching for something he just could not find.

On the Saturday Ben tried to focus his attention on going to the rugby match.

At least it will pass some time, he reminded himself. He did his weekend jobs and was eating a light lunch when there was a flash from his mobile phone. He gulped down his mouthful of sandwich and picked the phone up. His heart thumped hard when he read the message:

Ludmila Sat 8 Aug 12.46

• *Hi Ben. I am good & I hope u r 2. Thank u so much 4 Wed. I really enjoyed day & dinner. I love my new clothes & shoes. U r very kind. I really hope I can work in Oxford. I miss u 2. I hope u have nice wkend. I am @ airport now. I look 4wrd 2 cing u again when I come back. Ludy x*

Wow. Ben was overjoyed. He could have sung and danced on the spot. It was the first time that Ludmila had said that she missed him and it was also the first time that she had included a kiss in her text message. Surely their relationship had finally reached a new level. The anguish had all been worthwhile. He could now reassure himself that he had finally made some significant progress towards finding his Miss Right.

The afternoon at the rugby club passed nicely. Ben was more cheerful than usual for obvious reasons. Roger greeted him with a smile but said,

"I'm glad your timekeeping has improved."

Ben smiled but knew what Roger meant. He was introduced to a new client of Triangle Accountants, who was Roger's guest for that match. While watching the match Ben looked at the crowd. Yes, just as he had observed the previous year, there were still plenty of young ladies there: some in groups, some with their husbands or boyfriends. If he hadn't had Ludmila Ben would have felt awkward and resentful at still being single. However, now he smiled to himself, as none of those females interested him in the slightest.

Of course he so wished Ludmila could be there with him, but he hoped that she would soon be coming to live with him in Oxford and working locally. Ben laughed. How would Ludmila like rugby? And would he even try and explain the rules of the game to her? He knew that if she didn't like the game she would say so in her direct way. That day's match was a good one. Afterwards he had a couple of drinks with Roger and the new client and then went home, still in a good frame of mind.

On the Sunday Ben, very unusually for him, went to the office to make sure that everything he was working on was up to date. He then went to the gym in the afternoon and then drove over to see his parents for the evening meal. It was noticeable that the conversation was a lot more guarded this time.

Over dinner Mrs Smith asked,

"Have you arranged a holiday for this year?"

"No, not yet." Ben glanced from one parent to the other. Mr Smith was concentrating on the food on his plate. His mother persisted with her questions.

"Are you still seeing that young lady?"

"Yes, I am."

"Where is she?"

"On holiday with friends at the moment."

"I see." Mrs Smith's tone spoke volumes. Ben pulled a face full of exasperation. Mr Smith cleared his throat and intervened.

"Well, if you are going to be serious with her, perhaps we should meet her one day soon."

Ben smiled and nodded in agreement. At least his father was being diplomatic. Maybe Ben's parents had realised they had to stop trying to dictate what sort of girl he should be with. They might also have grasped that he would not let them be too judgemental before they had actually met Ludmila.

The following week started quietly. Ben made sure that he was not late for work again and, thanks to having gone in briefly at the weekend, he was completely on top of his workload. Inevitably, despite having enough work to keep him busy, his thoughts were constantly on Ludmila. He did wonder how her holiday was going. He wasn't overly worried about her meeting any other young men as she hadn't appeared to be too interested in attracting male company and always seemed to speak to everyone very formally. He knew his insecurity would most likely start when he and Ludmila hopefully became a proper couple. Equally, there was nothing to stop him messing around with other young ladies in Ludmila's absence – not that it was of any interest at all to him. He wondered if Ludmila ever thought about that.

On the Tuesday lunchtime there was some very sad news from the business group. The wife of one of the senior members had unexpectedly passed away that weekend. The funeral would be taking place on the Friday. Ben was shocked and upset. It was the first time that there had been any death relating to his working life. Ben discussed this with Roger. It was agreed that Ben would attend the funeral. At home he ironed his black suit. At the funeral the senior member's immediate family was there, as were most of the members of the business group. Ben stayed with Simon throughout the service. Out of respect he did not mention Ludmila or the charity dinner.

Over the following weekend Ben found that he was now missing Ludmila terribly. He had kept himself busy thinking about work and, understandably, the funeral had preoccupied him too. He sighed and decided that the old saying, *Absence makes the heart grow fonder*, was all too true. He had hoped that after the first week he would be able to cope with Ludmila's absence. Of course he had had periods of time away from Ludmila before, but not with her being abroad and not being easily contactable. Ben would have gladly called and texted her but didn't think he would get any response, and that it might also annoy her while she was with her friends.

At the Tuesday lunchtime the business group remembered the senior member's wife. That senior member was absent. The president agreed with everyone present that they would dedicate the first part of the meeting to her. There was a minute's silence and they then drank a toast to her memory. The second part of the meeting proceeded as normal. Simon was there but any chat would have to wait until they met up on Thursday evening for drinks. Meanwhile, a couple of members came to talk to Ben.

"Who was that very attractive young lady who accompanied you to the charity dinner?" asked Malcolm, a local printer, who was one of the few members of the group who had not got to speak to Ben or to Ludmila at the event.

Ben smiled.

"Her name is Ludmila. She comes from Moldova."

"Is she your girlfriend?" asked Malcolm.

"Well... we're very good friends," Ben said, somewhat hesitantly.

"Like that, is it?" laughed Malcolm, and winked at Ben.

Ben suddenly remembered Ludmila's CV. Just as the meeting was finishing he went to speak to Geoff, who worked in marketing.

"Geoff, can I have quick word, please? You recall the charity dinner last week and my good friend, Ludmila, who accompanied me."

"Oh, yes," said Geoff with a smile. "I remember her."

"Well, she's working as an au pair and doing an intensive English course. I'm hoping she'll come and live with me in Oxford soon and she would very much like to work in marketing locally, if possible. Sorry to be so forward, but would you possibly be able to help at all? If not, could you refer me to someone who can?"

"Err... well, there's nothing much at the moment," answered Geoff. Ben's heart sank. He knew very well what a huge difference it could make having someone to pull a few strings and open doors for Ludmila in order to get her a job locally in marketing as she wanted – and of course, for their possible future together.

Suddenly, on seeing Ben's reaction, Geoff smiled and put his hand on Ben's shoulder briefly.

"Let me have a copy of her CV and I'll see what I can do."

Ben could not conceal his delight.

"Thank you so much. I'll send you Ludmila's CV later today."

Ben had remembered that Ludmila's CV was in his flat, and he obviously could not go and get it and then be late back to work. He would scan and then email Ludmila's CV to Geoff that evening. He needed to be quick in case Geoff might regret his promise to help. After the meeting, and out of sight of any of the other members, Ben punched the air with delight. His dream of Ludmila coming to Oxford to live with him and work there was taking a huge step forward.

Ben and Simon met up for drinks on the Thursday evening. Ben was pleased to see Simon again away from the business group so that they could talk more freely and openly without any interruptions, or worry about excluding or offending anyone at the business group. They did briefly discuss the funeral. Ben admitted how much it had affected him. Simon was quite upset too. Inevitably the conversation got round to Ludmila. Ben told his friend about the impact Ludmila had made at the charity dinner. Without going into too much detail he indicated that he felt their relationship was heading in the right direction, particularly as there was now the possibility that Ludmila might be coming to live with him in Oxford and working locally.

"That's great," said Simon. "I'm very pleased for you. You deserve to be happy. I've noticed how much you've suffered being single. So where is Ludmila now?"

"She's on holiday abroad with friends and coming back this weekend," said Ben, a little awkwardly.

"I see." Simon frowned a little. He seemed about to speak but then shook his head and picked up his drink.

"She's changed my world, Simon. I never thought that I would meet anyone like her. She's made me feel good about myself and I've rarely seen anyone that beautiful," said Ben, and nodded very positively.

"But you are still not a proper couple yet. I still think you should still be a bit careful," said Simon, sounding like a wise old owl.

Ben felt awkward and defensive too.

"I accept that Ludmila is different from girls here but let's not forget that she does come from another country. I'm pleased that my parents would like to meet her."

"Well, that's encouraging." Simon tried not to laugh.

"Is something funny?" Ben was getting irritated.

"I really do hope it works out for you, Ben," said Simon diplomatically.

Ben smiled and nodded.

"Perhaps we can go out as two couples one day soon," continued Simon.

"Yes, that would be great – and I'm sure Ludmila would like that too."

They finished their drinks and agreed to meet up in a fortnight, work and other commitments permitting. Ben was aware of Simon's concerns about Ludmila and he did not need any reminding that they were still not in a proper, conventional relationship. But Ben nonetheless wanted to carry on believing that she was his Miss Right and that their relationship would eventually work out. At the moment he was desperate to see her as soon as possible after her return from holiday.

Ben decided he would text Ludmila on the Sunday and follow it up with a phone call early the following week to ask her how her holiday had been, and to arrange when he could see her again. Of course he had the potential good news about a job possibility for her. He was so impatient to see her that if she was free during the coming week he would risk taking an afternoon off work to meet up with her.

Chapter Twenty

It was the Saturday afternoon. Ben had been food shopping early in the morning, done his ironing and the housework and had then gone to the gym. He had entered an endurance competition at the gym, which was really aimed at those gym junkies who worked out five days a week or more. Ben had ended up doing nearly twice his normal workout. He was exhausted and, after trying to eat some lunch, he felt unwell. It didn't help that he was still feeling tense about Ludmila's return from her holiday that weekend. He flopped on the sofa, deciding he would wait until Sunday to text her. He would suggest that they meet up again soon, but he wasn't going to say anything about forwarding her CV to Geoff at the business group until he next saw her.

By the late afternoon Ben was having a nap to recuperate from his exertions at the gym. Suddenly he was half awake, and it was as though he could sense a presence in the bedroom. It almost felt like a human figure was floating over him, and it was as though Ludmila was there. Ben did not speak but instinctively smiled, and then the presence then seemed to disappear. Ben came fully awake a few minutes later. He wasn't particularly scared by what had happened, as he simply assumed that because his thoughts were constantly on Ludmila it was hardly surprising that he would be dreaming about her again.

In the evening Ben simply sat watching television. His eye was suddenly caught by the flashing of his mobile phone. He got up to see who was messaging him. His heart gave a mighty thump when he saw it was from Ludmila.

Ludmila Sat 22 Aug 20.09

• *Hi Ben. I hope u r good. I had nice hol in Italy & I am back now.*
Speak soon. Ludy x

Ben was delighted that Ludmila had contacted him straight away on arriving back from her holiday abroad and equally that she had put a kiss at the end of her message. Ben assumed their relationship could now progress from where they had left it two weeks earlier. His mind turned back to the presence floating over him while he was having his nap. Could that really have been Ludmila? Did she have some sort of sixth sense?

Stop being fanciful, he told himself. Anyhow, he would still wait to contact Ludmila until the Sunday.

On the Sunday morning Ben went out for a newspaper. Strolling back home, he decided he would text Ludmila. But on second thoughts, why not call her? He didn't wait to get back home.

"Hello, Ludy. How are you? I'm very pleased you had a nice holiday."

"Hello, Ben. I'm good, thank you. It was great holiday and so much to talk about."

Unintentionally Ben then said,

"I've some good news from the business group. One of the members has got your CV and will let me know soon if there is a job opportunity for you in Oxford." A bit hesitantly, he continued, "I really missed you, Ludy. Did you miss me too?"

There was quite an uneasy pause before she responded. Then she said,

"Oh, yes. I missed you." Ben smiled to himself. Ludmila continued, "Come and see me this evening."

Ben could have leapt through the roof. He had been nervous about not seeing Ludmila for another week and he would never have expected this.

"Of course, Ludy. What time shall I come over?"

"7pm."

"Perfect. See you then. Bye, Ludy." Ben was overjoyed. It would be no problem to sort out everything he needed to do, then shower and shave again before setting off for Bournemouth just before 5pm. The weather was nice and warm and he was wearing a red polo shirt and another new pair of chinos. He was now used to the drive to Bournemouth and, subject to traffic, could predict the duration of the journey fairly accurately. He still felt a little tense, but hoped that as soon as he and Ludmila saw each other they would be at the same point with their relationship where they had been a few weeks earlier.

He arrived at her host family's house in good time. He waited for quite a while, checking his mobile phone every few minutes. Eventually he texted:

Ben Smith Sun 23 Aug 19.21

• *Hi Ludy. I've arrived. Can't wait 2 c u again. Ben xx*

Ben then became concerned that Ludmila had not appeared nor responded to his text message. He was about to call her when suddenly she turned up.

"Ludy," Ben half shouted as he raced towards her. Ludmila looked a bit surprised, took half a step backwards and then smiled at him. Ben went to kiss Ludmila on the lips. She had begun to turn her head away but then let him kiss her properly.

"I've missed you so much. You are just so beautiful."

Ludmila blushed. She smiled but looked away. Ben took her hand. She let him hold her hand for a moment and then pulled it away. Ben felt distraught. What was she playing at? Had something happened during her holiday to make her behave like this towards him? Ben didn't know what to do so he turned to face Ludmila and made doe eyes at her.

"Vot? Vot?" she said very abruptly, almost comically

159

sounding like a Pekinese dog growling. Ben was shocked but suddenly he laughed to himself and responded,

"Vot? Vot? Vot?" mimicking her accent, but not her abruptness. Ludmila laughed and Ben laughed too. He held out his hand again and Ludmila took it and squeezed it.

"I have present for you." She took a small parcel out of her bag and gave it to Ben.

"Thank you, Ludy." Ben smiled. He unwrapped the present. It was a little of book of postcards of Florence. He very much appreciated the gesture and kissed Ludmila on the cheek to thank her.

"Take me to Christchurch now, please."

"Of course," said Ben. "You direct me there." As they walked towards the car, he said, "So tell me more about your holiday."

"It was wonderful. I saw so many special places. Weather was perfect. I show you photos."

As Ben drove towards Christchurch he suddenly felt Ludmila's hand on his knee. Ben was a little taken aback by this but his heart suddenly started racing. Were his somewhat inappropriate prayers about to be answered? Obviously, he had to struggle to concentrate on his driving. Ludmila's fingers stroked his knee. She then worked her way towards his thigh but suddenly took her hand away. Ben felt great excitement one second and then equally enormous disappointment that she had stopped her adventurous behaviour so quickly. Ben looked at her and smiled. She nodded back at him.

As they drove into Christchurch Ben saw a pub and suggested that they go there for a drink. Ludmila agreed. They sat outside. He had a lager and Ludmila asked for lemonade. Ben smiled at her for wearing flip-flops, as it was not as warm there as it would have been in Rome. Ludmila noticed and smiled.

"Go on. You want to play with my feet."

Ben smiled. He took her right flip-flop off and stroked her foot and gently pinched each toe. He enjoyed it. Of course he again wished she had painted her toenails. Ben carried on caressing Ludmila's foot. She suddenly looked uncomfortable and moved her foot away. Ben wondered if something was wrong but chose not say anything about it.

He remembered something that would interest her.

"Ludy, did I tell you that I spoke to one of the members at the business group about you wanting to work in marketing and that he told me to send him a copy of your CV?" Of course he knew perfectly well that he had already mentioned it to her.

"Oh, Ben, that would be wonderful. Thank you very much. You are so kind to me." Ludmila leaned forward and kissed Ben firmly on the cheek. They smiled at each other and then held hands. Ben looked at Ludmila intently, closer to believing now that she would be his Miss Right.

He wasn't really paying attention but he thought he could hear one of Ludmila's flip-flops falling gently to the ground. They were still smiling at each other when Ben felt Ludmila's foot against his groin.

Oooh, he thought. Was there still a possibility that this might actually be that special evening? He raised his eyebrows and then winked at Ludmila. She suddenly looked away and, to Ben's great dismay, she moved her foot away and put her flip-flop back on.

He stifled a sigh.

"Would you like another drink?"

She shook her head.

"There is nice walk near here. Take me there, please."

So they left the pub. They were holding hands but Ben noticed that it seemed a little forced and reluctant on Ludmila's part... but it was progress of a sort so he was not going to ask her what, if anything, was the matter. Spending time with her was still like a yoyo: one minute Ben was ecstatic whereas the next minute he would be left feeling very disgruntled. Maybe it was some sort of game to her or maybe that was genuinely how she was. Ben would have to accept it. He was delighted at the prospect of Ludmila coming to live and work in Oxford. And that evening they had finally had their first sexual contact, albeit a very minor one. It was a step forward and he was delighted nonetheless.

They walked through a park and came near to the sea. Ben saw that there was a church and graveyard nearby. It suddenly made him think about ghosts. He was not sure whether he believed in them or not. He thought he might once have seen a ghost in a dream many years earlier. He glanced at Ludmila and smiled. She was looking so beautiful as she walked along, staring into the distance.

"Ludy," he asked in a low voice, "Do you believe in ghosts?" although he had not remembered the supposed presence floating over him on the Saturday afternoon.

Her head whipped round towards him.

"Don't mention ghosts, please." There was a note almost of hysteria in her voice. She snatched her hand away and pressed it to her lips. She was almost leaping up and down.

"Why, what's wrong? Have you seen ghosts before?"

"My family had experience." Both her hands were covering her face. Ben pulled her away from the graveyard. Once they were well clear of it he took Ludmila's hand with both of his and said,

"Tell me, please. What happened?"

She stared at him in silence for a few moments. Her face seemed to be going whiter by the second. Ben had never seen her that scared before.

"OK. I tell you." Her voice was low and trembling. "Some years ago my mother's uncle, he died young. He was buried near river. His ghost came back and said,

'I'm cold.' My mother told her aunt and he was buried again in another place. She did not see ghost any more. But I am always scared of seeing ghosts now."

Ben listened intently. He had heard somewhere before that some Eastern European countries had a certain fascination with ghosts. Reassuringly, he gently squeezed Ludmila's hands and smiled at her. He said,

"It's OK, Ludy. I don't think there are any ghosts here. But I will protect you from any."

She stared at Ben for a moment as if she almost understood what he meant and then she looked away. As they walked on they admired the scenery. It was getting dark and too late for any ice creams. She then asked Ben to take her home. His heart sank yet again. With what Ludmila had done to him earlier that evening he wanted to believe that there was a chance that she might be spending the night with him, or that at least he would finally get to make love to her. Was this still some sort of endless game? What was her agenda and had she played this type of game with other young men before? Ben was perplexed. However, he did not feel brave enough to confront her about this. He just enjoyed her company. But he soon saw that she had noticed the change in him.

"You OK?" she enquired.

"Yes. Just sad that we're going back now."

"I know, but work tomorrow."

Ben walked silently back to the car, making sure they passed the graveyard very quickly and only holding Ludmila's hand very loosely. She suddenly put her hand in her pocket. Ben had almost switched off and didn't actually notice for a few moments. He carried on walking, then realised and looked at her.

"You trying to make me unhappy?" she snapped.

"No. I… " Ben could not take the opportunity to say what was really bothering him. He then smiled at Ludmila and leaned forward to kiss her. Ludmila turned her head away, just allowing him to kiss her on the cheek. She held out her hand and he took it again, this time taking care to hold her hand tightly as they walked on. They got back to Ben's car soon after and then drove back to Bournemouth. Ben glanced at Ludmila.

"So what are you doing this coming week, Ludy?"

"I am very busy. Tomorrow I am working. Tuesday and Wednesday, college too. There is English exam soon and I must prepare."

Ben nodded. He acknowledged that he could not be her priority when he was not there but he really wanted to see her more often – and, now, for her to spend a night with him – as their relationship desperately needed that to happen for it to be able progress to the next level.

"Will I see you again soon?" he asked, looking into Ludmila's eyes and smiling – but with difficulty, as he was already anticipating a negative response.

"I don't know yet, Ben. We see."

He knew she could see his disappointment but she was not going to say anything soothing. However, she ran her finger up and down Ben's cheek. He smiled but still felt both sadness and frustration that he would have to wait a while now before he could see her again and before the possibility of any further sort of adult contact. They arrived at her host family's house. Ben stopped outside. Before getting out of the car, he turned to her, took both her hands and said,

"It was a lovely evening, Ludy. I will miss you now until the next time I see you, Beautiful."

Ludmila smiled. She gave Ben a kiss before saying,

"Goodnight." She opened the car door to get out. Ben remembered again about the CV.

"Oh, I will see if there is any news about your CV too," he said.

She turned back and gave him a proper kiss. It felt amazing. Ben then had a rush of blood and for the first time, he could barely control himself physically in front of her. He looked at her chest and then put his hands on her breasts and gently caressed them. Ludmila looked very surprised but put her hands over Ben's. She let him carry on for a couple of moments but she then firmly pulled his hands away. Ben felt disappointed, but had already reluctantly accepted that that was how Ludmila behaved. She got out of the car and walked to the gate.

Ben followed her swiftly and took her hand and kissed it.

"Goodnight, Beautiful. Sleep well. I will miss you so much until I see you again."

"Goodnight, Ben. Thank you for lovely evening. I miss you too."

They kissed again and Ludmila walked to the door and waved. He waved back and watched for several moments. At last he dragged himself away and drove off. He wanted to believe that he had made some significant progress in his relationship with her, yet every time they made any advances she backed off promptly. And, yet again, she had not said anything about the next time that Ben would see her.

He got home at around midnight. Unsurprisingly, he felt very restless. He now totally adored Ludmila. His heart wanted her to be with him all the time while his head just about managed to control his thoughts and actions to a certain extent, and also made him very reluctantly accept that there was still quite a way to go to capture her heart (and before they became a proper couple). He had a glass of milk and made himself read for a little while. It took him until 3am before he finally managed to drift off to sleep.

Unsurprisingly, he dreamed of Ludmila that night. They were running round and playing on a beach and then went to where Ben was staying to spend the night together. Ben woke up with a huge sigh of disappointment afterwards.

Chapter Twenty-One

It was very much a case of after the Lord Mayor's show for Ben on the Monday morning. He was still delighted at the progress he had made with Ludmila but, at the same time, their relationship was surely a long way behind what it would have been if he been seeing an English girl. However, Ben had not forgotten the trauma of the dates he had had only a few months earlier. He shuddered. In Ludmila he saw a young lady who was beautiful, genuine and, although different in so many ways from girls here, at least seemed to accept him as he was. There was still no question of him ever letting go of her or of him wanting to meet any other young lady.

He did not text her at the beginning of the week. She was busy, and as she did not play text tennis so neither would he. On the Tuesday work was very busy. At lunchtime he popped out briefly for a sandwich. Then he felt the urge to contact her, so sat down at his desk and wrote:

Ben Smith Tue 25 Aug 13.12

• *Hi Ludy. I hope u r well. Thank u 4 a wonderful eve on Sun. U make me so happy. I hope u r having a nice week. I look 4ward 2 cing u again soon. Missing u so much. Ben xx*

He hoped she might respond fairly soon. After work Ben had a snack, read a newspaper and then went to the gym. He did keep a close eye on his mobile phone, and in fact he was almost relieved to be able to put it away for a couple of hours. Anyhow, Ben was somewhat disappointed to find that after his gym session there was still no response from Ludmila. After returning home and just before going to bed, Ben tried to convince himself that it would all be fine and that Ludmila would send him a nice text message the following day. Despite his concerns Ben did sleep better that night, but that was mainly due to his session in the gym.

Ben was working on a task for Jonathan on the Wednesday. He felt considerably more anxious now. Possibly Ludmila might not be feeling the same way about him. He still did not feel particularly jealous that Ludmila might be interested in any other young man. Ben had already worked out that someone with Ludmila's looks would surely attract constant male attention but, as he had noticed, she was not flirtatious – at least, not in front of him. He also took comfort from the fact that she seemed quite willing to spend a lot of her free time with him.

Ben did find it increasingly difficult not to keep checking his mobile phone every few minutes. At one point Roger came into Ben's office to explain something. At that moment Ben saw his mobile phone flash. Without listening to Roger Ben, almost losing a heartbeat, checked his mobile phone. His heart sank immediately when he saw that it was just an advert.

Roger shouted,

"Ben, put that mobile phone away immediately and pay attention when I am explaining something to you. Do you understand?"

Ben felt his face reddening. He went to cover his mouth.

"I'm so sorry. I was expecting… "

Roger shook his head.

"Whatever it is, it will have to wait. This is far more important. Please do not do that again. And never ever do that in front of clients. Do you understand? Thank you."

Ben felt awkward and embarrassed for the rest of the time, even though Roger did compliment him on the good work he'd done. How could he have been so foolish? Of course he should not have been checking his mobile phone when Roger or anyone else at work was talking to him, and certainly not when they were explaining things to him.

There was still no text from Ludmila, even after work. Ben started to feel very upset and tense. He paced up and down in his flat, his heart swaying between hope and despair. Of course the obvious thing to do would be to call her but for some reason he didn't want to, and his heart seemed to keep telling him that she should respond first before he contacted her again. As he would be seeing Simon the following day Ben decided to stay in that evening rather than go to the pub and he read a little, and he also watched the news on television before going to bed. He didn't sleep well, worrying both about Ludmila and also about Roger telling him off at work.

The following day Ben was careful not to be caught out again with his mobile phone. He cleverly decided to put his mobile phone between a couple of books and some files so that nobody passing outside his office would see him checking it. He would also try and make an effort not to check it too often. By now he was almost certain that Ludmila had decided not to have any further contact with him. He forced himself to wait until Friday, and then he would call her if she had not responded to his text message in the meantime.

The Thursday passed reasonably quickly, although there was still no message from Ludmila. At least Ben could look forward to seeing Simon that evening. They met up for drinks in a quiet pub. Simon was very cheerful and told Ben in great detail about a speedboat that he had recently purchased and how he and Natalie would also be going on a cruising holiday to Norway at some point in the following year. The conversation then turned to Ben's affairs.

"So how are things with Ludmila?" asked Simon.

"Fine," Ben hesitated before continuing. "I saw her last

Sunday and we spent a lovely evening walking near Christchurch."

"When are you seeing her again?"

"She's busy at the moment so I'll probably see her next weekend." Ben found it hard to meet Simon's eyes as he said that.

Simon raised his eyebrows and frowned a little.

"Like that, is it?"

Ben looked away.

"I appreciate it's taking a long time but I'm sure it'll work out fine fairly soon. I'll tell you in the strictest of confidence that Geoff at the business group has a copy of Ludmila's CV. I'll check with him shortly as to whether there are any job prospects for Ludmila in or near Oxford. That would be fantastic if he could find her a job locally, then we could live together." Ben now sounded very excited.

"Ah, but... " Simon stopped himself. He seemed to want to say something very important but looked as if he realised that it was surely not what Ben would want to hear.

"What?" asked Ben uncomfortably.

"Oh, nothing. I'm sure it will all be fine for you with Ludmila."

Ben nodded. However, he sensed that Simon was aware something was troubling him but was trying not to upset him. Otherwise, they spent a pleasant evening. They finished their drinks and as they said goodbye they agreed to meet up again in a couple of weeks' time. Ben had taken care not to check his mobile phone in front of Simon. Now he pulled it out and his heart sank again. Still no text message from Ludmila. That was it. He would phone her on Friday. Anyone else in his position would have phoned her before now but something inside him had prevented him from doing so every time he had wanted to contact her again.

Yet again Ben did not sleep well. He didn't dream about

Ludmila but had a strange dream in which he was twenty-one again, although he was conscious of actually being ten years older. Ben woke up with great difficulty the following morning. Of course he knew that he was still young but maybe that dream had pointed out to him that he needed to enjoy and to sort out his life while he was still young. For immediate purposes that meant speaking to Ludmila straight away. Quite simply, Ben had agonised for far too long over why she had not responded to his last text message.

At work Ben was doing some payroll accounting and working in his usual conscientious manner. He did check his mobile phone occasionally. At around 11.30am he checked that there was nobody around or likely to come in on him and he half closed his office door, after establishing that there were also no telephone calls for him to make or receive. He picked up his mobile phone and called Ludmila. His heart was beating very fast. He was concerned to see that she was OK and that they could carry on with their relationship.

However, much to his surprise and disappointment, there was no answer. Surely Ludmila would have seen that he was trying to call her. She had always answered his calls previously. Ben felt really troubled now. He walked up and down in his office, not really caring if anyone could see him or not. A few minutes later he called again. There was still no answer so Ben left a voicemail:

Hello, Ludy. I hope you are well. I am very sad that I have not heard from you recently, and I hope everything is OK and that I haven't upset you in any way. You know how important you are to me and I miss you so much and I can't wait to see you again. Please, please contact me as soon as you can. Hugs and kisses. Ben.

Ben didn't notice that Roger had come into his office. Ben didn't jump or look embarrassed or even try to apologise. Roger looked at Ben's mobile phone and then reminded him about the rugby match on Saturday afternoon. He added that he would be entertaining some potential clients and asked Ben to wear a suit and to come a bit earlier. Ben nodded and Roger explained that those potential clients ran a building company near Woodstock. Ben carried on with his work afterwards, checking his mobile phone every few minutes or so.

Lunchtime came and still there was no response from Ludmila. He went out for a pub lunch and almost managed to spill his food down his suit as he incessantly checked his phone. When he got home Ben decided to go to the gym as he would not have much time tomorrow due to the rugby match. His anxiety had increased and he called Ludmila again. He was saddened but not surprised that there was still no answer. Ben covered his face with his hands. Obviously something was seriously wrong. Why hadn't she contacted him before then? He felt close to tears. He could not bear the thought that he might have lost her. She had already changed his life and now nothing else apart from his immediate family and − to a lesser extent, his job, really mattered to him.

Needless to say Ben spent an uneasy session in the gym, and although he accepted that he was spared the torture of not having to check his mobile phone every two minutes or so for at least for a couple of hours it was going to be an agonising weekend until he could find out what was wrong with Ludmila.

Ben had a lie-in on the Saturday morning. He certainly needed it after his exertions at the gym the previous evening, and with the constant worrying about not hearing anything from Ludmila. He decided that he would iron his suit and shirts and have brunch before going to the rugby club in the early afternoon, and then do his food shopping and housework on the Sunday. Ben switched on his mobile phone. This time, after his heart had sunk at there still being no messages from Ludmila, he felt angry. Why was she doing this to him? Ben was desperate to find out the reason. He called Ludmila but again there was no answer from her. Ben tried very hard to compose himself as he left her a further voicemail:

Hello, Ludy. It's Ben again. I am now extremely sad and worried not to have heard from you. I can't help you if you don't tell me what's wrong. You know how much I care about you and I can't be happy without you. Please, please, please call me back as soon as you can. Hugs and kisses. Ben.

Ben shrugged his shoulders. He felt somewhat annoyed that he was practically having to beg Ludmila to contact him, but he knew how he felt about her and he almost had to wipe away a tear. But he could not keep calling her. Ben would go down to Bournemouth on Sunday, although the thought that Ludmila might not want to see him was unbearable. He forced himself to put his mobile phone away and get on with the day as best he could. Of course he could not let any of this show in front of Roger, nor the potential clients at the rugby match.

It was an important afternoon at the rugby club. Ben arrived promptly to find Roger already there. The potential client guests arrived shortly afterwards. Roger had been put in contact with them by a retired ex-colleague of his and was hoping to make them clients of Triangle Accountants. Ben listened carefully as they explained about their business and what sort of accountancy services they were looking for. They all had a drink together in the rugby club bar.

After a little while the conversation got round to Ben. He told them how much he was enjoying working for Triangle Accountants and also about how much he enjoyed living in Oxford. Roger commented that Ben was making his mark at Triangle Accountants. Ben smiled at this.

Ben was then asked whether he was married. He smiled and shook his head.

"No girlfriend, either?" said one of the potential clients jokingly.

"I'm seeing someone but it's rather casual at the moment," Ben replied, and hoped they would leave it at that. It was not their business, anyway. Of course, he was not going to discuss anything about Ludmila – particularly not at this difficult time, either with Roger or with strangers – even if they were going to become clients of Triangle Accountants. Ben was thankful that the conversation then turned to the rugby match. It was imperative to put his concerns about his private life to one side and to concentrate on the task in hand, which was to try and impress those potential clients. Therefore, while politely waiting his turn, Ben commented on the rugby team and what a good match it promised to be this afternoon, and asked the potential clients about their interest in rugby.

But of course it was impossible for Ben not to think about Ludmila. He did look at some of the couples in the crowd. There were only a few younger than him. He didn't feel any jealousy or resentment towards them, yet seeing those couples did remind Ben of how much he adored Ludmila and how he longed to have her there with him all the time.

The match went well and it was still a sunny and slightly breezy afternoon. Ben cheered quite loudly for the home team without getting too carried away in front of his firm's potential clients. Suddenly in the second half Ben's mobile phone flashed. He knew exactly who the text message was from. However, he realised that in front of Roger and the potential clients he needed to stay entirely focused on entertaining them and watching the rugby match.

It transpired that it was an agonising further couple of hours for Ben. He racked his brains regarding what Ludmila might have meant in that text message. Did she still want to see him again or not? Roger, Ben and the potential clients had another drink after the rugby match. It was then agreed that Roger would meet them during the following week to play golf and, Ben assumed, to discuss how Triangle Accountants could help them. Ben was not invited to play golf. Roger thanked Ben and they then left the rugby club. Ben sighed deeply as he was finally able to check his mobile phone. Ludmila's text message read:

Ludmila Sat 29 Aug 15.02
• *Ben, I don't know why u make me do bad things! I am so scared & worried. Ludy*

Ben read that text message with total disbelief. What on earth was Ludmila talking about? And why had she taken so long to reply to his last text message? It also hurt him deeply that the affectionate kiss was missing from Ludmila's text message as well. She hadn't said she did not want to see him again, but surely that could be inferred from what she had written. Ben went home feeling even more upset and bewildered.

By the time he walked into his flat Ben had become very angry as well. What was the matter with that young lady? Why had she suddenly turned funny on him? Hadn't he always been remarkably polite and tolerant towards her and always treated her like a princess? Also, what did she mean by *bad things*, and what was she worried and scared about? Was there someone else involved? He gnashed his teeth. He was not going to reply to her that evening: rather, he would sleep on it and call her on Sunday morning to try and get to the bottom of her strange behaviour towards him.

Ben did manage eventually to get to sleep that night. He was still very troubled by Ludmila's text message, and only very slightly relieved to have actually heard from her. Ben then remembered an ex-colleague a few years earlier in the City who had been in a serious relationship for several years, but when that relationship had ended he had said to Ben on a drinks night out that when females started to get funny with you for no apparent reason then it usually meant that your relationship with them was over. But Ben knew that Ludmila was different. Therefore, it was imperative to establish what exactly was wrong with her before he could decide what to do next.

On the Sunday morning Ben decided to call Ludmila at around 10am. He didn't plan anything in particular to say to her other than to establish what the problem was and to try and deal with it. He would not be unpleasant or lose his temper. He paced up and down in his flat and was unable to concentrate on either watching television or reading a book or anything else. Promptly at 10am Ben puffed his cheeks and called Ludmila's mobile phone.

"Hello," Ludmila said.

"Hello, Ludy. It's Ben. How are you?"

"Oh. Hello, Ben. Why you didn't call me yesterday?"

"Ludy, I was worried sick all week when I did not hear from you. What's the matter? Why didn't you contact me sooner and why didn't you answer my calls? I was so upset." He was finding almost impossible to keep calm.

"Err... you see, I had big problem. I was very worried... "

"What problem?" He had to struggle not to give in to his temper.

"It is difficult to explain." Ludmila was sounding anxious and flustered.

"Why did you get funny with me? You know how special you are to me and I would do anything for you."

"I know, but... "

"What, Ludy? It's very difficult to understand you." Ben knew he sounded impatient.

"Please, Ben, try to understand. I had big problem... "

"But I don't understand. If something was wrong, why didn't you tell me immediately? Of course, I would have done anything possible to help you. You should know that by now."

"I know. But sometimes you can't help."

"If you don't tell me what's wrong then I can't help you, can I? This is just getting silly now. Why on earth did you say that I made you do bad things? You are not a child. We have done things much slower than most girls here."

"Don't compare me with other girls, Ben," Ludmila snapped.

"OK. Look, we are both upset. I will call you again later." Ben hung up. In a very few minutes he was tearing at his hair. He realised that he had not handled that conversation at all well, but by the way she had reacted she hadn't really given him any other choice. Also, he still could not understand what she meant by a *big problem*.

Was somebody after her? Had she become involved with undesirable people, or did she have financial problems? All these thoughts were still flying around inside his head. Was that why she had made that bizarre comment about him making her do *bad things* when it was quite simply not true... and, yes, Ludmila did need to grow up. He swung round again. He had to calm down too. Of course he would not give up on her but she had ruined that last week for him and she was now spoiling the weekend as well. All right, he would go out now and find something to do. He was not going to call her again until that evening.

As he didn't fancy walking around Oxford Ben decided to drive to Banbury. It took just over half an hour to get there. When he parked in Banbury town centre, the heavens opened. Typical. And he didn't have an umbrella.

Too bad, he thought. Ben wandered through the shopping centre before stopping for some lunch in a cafe after a while, but he was still too annoyed and confused about Ludmila to fancy the sandwich he'd bought.

After Ben had finished a second cup of coffee he noticed that the weather had improved, so he set off for a long walk. There weren't many people out walking, perhaps due to the rain earlier. In any event Ben hardly noticed them, not even the younger couples holding hands. He simply could not fathom out what the matter was. In fact he wasn't sure that he actually wanted to speak to Ludmila again that evening.

By mid afternoon Ben felt ready to go home. He wasn't much calmer than when he'd gone out in the morning but it was better than driving himself to despair by staying at home. When he reached his flat three-quarters of an hour later he was so shattered that he threw himself on the bed to sleep. He realised that he was avoiding answering his own question.

Did he love Ludmila? Ben knew that in life you could kid other people as to your feelings, but it was a very foolish game not to be honest with yourself where your feelings for another person were concerned. Ben rolled over, sighing. Fortunately, he was so tired that even those endless troubled thoughts about Ludmila and his extra cups of coffee earlier that afternoon did not prevent him from falling asleep.

It was in fact a very deep sleep, and Ben did not wake up until nearly 6pm. He had an amazing dream. Ludmila was lying there beside him in his bed and they were so close and Ben was feeling ecstatic. He then woke up with a broad smile and turned to kiss her, only to find she wasn't there. Ben gasped and put his head in his hands. Anyhow, that dream had served its purpose. Ben would not avoid the question nor try and pretend that he did not love Ludmila. He called her straight away.

"Hello, Ludy. It's Ben again. How are you now?"

"Hello. I'm very sad because how you spoke to me and you didn't call again before."

"I am really sorry, Ludy. I was very upset. Anyhow, how are you feeling?"

"I thought I might have very bad illness. I was in so much pain. And was afraid it was a cancer. I can't tell you – too embarrassing – but the hospital did tests. It should be OK but I must see doctor again on Wednesday."

"Oh, my God. Ludy, that is terrible! So that was why you

were so scared. But why didn't you tell me? I would have come running to see you and help in any way I could."

"I know, but it was very difficult. I have final check on Wednesday."

"I will pray for you, Ludy. But I am sure it will all be fine for you." Ben was trying not to cry. "Ludy, I would love to see you again as soon as possible but I guess it is too late for today now."

"Actually, I wish you called me again earlier and you could have come to see me. I am busy tomorrow morning now."

A cancer scare. Between shock and shame at the way he had spoken to Ludmila that morning Ben was trembling. He felt devastated. Why couldn't he have been kinder towards her?

"I'm so sorry, Ludy," Ben continued. "Please forgive me. It's because I… " Ben knew what he wanted to say but couldn't bring himself to say it, and knew that perhaps it wasn't the right moment.

"I know, Ben." Ludmila then sounded happy. Maybe it was because she had understood what Ben had meant to say.

"OK, Ludy. I hope you can have a nice quiet evening. I do wish you were here with me. I hope and pray that it all goes well for you on Wednesday. Please let me know afterwards. Of course, if you need me on Wednesday, I will come down to Bournemouth."

"Thank you. Ben. Yes. Perhaps you take me to nice place next Sunday."

"Of course, Ludy. I will surprise you and make it a very nice day for you. Goodbye and many kisses."

"Thank you, Ben. Goodbye. I kiss you too."

Ben was touched by Ludmila's last comment and also impressed by her optimism in relation to her cancer scare. He was very relieved that he had spoken to her again and had finally cleared up the problem. He had been far too rash. If he hadn't made such an issue out of how she had behaved towards him during that past week he would have seen her that day. Worst of all, Ludmila with a bad health scare. It simply did not bear thinking about. Could the best thing that had ever happened to Ben now about to be taken from him? Surely not. Ben tried to watch some television but he was worn out and wanted only to sleep.

However, sleep wouldn't come. He was still very alarmed by Ludmila's cancer scare. He would certainly pray for her to be given the all-clear on the following Wednesday. But then a doubt crept into his mind.

What if she wasn't telling the truth? Did she not want to see him that weekend and had she only mentioned that he could have seen her when she knew it was too late? Ben felt concerned by those thoughts too, but calmed himself down by reasoning that maybe Ludmila was testing him to see how much he cared for her. Well, now she knew the answer. For present purposes, Ben would go along with the cancer scare. Hoping and praying that she would get the all-clear, he knew exactly where he would take her the following weekend.

Chapter Twenty-Two

Ben felt better the following morning. If it was indeed a genuine cancer scare he was still extremely concerned about Ludmila's health. But at the same time he was not sorry that he had revealed to Ludmila how he felt about her. Provided all went well on Wednesday he knew things would get better now for him and, hopefully, for Ludmila too.

Arriving at work in good time he went straight to see Roger, who thanked him for Saturday afternoon. Roger didn't mention playing golf with the prospective clients on Wednesday nor what involvement Ben would have if they did become clients of Triangle Accountants. Nonetheless, Ben felt satisfied that he had done what Roger expected of him. Ben then got on with his work.

Far more importantly, Ben resolved there would be no more silliness – at least, not from him – where contacting Ludmila was concerned. He would text her on Tuesday and if she did not reply he was not going to leave matters very long before finding out what was going on.

It was the fortnightly meeting of the business group the following day. Some members asked Ben how Ludmila was getting on. Ben certainly didn't mention her health problem, knowing what the inevitable consequences might be for any prospective employment for her in Oxford. He simply said that she was busy with her studies that week and so he would not be seeing her until the following weekend. That much at least was, hopefully, correct. Ben also went to speak to Geoff to see if there was any news on job prospects for Ludmila in marketing. Geoff replied,

"I've tried a few people, Ben. Unfortunately they did not have anything. However, a friend of mine who runs a small marketing company said that he might have something in a couple of weeks' time which may suit Ludmila. But that is strictly *entre nous* at the moment. OK?"

"Absolutely. Thank you so much." Ben smiled broadly. Was the dream of Ludmila coming to live with him about to take a huge step towards becoming a reality? Of course Ben understood that nobody else was to know, and that included Ludmila as well at the moment. First and foremost they had to deal with her health scare, and hope that it would be over on the Wednesday. On his way back to work Ben texted:

Ben Smith Tue 1 Sep 14.17
• *Hi Ludy. I'm still v sorry about Sun. I am praying that all will be well 4 u 2moro @ doctor's. I miss u so much & I can't wait to c u again next Sun. I hope u'll enjoy the day out I'm planning 4 u. Of course, I will come & be with u 2moro if u need me. I'll be thinking of u. Speak soon, Beautiful. Ben xx*

Ben didn't know whether to laugh or cry. He was so happy now that he and Ludmila had sort of reached an understanding about their relationship, but he was very worried lest anything should spoil it now.

What if Ludmila did have an incurable illness? Ben could cry at the thought of it. Of course he would look after her regardless, even if she went bald and ended up in a wheelchair. As far as he was concerned she was his, and he hoped that that was what she wanted too. Nothing and no one could change how he felt about her.

Ben then briefly thought about Rebecca, Emma, Selina and Jess.

What had happened to them since? Was Rebecca still with that young man he had seen her with in the Ashmolean Museum? Had Emma,

Selina and Jess found their Prince Charmings or were they still behaving as rudely to every man that they had a first date with? Ben could not quite bring himself to laugh about it, as it had upset him greatly at the time. But, thankfully, they no longer had any importance to him now that Ludmila was part of his life.

After work he went to the gym. He wasn't too concerned about hearing back from Ludmila straight away. He would call her by the Wednesday evening to see how her medical appointment had gone. However, just as he was leaving the house his mobile phone bleeped:

Ludmila Tue 1 Sep 19.39
• *Hi Ben. Thank u 4 yr txt. I am v worried about 2moro but happy that u care so much about me. I will call u 2moro eve. Look 4ward 2 cing u again Sun 2. Ludy x*

Ben nodded and then sighed on reading Ludmila's text message. Yes, it was great that she had fully understood his feelings towards her and that they both needed to make more effort in how they behaved towards each other. It was also very pleasing too that, despite her medical worries, she was looking forward to seeing him again as well. Ben briefly toyed with the idea of calling her but decided to wait for her call and continue to pray in the meantime that tomorrow she would be given the all-clear.

After a routine session at the gym Ben went home and decided to go to bed early. He still felt very nervous, but something inside seemed to tell him that everything would be all right for Ludmila the following day.

Ben got to work quite early on the Wednesday. He knew that it could be a very long day and he would have to avoid checking his mobile phone every couple of minutes if possible. The day started with a very rare staff meeting. Karen was there and she nodded at Ben but did not say anything. Ben wondered if Karen knew about Ludmila, but he was certainly not going to ask her. Roger made an announcement:

"Due to the effects of the current recession as well as the lack of a sufficient amount of new work coming in, I would appreciate everyone at Triangle Accounts doubling their efforts to try and get new clients for the firm so that we are able to carry on as we have been."

That was worrying. Ben had not realised that Triangle Accountants was struggling financially to that extent. Certainly nothing had been said to him about it, and he had always thought that he had had enough work to do. He would do what he could do although, other than his business group, he didn't have any other contacts locally. Surely it was up to Triangle Accountants to increase its marketing campaign to attract new clients?

Ben shrugged his shoulders after the staff meeting. Of course, Ludmila was still far more important than his job. However, he did nonetheless still feel a little concerned. Other than the few occasional hiccups he thought that he had done well in his job since he had joined Triangle Accountants, as evidenced by his successful first appraisal. He also felt that if there had been any serious problems concerning him or his work then Roger would almost certainly have told him straight away. Ben checked his mobile phone discreetly and then carried on with his work. He had lunch with Tony, who asked,

"What did you think about the staff meeting today?"

"I was very surprised. I wasn't aware things were that bad, as nobody had said anything to me before. I'll just carry on with my work as normal but will see if there is anything I can do to get new clients," Ben replied.

Tony raised his eyebrows and looked a bit puzzled but continued,

"Yes. Let's hope there are no adverse consequences and that Triangle Accountants can continue as it has before. But you're still happy here?"

Ben was shocked by that question.

"Of course. I love working at Triangle Accountants. It's like a second family to me. It's been a great year for me and I look forward to many more years here."

Tony nodded. They finished their lunch and the conversation turned to more general matters as they walked back to work. Ben checked his mobile phone as soon as he was back in his office. There was still nothing from Ludmila. Ben started to feel more apprehensive. Would she tell him if there was a problem? After their last telephone conversation, surely that should not have been an issue. He was prepared to drive down to Bournemouth straight after work if necessary. However, after the staff meeting – and despite assuring himself that he had nothing much to worry about, Ben realised he could hardly ask to leave work early that day.

It proved to be a very tense afternoon for Ben. He was waiting for a phone call or a text message from Ludmila. He knew very well that to contact her first – particularly at the wrong moment, and if the news was bad – could be fatal to their relationship. Equally, if the waiting was agonising for him, he could imagine how Ludmila must have been feeling. It was virtually impossible for him to concentrate on his work but he struggled through it, hoping and praying for Ludmila all the time.

At 5pm there was still nothing from Ludmila. Ben was starting to go out of his mind with worry. It could only be bad news now. How could the world be so cruel to him and his dear Ludy? After nearly a year of agonising over whether he would ever find a suitable young lady – as well as the bad experiences with other young ladies, which had even led Ben to doubt himself – he could not begin to even think of losing Ludmila. Given the staff meeting that morning, Ben decided to stay an extra hour at work just to tidy up his files. Then at 7pm he would call Ludmila.

About an hour later, after Ben had left work and walked home, he was not sure what to do. He had no appetite, nor could he contemplate going to a pub. He wanted to telephone his parents and explain Ludmila's problem to them but he could not bring himself to do so. Sitting in his flat with his head in his hands Ben played some music and prayed again for Ludmila. He tried to smile, remembering how Ludmila had inspected him when they first met and how they had embraced and become closer. It was still unimaginable that he might lose her. It took a huge effort to keep calm in spite of his fear and frustration.

Suddenly his mobile phone rang. It was Ludmila. Ben's heart pounded against his ribs as he croaked,

"Hello, Ludy. I have been so worried about you. What has happened?"

"Hello, Ben. Thank you. It's OK. The consultant said it is clear. No cancer."

Ben soared with delight.

"Oh… my dear Ludy. That's wonderful news! Thank God. I was so worried and scared for you." Ben's voice was excited and trembly at the same time.

"I know. I am so happy that you care about me."

"Of course I do, Ludy. What are you doing now?"

"I have quiet evening. I know you want to see me again soon. I know. You surprise me on Sunday."

"Thanks, Ludy. I know the perfect place to take you. I hope you will like it."

'I hope too.' Ludmila laughed.

Ben was beaming. His prayers had been answered. Ludmila was well.

"OK, Beautiful. You have a nice, quiet evening and sleep well. I can't wait to see you again on Sunday. I am so pleased that you are OK. Goodnight, dear Ludy."

"Goodnight, Ben."

Ben cried hard. Someone up above was looking after them. All his negative thoughts from the past few days suddenly disappeared. He even thought that the staff meeting at work had been a storm in a teacup. What was important was that his prospective Miss Right had been given the all-clear by the doctor and hopefully in the next month or so she might even be coming to live with him in Oxford. Ben could not have felt happier.

Chapter Twenty-Three

Ben slept soundly that night. He went to work with a broad smile on his face. He knew exactly where he would be taking Ludmila on the following Sunday. Ben saw his secretary Karen, who smiled back at him. Ben wondered what Karen might know. Anyhow, given how happy he was feeling, he went to speak to her.

"How are you today, Karen? I meant to tell you before that I'm still seeing Ludmila. I can't say how indebted I am to you as I would never have met her otherwise. She's such a wonderful young lady. I'm really happy with her. Thank you so much again."

"That's OK," smiled Karen, "I'm very pleased you're happy. I hope it works out for you." But she then went off quite quickly, much to Ben's surprise. He shrugged. Maybe it was because there was something urgent that she needed to do for one of the partners.

Ben's favourite great-aunt had lived in Aberystwyth. He had always loved going to Wales with its beautiful scenery, friendly people and relaxed way of life. Aberystwyth was an amazing town with its seaside, pier, cable car ride and the castle ruins. It would make a perfect day out for Ludmila. Ben had often dreamed when he was younger of walking along the beach there hand in hand with a beautiful girl. Now it was really going to happen for him.

Ben was careful to carry on diligently at work. He made sure that his mobile phone was out of sight and that he would not be caught out by anyone checking it too often. During his lunch hour he used it to check out journey times. It was a long drive each way but it would certainly be worth it. He could not do Saturday because of the rugby club match. He very much wished that he and Ludmila could drive down to Wales on the Saturday and then spend the night together there. Surely it would happen soon, but unfortunately for Ben it didn't seem likely that it would be that coming weekend. He checked that nobody was around and sent Ludmila a text message:

Ben Smith Thur 3 Sep 14.17
• Hi Ludy. I can't tell u how happy I am & relieved that u r better & had the all-clear on Wed. I was so worried 4 u. I am planning the perfect day out 4 u on Sun. I will tell u more about it on Sat. I miss u loads & can't wait 2 see u again. Ben xx

Ben smiled to himself. He didn't mind when Ludmila answered as long as she did answer and said something nice. He carried on with his hard work in the afternoon and stayed behind for the best part of an hour checking local business directories for companies to contact regarding their becoming potential clients of Triangle Accountants. He reached home and was getting ready for the gym when he got a reply:

Ludmila Thur 3 Sep 19.51
• Hi Ben. Thank u so much 4 nice txt. I feel better. I am so happy that u care 4 me. I look 4ward 2 Sun. Talk again soon. Ludy x

Ben was delighted. Things seemed to be improving with their relationship. So who knew now what might happen that weekend? If this had been any other girl then the waiting would have already driven him out of his mind but Ludmila was still definitely worth waiting for.

The Friday passed quietly. Ben gave Roger a list of the local companies he recommended contacting as potential clients.

Roger thanked Ben and said he would come back to him shortly about them. He also asked Ben to check with the local newspapers about the cost of adverts and also to see if any special offers were available, which Ben dutifully did. He left work at about 5.30pm feeling very cheerful and smiling to himself about the weekend ahead. All of sudden, in the next street to Triangle Accountants, Walter and Josh called him and beckoned him into a pub. Ben was taken aback but went in. Ben was surprised to see some of the other staff from Triangle Accountants there too. They all stared gloomily at him.

"Why are you looking so cheerful?" Walter asked. "Aren't you worried for your job like the rest of us, or do you maybe know something we don't?"

"Not at all," Ben was offended. "I love my job here. I've worked hard and done my best to please the boss and to respect Triangle Accountants and its staff." They all nodded and Ben could see his words had sunk in. "Are things really so bad?" he asked, still alarmed by all this. Everyone nodded. They discussed how they could all try and get more work in for Triangle Accountants and Ben explained what he had been doing. It was agreed that everyone else would contact family and friends locally and then propose to Mr Hudson that it might be a good idea to offer some sort of discount or special offer to new clients. Ben then had a quick drink with his colleagues. He noticed that Sarah was there, but not Mark or Karen.

"Please don't mention any of this to Mr Hudson or the other partners, Ben," said Walter as Ben was leaving.

"Of course not," Ben replied. On his way home, Ben shook his head about that meeting. Surely there was still nothing to worry about. He was doing his best, and Roger could see that. If there was a problem and he really was at risk of losing his job then he would have expected Roger to warn him first. Ben thought no more of that odd meeting other than he hoped there wouldn't be any more meetings like that, and that nothing would get back to Roger or the other partners about Ben being at the pub.

The Saturday morning went by as usual. Ben did all his chores. He got to the rugby club in good time in the afternoon. However, very surprisingly, Roger was not there. Ben wondered why, as it had not happened before. Was Roger unwell? Had he had an accident? Or was there something more important going on? Ben just carried on as normal. He cheered quite loudly for the team without drawing attention to himself. Roger did turn up at half-time. He seemed a bit flustered, and Ben also noticed that he even appeared a little surprised to see Ben there. Roger nodded to Ben and took his seat, and then they watched the second half of the match with Ben a bit quieter in his cheering for the home team. They had a drink afterwards in the rugby club bar and Roger thanked Ben as usual, but did not say why he had been late in coming to the match.

By now Ben had got used to fitting the rugby club into his life in Oxford. He hoped that either Ludmila would come to the matches with him or, if they got married, he might be excused attending some of the home matches when family matters arose. Ben chuckled to himself that this had seemed impossible only a few months earlier. Who knew? Perhaps Ben would one day be attending the rugby club as senior partner of Triangle Accountants.

Anyhow, his rugby club duties were over for another fortnight and he could focus on the most important thing in his life which was – of course – Ludmila. He had planned as much of Sunday as was possible in advance. At 7.30pm he called her.

"Hello, Ludy. How are you? What have you been doing today?"

"I look after children. Also I study for English exam. So where you take me tomorrow?"

"It will be a surprise for you,' Ben laughed. 'I'm sure you'll love it."

"OK. So vot happens then?' Ludmila sounded intrigued.

"Have a good night's sleep. I will pick you up at about 9am, so you'll need to be up early and get a good night's sleep tonight. OK?"

"OK," she sighed. "But that is early."

"Ludy, I am sorry to mention it again but I am so happy and relieved that you are better."

"I know, Ben." Her voice faded to a whisper.

"Sleep well, Beautiful. I can't wait to see you again."

"Goodnight, Ben. I look forward to tomorrow too."

Ben could not stop smiling for the rest of that evening. He busied himself checking that he had everything ready for the journey. He got himself to bed at 10pm, knowing how early he would have to get up on the Sunday. He read a little before drifting off to sleep.

Ben jumped out of bed promptly to the sound his alarm clock at 6am. Very speedily he showered and ate some breakfast. Picking up the rucksack he had filled with some towels and CDs, he left his flat and was on his way before 7am. He drove quickly and stopped at a petrol station just before Bournemouth where he filled up and also bought some bottles of water and some sweets that he hoped Ludmila would like. He had a little time to spare so he had a coffee, then freshened up and sprayed on his aftershave.

He looked for a present for Ludmila but decided he would treat her to something nice in Wales, whether it might be a souvenir or something else of her choosing. He got to Ludmila's host family's home just before 9am. He got out of his car and walked up and down. Suddenly came the sound of the front door opening and closing. It was Ludmila. Ben felt his heart pounding. As she closed the front gate he raced towards her. He stopped dead in front of her and looked at her intently.

"Vot? Vot?" she asked, somewhat bewildered. Ben laughed and looked at Ludmila's pockets and then pointed to his own pockets in jest, remembering how Ludmila had inspected him when they had first met. Ludmila smiled back and then Ben instinctively put his arms around her and they embraced very passionately. Ben didn't know whether to laugh or cry. He obviously did not want her to see him upset, particularly after what she had just been through. Even so, he felt a tear run down his cheek. Ludmila smiled and wiped it away with her finger.

"Thank you, Ben," she said.

He swallowed and nodded. The weather was quite warm that day. Ludmila was wearing a nice pink top and jeans. Ben had on a light green shirt and jeans. He smiled at her.

"Ludy, it will take a while to get where we are going but I am sure you will love the scenery and the seaside."

"But we have seaside here," Ludmila said sharply.

"I know but I'm taking you to see my seaside. It's very nice there." Ben chuckled to himself. He was sure she would love Wales.

"I got some bottles of water, some sweets I hope you'll like and I brought some extra CDs too."

"Thank you. That is nice." Ludmila smiled and they held hands briefly before getting into the car and setting off. It wasn't long before Ben noticed that Ludmila's head was nodding.

"Grab a cushion from the back seat," he told her. "Go on. You'll feel better after a nap."

She smiled at him and went to sleep quite quickly. Ben noticed that her mobile phone flashed a couple of times and he wondered who was texting her, but he wasn't going to wake her up to find out. When Ludmila woke up they had already reached Bristol. She looked a little embarrassed but Ben reassured her.

"It's OK, Ludy. I can imagine how tired you must be after the past week or so."

"Thank you, Ben. You are so kind to me."

Ludmila was both fascinated and impressed by the Severn Bridge. She then asked about lunch. Ben laughed.

"It's going to be a Welsh restaurant. We'll find something

soon." As it happened, they found a cafe as they reached the Brecon Beacons. Ludmila seemed quite tearful as she observed the impressive mountain range.

"Whatever's wrong, Ludy?"

"I am sad. I remember my grandfather. He took me to hills when I was small girl. I feel very emotional."

Ben smiled and nodded. He quickly leaned his hand across and touched her arm reassuringly. They went into the little cafe on the edge of a village, with a splendid view of the grey-green hillside. They both had a hot dog and lemonade to drink and some fruit afterwards. Ludmila surveyed the scenery.

"It is so nice. I hope to come again."

Ben's heart jumped. He knew a hint when he heard one.

"Of course, Ludy. I am sure we will come here again many times." He could hardly conceal his eagerness. Ludmila looked at him for a moment before smiling. As they walked back to the car Ben told her the legend he had heard as a child about the origins of a family of doctors in the Brecon Beacons. She listened carefully and looked at Ben as if to say that he had invented that story to try and impress her. Ben smiled. It really didn't matter whether the legend was true or not. It was far more important for him to have his future Miss Right with him and to be concentrating on having a good time with her and improving their relationship.

After lunch they drove through Rhayader and the Elan Valley on the old road through the hills to Aberystwyth. Ludmila gasped at the wild hills and the fast-flowing rivers. However, by now she had listened to all the CDs she wanted to and she was becoming impatient.

"Ben, how long? I want to get out of car now."

"OK, Ludy. We're nearly there."

In fact it was still a while before they reached Aberystwyth and had parked the car. Ludmila raced to look at the sea. She smiled and said,

"It is so beautiful. It was long journey but worth it." She kissed Ben on the cheek. They then decided what they would be taking with them. Ben took his rucksack. Ludmila had a little bag with her. They would take pictures with their mobile phones. Ludmila saw a bench facing the sea and asked Ben to come and sit down on that bench with her.

"I like looking at sea," she told him with a broad smile. She seemed lost in her own world for a few moments so he leaned his head gently on her shoulder and put his hand on her long, dark blonde hair. This was absolute bliss for him: a lovely seaside and a beautiful girl with him whom he loved so much, and hoped that she loved him too. Ludmila seemed to carry on being preoccupied with the sea. She did then appear to realise what Ben was doing. She smiled and kissed him on the forehead but then stood up quite quickly – so that Ben, quite comically, almost fell off the bench.

Ben remembered that there was a crazy golf course next to the seafront. Ludmila was very keen to have a game. This time it was a closer game than when they had played in Bournemouth on their first date but Ludmila still won – not that Ben minded in the least.

They stopped for a cup of tea afterwards. Ludmila's mobile phone flashed a couple of times. She answered the text messages straight away. Ben could not restrain his curiosity.

"Is that your friends who keep texting you, Ludy?"

"Yes."

"Did you tell them about me and where you are today?"

"No."

Ben was shocked. Why wouldn't Ludmila have told her friends about him? Was he not that important to her, or did she want to keep their relationship secret? Ben pressed his lips together in irritation. It didn't bear thinking about if Ludmila did not actually value their relationship.

"Vot? Vot? It's OK. I am private person." Ludmila had spotted Ben's anxiety.

Ben perked up on hearing that. He reminded himself that she came from Moldova and although he still knew next to nothing about that country, he accepted that she might not have been as free as girls here and that she might well have to be more discreet about any relationships with young men.

After visiting the castle ruins they walked round the shops. Ben told Ludmila that he wanted to buy her a present. Ludmila smiled and Ben noticed that she did not hesitate in finding quite an expensive painting of the local seafront.

"Thank you so much, Ben. Very kind," she said appreciatively.

"You're very welcome, Ludy. I hope you like it and that it reminds you of today." Ben smiled helplessly at her.

Then she said she wanted to try the cable car. Ben hadn't been on the cable car for years but didn't mind having another ride. He bought their tickets and they got on. As the cable car was ascending the hill Ben suddenly felt nervous. He seemed to have a totally unexpected attack of vertigo. He couldn't say anything but he instinctively clung to Ludmila. She giggled and the other passengers started laughing as well. Ben felt embarrassed but shrugged his shoulders and did his best to try and laugh it off.

At the top of the hill they walked off the path. They were suddenly amazed as they saw a second bay. Despite all his visits to Aberystwyth, Ben had never seen this before. The view of the second bay completely took their breath away. Ben put his arm around Ludmila, who snuggled up to him.

"It is just so beautiful, Ludy." Ben's voice was hushed.

Ludmila smiled and nodded.

"Just like you, Beautiful," Ben added, kissing Ludmila passionately on the cheek. It was another special moment for him. He could have again put his hands above his head as if in prayer and given thanks. He could hear 'The Miracle' playing in his head. They took pictures of the scenery on their mobile phones. Ben also took some pictures of Ludmila and she took a couple of photos of him. Ben gave his mobile phone to a passer-by, who kindly took a photo of Ben and Ludmila snuggling up together.

Ludmila looked down again at the pier and the beach and suggested that they should walk down there and then along the seafront. It was still quite warm, although it was getting late in the day. They walked slowly along the seafront and Ludmila then wanted to walk on the beach and sit on the sand. Ben was a bit surprised – and he didn't have a beach mat but did have a spare towel, so they sat on that.

Ben had forgotten to mention the possible good news from his business group contact. He suddenly remembered it and was about to tell her that there was a potential job in marketing for her, when much to his surprise, Ludmila moved and sat behind him with her hands around his chest. Ben tingled with excitement and leaned his head gently backwards into Ludmila's chest.

"Vot your intentions towards me?" Ludmila asked unexpectedly.

"I hope you will come and live with me and be with me forever," Ben said somewhat nervously, even though he had rehearsed that sentence many times previously.

Ludmila did not say anything further, but kissed the back of Ben's head. Suddenly Ben felt his heart pounding with excitement and anticipation as Ludmila's hands started rubbing his stomach, and then her fingertips stroked his groin. Ben shut his eyes, breathed deeply and savoured every second. Ben had forgotten that people might have seen them but that was totally irrelevant to him. He wondered what else she might do. Surely she would not go that far, and not on a public beach? Ben could have laughed at the very thought of that happening there.

So much for Ludmila coming from a stricter culture, he thought. He didn't turn round but continued his deep breathing and feeling ecstatic. However, just as he was preparing himself for the impossible, Ludmila stopped and got up.

"Home now. I am tired. We eat on the road."

"OK, Ludy," Ben said obediently. How could he be anything else after what had just happened? They walked quietly back to the car. Ben noticed that Ludmila wasn't holding his hand, but he could hardly complain. He accepted that they would not be making love that evening but he nonetheless felt ecstatic by what Ludmila had just done to him.

Ben worked out the journey back in his head. He would drive as far as Bristol if possible and then get petrol and they would stop at a motorway services. Ludmila was quiet in the car. Ben smiled at her frequently. She answered a few more text messages and then put her car seat back and slept for a while. Ben turned the CD player down and thought over the events of this special day out with Ludmila. What had also made it extra special for him was sharing his past by bringing her to his favourite childhood place. He had even managed to forget about being irritated by Ludmila's friends frequently texting her.

They made good time as there was not much traffic. Ludmila dozed off and woke up. Ben got petrol and then woke Ludmila up at a motorway service station near Bristol. She smiled and willingly held his hand as they then went for a light dinner. Ben did not mention what had happened on the beach and neither did she.

For the rest of the journey Ludmila listened to a couple of the CDs she liked again, but did not say much. Ben guessed that she was a little embarrassed but there was really no need for her to be. He judged that in such situations it was best not to say anything. It was after midnight when they finally got back to Bournemouth. Ben very politely opened the car door for her and got her bag from the boot.

"Oh, Ben. Thank you so much. It was lovely day."

"It was a lovely day because of you, Ludy." Ben kissed

Ludmila's hand before kissing her on the lips. Ludmila hugged Ben. His happiness suddenly turned to sadness and despair at the thought of being parted from her. He had not asked her when he would see her again but hoped that it would be the following weekend.

"Ben, you look very tired. I hope you get sleep tonight." Ludmila sounded concerned.

"That's OK, Beautiful. You need your rest more. Sleep well. I hope I see you again soon. I will miss you terribly in the meantime."

Ludmila smiled. She pinched Ben's cheek then kissed her finger and pressed it against his lips. He immediately kissed her finger back. He was struggling to keep back his tears. Ludmila waved and then walked into her host family's house. Ben really didn't care about the time or that he would be exhausted for work on Monday morning. It had been a wonderful day with Ludmila. He was still delighted, too, about her touching him on the beach. He would be very sad now until he saw her again. However, they were closer now and Ludmila was over her health scare and that was all that mattered. It was nearly 3am when he got back to his flat.

Chapter Twenty-Four

It was 9am when Ben woke up the following morning, despite having set his alarm for 7.30am. He jumped through the shower, shaved, got dressed, grabbed a couple of cereal bars and ran to work. Roger was waiting for him. He pointed to his watch and said rather crossly,

"And what sort of time do you call this, Master Smith?"

"I'm really sorry," Ben said very apologetically. "I certainly didn't mean to be late. I unfortunately overslept.'

"It's all right." Roger cleared his throat. He gave Ben an additional task to do that morning. Ben got on with it straight away. He felt a bit annoyed about being late for work but there was a spring in his step. He was still elated about the day he had just spent with Ludmila, and nothing was going to spoil that. The day, in fact, passed quickly and quietly. Ben had planned to go to the gym on the Tuesday evening. He also looked forward to seeing Simon again on the Thursday evening for drinks. But, most importantly, he wanted to know when he would see Ludmila again.

Ben was still delighted with what had happened that weekend, but he did wonder what would happen the next time they met up and whether he would ever get to make love to Ludmila. It was concerning Ben now. Much as he worshipped her and had convinced himself that she would become his Miss Right in due course, it still felt odd that they had not consummated their relationship. Perhaps he might even have to wait until he married her. Ben was not too concerned that Ludmila had not responded to his indirect marriage proposal the previous day: the main thing was that he had said how he felt about her and she now knew it.

Further, he didn't need to bombard her with text messages at present as she was concentrating on her English course – with an important exam coming up shortly. He could wait until the Tuesday to send a message. If she responded positively he would suggest that they meet up again the following weekend.

Late on the Tuesday afternoon, just as he was finishing work, Ben texted Ludmila:

Ben Smith Tue 8 Sep 17.42
• *Hi Ludy. I hope u r well. I had such a great time on Sun. Thank u so much. U know I went to Wales many times as a child & I never thought I would go there with someone as beautiful & special as u. Wales is a beautiful country but not as beautiful as you. I hope everything is OK 4 you. Miss u loads, Beautiful. Speak soon. Ben xx*

He smiled to himself. It was perfectly true that he had never taken either of his previous girlfriends to Wales, and he had never thought he would be accompanied there by any young lady as beautiful as Ludmila. However, the concern did remain about as to whether and when Ludmila would want him to take their relationship to the next level. Yet he was still very anxious to see her again as soon as possible.

The week carried on as normal but there was still no message from Ludmila, so Ben made up his mind to call her on Thursday. He most certainly did not want a repeat of what had happened a couple of weeks earlier. However, on Thursday morning, there was a text message from Ludmila:

Ludmila Thur 10 Sep 10.08
• *Hi Ben. I am good, thank u. I really enjoyed Sun & Wales is beautiful. Thank u 4 special day. Talk soon. Ludy x*

Ben was very pleased that she had enjoyed Sunday and considered it to be a *special day*. On the other hand, there was no mention of when they would next meet up. He stood up in his office and his head trailed the ground for a little while before he got back to work. What was he going to do for the coming weekend? That evening Simon remarked that Ben seemed a lot more cheerful than he had done on the last occasion, but still did not quite appear to be fully contented.

"How are things going with Ludmila?" asked Simon, looking at Ben intently.

"Fine. We had a lovely day out in Wales last Sunday."

Simon nodded.

"When are you seeing her again?"

"I don't know yet." Ben couldn't keep the disappointment out of his voice.

"Keeping you on your toes, is she?" joked Simon.

Ben raised his eyebrows but did not answer. He then remembered the photos of Ludmila he had on his mobile phone and showed them to Simon.

"Here, have a look at these pictures of us from last weekend."

Simon looked at the photos and was speechless for a few moments.

"Oh, my. She looks fantastic. I understand now." Simon was nodding his head. "I look forward to meeting her soon," he added with a grin. Ben nodded.

Simon then talked about his next holiday. Ben felt a little envious, as Simon could afford so many lavish holidays – and being self-employed, there seemed to be no restrictions as to when he could take them. Simon would be going to the Caribbean next. He told Ben he would see him again in about a month's time.

Friday passed as usual. Ben hadn't given much thought to what he would do for activities that weekend. He decided to go to the gym on Friday evening. He would carry out his normal tasks on Saturday morning before going out somewhere. He wasn't going to spend the entire weekend in his flat, and the weather forecast was very good. As far as Ludmila was concerned he would text her on Saturday. He did not expect to see her then. Perhaps there might be a chance of seeing her on Sunday, but Ben would not force it.

It was around Saturday lunchtime. Ben had just finished the housework and was watching some television. He was planning to check online for an activity to try out or an event to go to locally that afternoon. Unexpectedly, his mobile phone rang. It was Ludmila.

"Hello, Ben. How are you? What you are doing now?"

"Nothing much. Just finished the housework and watching a bit of television."

"OK. Come down to Bournemouth. I wait for you."

Ben could have jumped six feet in the air. It was perfect timing from her.

"Thanks, Ludy. I'll be down straight away. See you shortly," he said, almost out of breath.

Ben quickly changed his clothes. He decided to take a smart shirt and trousers on the off chance that they might get to have dinner somewhere nice. Ben took his aftershave with him as well. He raced down to Bournemouth, getting there in just under a couple of hours. He was so excited about seeing Ludmila again that he had forgotten that he had never previously seen her on a Saturday.

This time, much to his surprise, Ludmila was waiting for him at the front gate of her host family's house. Scarcely had Ben got out of his car when she walked across the road towards him and kissed him passionately on the lips and then stroked her hand across his face.

"Hello, Beautiful. It's great to see you again." Ben hugged her very tight.

"Thank you, Ben. I am very happy to see you too."

Ben beamed at her. The only slight disappointment was that she was wearing a light cardigan and jeans. He would have liked to see her in less clothing, but then so – surely – would plenty of other men. He smiled helplessly at her. He was still so excited by this lovely surprise.

"Let's go and play crazy golf," Ludmila said domineeringly.

"Of course, Ludy." Ben smiled to himself at Ludmila's constant direct manner. She certainly still knew what she wanted and didn't hesitate to say so. They drove to a town centre car park and then walked to the crazy golf course. Once again she evidently enjoyed the game and won it fairly easily.

"I win," she declared triumphantly.

Ben burst out laughing. Ludmila started laughing too.

"Vot? Vot?" Ludmila looked intently at Ben. Ben stood silent for a moment and then covered his mouth with his hand and started laughing again. Ludmila shook her head but smiled.

"Shall we walk along the seafront now?" asked Ben.

She looked surprised but nodded agreement. They walked towards the seafront. Ben had his arm around Ludmila. Many people looked at them as they walked past. Ben felt very important, and also knew that he would be the envy of many men. They reached the seafront. It was very busy with people there but they had space to walk. At that moment Ben was feeling contented but he did wonder what would happen with Ludmila that afternoon. It was very likely that she would go off at some point, and it would be another week at least before he saw her again. He would have to face up to asking her about where their relationship was going.

They were in a quiet spot without other people. Totally unexpectedly, Ludmila said, "Sing me a nice song, Ben."

Ben was dumbfounded. Apart from occasionally humming along to some of his favourite pop songs, he hardly sang at all.

"Um… I'm not really much of a singer, Ludy. Why do you want me to sing to you?"

"Please. I want you to sing."

"OK, then." Ben raised his eyebrows. He would have to think of an appropriate song promptly. He decided on 'Morning Has Broken' and sang the first verse. As he sang he actually almost enjoyed it. Despite her sharp manner he felt he could relax in her company. When he finished singing, Ludmila said,

"Thank you. That was not so bad."

That was praise indeed! Ben wondered how any of the other dates he had had would have reacted to him singing. Would they have just sneered or made out that there was something wrong with him? But, equally, would any of them have wanted to hear him sing in the first place? That was part of the appeal of Ludmila – after her appearance, of course.

They then came to the pier and they walked along it. Ben wanted to go into the penny arcade. He checked his wallet and went and changed some money for the one-arm bandits. Ludmila was cross.

"Why you waste money?" she said. Ben had always liked one-arm bandits. He squeezed her arm gently.

"It's OK. I'm not going to spend a fortune. It's just a little flutter. You'll see. It is fun."

Ludmila frowned and did not watch Ben play on the one-arm bandits. Unsurprisingly Ben did not win anything, so he ended his games quickly and said no more about it. Outside on the pier they came to a stall offering cuddly toy prizes for hitting the bullseye on the dartboard. Ludmila was very interested.

"Please, please, Ben, can we try? I like prizes." She again clearly knew what she wanted.

"OK. I'll try for you." Ben smiled. He hadn't played darts for quite a while. He didn't mind having a go, as it was still very important for him to show Ludmila that he would do anything for her.

"Thank you," said Ludmila, kissing Ben on the cheek.

Ben went and paid to have a go. It was three attempts to hit the bullseye to win a prize. He tried valiantly but couldn't manage it. He looked at her.

"Sorry, Ludy," he said a little forlornly and shrugging his shoulders.

"Let me try," demanded Ludmila.

Ben was taken aback. But he nonetheless went and paid for her to have a go. The first dart she threw missed the board completely. Ben tried not to laugh. The second dart she threw then hit the bullseye. Ben could simply not believe it. Had she played darts before? Ludmila then looked at the cuddly toy prizes. Ben would have chosen one fairly quickly. However, Ludmila had to inspect nearly all of them. After a while the stallholder glanced at Ben, who jokingly put his head in his hands and looked away muttering to himself, "For goodness' sake, just choose one," he said, but while making sure that Ludmila could not see him doing that.

The stallholder laughed and Ludmila eventually choose a cuddly rabbit toy. She then walked them back towards the town centre and the car park. Ben was very concerned by this and wondered what might be wrong with her now. He made up his mind that it was time to ask her where he stood with her and where their relationship was going. Just as he was about to ask, she said,

"Take me home now, Ben."

Ben could have cried out loud. It was not even 5pm.

"Why, Ludy? Is something wrong?" He could hardly conceal his disappointment.

"It's OK. Don't worry." She patted his arm reassuringly.

Ben still did not understand. Moodily, he walked back towards the car park. He carried on holding Ludmila's hand, but only very lightly. When they reached her host family's house, Ben got up to let her out of the car. He made no attempt to kiss or hug her. This really was too much for him. But Ludmila looked at him and smiled.

"OK. Come back in thirty minutes, and change your T-shirt." She kissed her finger and pressed it against Ben's lips.

He kissed her finger hard. He nodded and beamed as he now understood what was going on. Ludmila wanted him to take her out for dinner. He decided quickly that he would drive to any nearby pub, and would put on his smart shirt and trousers and use his aftershave. There was simply no escaping the fact that Ludmila certainly was still different but, equally, very intriguing in her manner.

Ben was back at Ludmila's host family's house well within half an hour. He waited with mounting impatience for her. Half an hour soon became three-quarters of an hour. Ben listened to music and constantly checked his mobile phone. He was about to call Ludmila when suddenly there she was. Ben could have fallen at her feet. She was wearing a beautiful dark blue evening dress and grey sandals. She had tied her hair back and she had even painted her toenails this time as well. She really was Miss World that evening!

Ludmila was also carrying what looked like a sports bag. A tiny part of his mind wondered why she had brought that with her, but he was concentrating more on taking in her stunning appearance. He raced over and almost went on his knees. He took her hand and kissed it, jokingly saying,

"My lady."

Ludmila laughed and ruffled her hands through Ben's hair. She handed him the bag.

"Put my bag in car boot," she said.

Ben obliged straight away. Did that mean what he thought it meant?

"Where would you like to eat?" he asked, once they were in the car.

"You find nice restaurant."

"Of course." Ben thought it would be good to find a well-known chain restaurant, so he needed to look on the outskirts of Bournemouth. It was extremely hard to concentrate on driving with Ludmila beside him, and with her so beautifully dressed. He had to struggle not to keep looking at her.

"Be careful with driving," she warned him abruptly.

Ben nodded obediently. Suddenly he felt a gasp of satisfaction as Ludmila put her hand on his thigh. He blew Ludmila a kiss from the side of his mouth the same way he had done in the cinema on their first date. Ludmila laughed and left her hand on his thigh. After a little while they found a large restaurant. They were both hungry. Unsurprisingly they got a lot of stares on arriving and going inside and Ben was enjoying his celebrity-like status. Once inside and having ordered their dinner, Ben said,

"Ludy, you look so beautiful. I am so happy to be with you now."

"Thank you. It's OK. Enjoy evening."

Ben felt Ludmila's sandal against his leg. He smiled rather than let his obvious emotion show. When they had started their dinner, Ludmila asked,

"What happens now with job?"

Ben had forgotten about that in the last few hours.

"I'll ask on Tuesday. Hopefully there will be an opportunity for you next month."

"Oh, Ben. That's wonderful." Ludmila went quite pink with delight. They clinked their glasses and carried on with their meal. The restaurant had a nice garden and it was still warm and light. They had a walk and sat down on one of the benches still receiving a lot of attention from the other people there. How Ben would have loved to have presented Ludmila with a red rose and even to have serenaded her. They sat there quietly looking towards the sea and watching the setting sun. To him it was absolutely perfect.

The air cooled rapidly. Ben could see that Ludmila was becoming a little chilly and that he did not have a cardigan to offer her.

"Let's go to Oxford," she said suddenly.

"Oh… of course," replied Ben, beaming at her.

They set off. Ben did not drive particularly fast, knowing that the longer he took the more time he would spend with Ludmila. He was not sure whether she might want to go back to Bournemouth later that evening but he certainly hoped that she didn't.

"Why you drive slow?" Ludmila frowned at him.

"Well… " Ben covered his mouth and tried not to laugh.

"You funny," she said, patting his shoulder.

As they arrived in Oxford Ludmila said,

"Take me to your flat."

Hallelujah, thought Ben. Was the second part of Ben's dream now finally going to come true?

They got to Ben's flat and he turned the heating on slightly, hoping that Ludmila would not need to put anything on over her stunning dress. Ben checked. He did have some white wine in the fridge but, unfortunately, no champagne. He asked her whether she would like anything to eat or drink.

"Tea, please," said Ludmila.

That was hardly the answer that Ben wanted to hear. Anyhow, he made tea for them both. Worse still, he noticed that Ludmila sat away from him and had put the television on and was watching the news. Ben was concentrating on Ludmila rather than on the television. How could he have done anything else?

"Vot? Vot?" asked Ludmila.

"Nothing, Beautiful." Ben did just about manage to conceal his frustration.

After the news had finished Ludmila turned the television off.

"Play some music," she told him.

Ben looked through his CDs and found a collection of love songs, so he decided to chance his luck. He put that CD on quite loudly.

"Come and dance with me," was her next order.

Ben was delighted. This was another first. He danced very close to Ludmila with his arms around her and she then put her arms around him too. The music was slow and soothing. Ben smiled at her and she smiled back at him. They kissed and then she put her head on Ben's shoulders. They danced to a few songs. Then Ludmila stopped to take her shoes off. She laughed and enquired,

"You like my feet now?"

"Oh, yes," sighed Ben and he grinned, remembering the time in the shoe shop when they were looking for a pair of shoes for her – and the time when she had let him play with her feet. It did make a difference seeing her with painted toenails but she was beautiful regardless – and Ben was madly in love with her, anyway. They then danced to a few more songs.

"You got wine?" was her next question.

Ben went and got the bottle of white wine from the fridge and two wine glasses. This time Ludmila sat on the sofa next to Ben. She had some wine and then sat with her legs over Ben's lap. He shut his eyes and tried to breathe deeply although his heart was beating furiously. Ludmila poured them both some more wine and let her hands wander freely. Ben shivered with delight. She then looked sideways at him and gave him a saucy smile and looked at her dress. Ben took the hint and ran his hands gently along her legs. He jokingly squeezed her toes. She laughed loudly but then looked at Ben intently as his hands reached her underwear. She jumped up and sat on his lap. She pressed herself into him and her eyes widened as she noted his arousal. She unzipped him and let her fingers freely caress him. Ben was in heaven. He closed his eyes again and was convinced that Ludmila was as turned on as he was.

"You take shower," Ludmila said, quite abruptly and equally unexpectedly.

Ben was shocked. There really was no predicting this young lady. Ben's second thought was to ask her to join him in the shower, but she would have obviously have had a shower while he was waiting for her earlier. Nonetheless, she always seemed to cut him short whenever he was getting close to her.

"OK," he croaked, trying to get his heart to beat at a more normal pace. "Stay here and I'll be back shortly."

Ludmila nodded and raised her glass to him. Ben showered as quickly as he could. As he dried himself he was afraid the evening might be over now and she would want to go home. There was no question of him forcing himself on her. Towelling his hair, he walked to the bedroom and stopped dead with shock. Ludmila was waiting for him there. She was lying under the bed sheet and her dress was on the chair.

"Now make me woman tonight," said Ludmila in a very domineering voice.

"Certainly, Beautiful." Ben would have loved to have added, *I thought you'd never ask*, but with her abrupt temperament that might well have gone badly wrong. His mouth split in a huge grin. It felt as though he was entering paradise. Ludmila smiled and suddenly threw her underwear from under the bed sheet at Ben. He laughingly dodged it and turned off the lights and jumped under the sheet with her.

It was unbelievable. They made love several times. They kissed incessantly and Ben also kissed Ludmila from head to toe. A long time afterwards, she lay quietly in Ben's arms. She smiled and kissed his neck and snuggled closer still. Ben held her tightly against him.

"Thank you for today, Beautiful. I can't tell you how precious you are to me."

"Ben, you are my king."

Ben swallowed a sudden lump in his throat. While Ludmila might not have said in exact words what Ben wanted her to say, calling him her king hopefully meant that she loved him too. They kissed again for several minutes before going to sleep.

It was very early in the morning when Ben woke up. Seeing

Ludmila asleep with her head on his arm he smiled helplessly. Miracles did happen in life! He could have sung, 'You Make Me Feel Brand New' but he didn't want to disturb her. Yet he couldn't resist. He kissed her and whispered,

"I love you, Ludy."

As he closed his eyes he heard her murmur,

"I love you too, Ben."

This time he couldn't stop the tears that squeezed out of his closed eyes. He wiped them away before pulling her closer and kissing her many times again before they both drifted back to sleep. It was very late in the morning before they woke up again. Ben felt very touched that they had been holding hands in their sleep. Ludmila turned towards Ben, kissed him and was on top of him. It was just as amazing as it had been the previous night, and she was still working her magic on him.

Afterwards she slipped straight into the shower. When Ben came out of his shower he found her looking around in the kitchen and declaring that she was hungry. They ate a breakfast that was more of a brunch. Then they took some bread to feed the ducks and set off for the park. What a contrast with his walks through parks over the last year. Now he was certain that he had finally found his Miss Right and, despite her different behaviour, it had certainly been worth the wait and all the anguish. He would still need to take things slowly with Ludmila but he was now dreaming of getting engaged to her soon, if possible.

They walked happily along hand in hand. Ben still noticed all the attention Ludmila got even though she was back to wearing her sweatshirt and jeans. She enjoyed feeding the ducks. What a pleasure it was to do such simple things together. Yet Ben couldn't help but wonder if all that would change for the worse once Ludmila started working in business.

They talked more about their respective families. Ben laughed to hear that Ludmila's older brother was a bit of a bully and how beautiful her younger sister was.

"Is your sister as beautiful as you?" he enquired.

"Oh, Valeria is more beautiful," she answered earnestly.

"I find that very hard to believe."

She laughed.

"No, no. It is true."

Ben nodded politely.

"I hope you'll come and meet my parents soon. Perhaps we could all go out for dinner."

"Yes. I would like to meet your parents."

Another important step on the way, thought Ben. He didn't doubt that his father would be won over by Ludmila's looks but it would inevitably be much harder for Ludmila to impress his mother. However, if she had already begun working in Oxford before she met his parents then that would no doubt help matters.

"Will you introduce me to your friends?" asked Ben.

"Err… OK. Maybe."

Ben was a bit surprised at this. What was the reason for her reluctance? They then stopped for a coffee. He told her more about Simon and what a successful business consultant he was. Ludmila seemed impressed, particularly when Ben mentioned the frequent foreign holidays Simon had – and his speedboat. She was enthusiastic about having a ride in the speedboat and said she would be happy to go out as two couples with Simon and Natalie.

Suddenly Ludmila checked her watch and gasped at the time. She needed to go back to her host family. Ben covered his hand with his mouth. He didn't make any attempt to hide his sadness.

"I understand," said Ludmila, rubbing Ben's cheek with her hand.

"All right." There was one important thing to do before he took her back.

"Please let me show you something before we go."

"Vot?" asked Ludmila a little impatiently.

"You'll see in a minute," answered Ben. He put his finger over his lips. She shook her head gently in bewilderment. They walked back but instead of going straight to Ben's flat, he took her via the shopping centre and to a jeweller's shop.

"Why?" Ludmila still seemed puzzled.

"Which ring do you like?"

She appeared awkward but looked at the rings and eventually pointed to an emerald ring.

"I like that ring."

"Right. I'll remember it for you." Ben beamed at Ludmila but he could not quite understand why she looked away rather than smiling back at him. They got back to the flat. He felt extremely sad that Ludmila didn't want to spend any more time there and after a quick glass of water was still anxious to get back to her host family. Ben carried her bag to the car.

Ludmila was quiet in the car but Ben noticed that she didn't get any text messages or calls on her mobile phone. He was equally sad that she didn't talk about the previous night or even that morning. He tried to start up a conversation.

"So what will you be doing this coming week?"

"Oh, I have work – and don't forget my English exam soon."

"I'll let you know about the marketing job after my next meeting at the business group."

Ludmila smiled and she put her hand on his thigh. At last she seemed to be getting back to how she had been yesterday evening and that morning, but Ben still felt slightly uneasy. He wondered what had happened to change her since the morning. They arrived at her house all too soon for him. It was obvious that she was still very conscious of the time. Before Ben got out of the car to let Ludmila out and get her bag he said to her, holding both her hands,

"Ludy, thank you so much for a perfect weekend. I loved

213

every second of it. You are such an amazing person. You make me very happy and I love you so much. I can't be happy without you and I hope that you will be coming to live with me."

"Thank you, Ben. It was lovely weekend. I love you too. I hope we live together soon."

That was exactly what Ben had dreamed of her saying. They embraced for a couple of minutes but he knew he could no longer delay her. He got out of the car, fetched her bag and opened the passenger door for her. They walked across the road hand in hand. Ben stopped at the front gate. He knew he could not go any further. There were tears in his eyes. He choked.

"Ludy, you'd better go now or I won't be able to let you go."

"I know, Ben."

They kissed again and Ludmila reached into her bag and gave Ben a present. It was a fridge magnet with the Moldovan flag. Ben was touched.

"Thank you, Beautiful," he said, kissing her on the cheek.

Suddenly, Ben was overcome. Impulsively he put his hands on Ludmila's shoulders and asked her to close her eyes. She looked surprised but obliged. Ben then kissed Ludmila a hundred times. Ludmila couldn't move. She seemed enchanted and then smiled broadly.

"Oh, Ben. That was so special," she said.

They kissed again and then Ben watched Ludmila go towards her host family's house. She turned round at the door, waved and blew kisses at Ben. He waved and blew kisses back but made himself drive off, torn between laughter and tears. Could he dare to consider that she was now indeed his Miss Right? She had not mentioned anything about meeting up again, which was surprising after the weekend they had just spent together. But he was sure he would get a positive response from her, especially if he had good news on the job front for her.

Back in his flat, Ben felt very lonely. He could have kissed everywhere Ludmila had been. He also had great difficulty believing that that weekend had actually just happened. He really wanted her to be there all the time. It would be difficult initially living together as Ludmila did things her own way and reacted differently to things from the way people here did, but they would surely get used to each other.

After a cup of tea Ben made himself go to bed early. Although work was a very poor second to Ludmila, he didn't want to be late in again. He lay in bed for a while, his thoughts now totally dominated by Ludmila... how he loved her and how he wished she was there with him right now. Ben looked at the pillow she had slept on. He put his hand on it. It had become a precious object. Before he finally went to sleep he remembered the old saying:

Good things come to he who waits. Ludmila had certainly proved that!

Chapter Twenty-Five

Ben woke up early on the Monday morning. He found that he had been clutching the pillow that Ludmila had slept on. He smiled and clasped it even tighter. The significance of that past weekend was only now starting to sink in. He got to work in good time. Although he still did not think that there were any major problems at work he didn't want to be late again. Ben walked in to work with a big smile and greeted everyone more vocally than usual. In his happy state he had forgotten how tense most people were about the current situation at work.

He wanted to contact Ludmila just to hear her voice, but even after such a perfect weekend she might not respond immediately. Her long silences would not be an issue once they were living together. In any event, Ben was quietly confident he would have good news for her from the business group the following day. That would be the perfect time to contact her. Monday proved to be a straightforward day at work and Ben went to the gym in the evening.

On the Tuesday morning Ben woke up, not having slept particularly well. He had suddenly become concerned about the business group and whether there would be a job opportunity for Ludmila in Oxford after all. For some reason his earlier confidence had disappeared. Given the current economic climate there would not be many opportunities for Ludmila to work in marketing, especially as she would have to start from the very bottom.

To Ben's relief, Geoff was in attendance at the business group meeting. Ben sat near him. He planned to wait until the end of the meeting to ask if there was any news. However, Geoff approached him first.

"Ben, I have some very good news for Ludmila."

"Yes?" Ben was all ears.

"My friend has an opportunity for a trainee marketing assistant in his firm starting in a month's time and has emailed me a job application form, which I will forward to you for Ludmila to complete."

"That's wonderful news." Ben made no effort to conceal his delight. He could have cheered as loudly as he had done for the rugby club, but for the right reasons this time.

Geoff winked at him.

"Between you and me I don't see any difficulty with Ludmila getting that job, but that is still strictly *entre nous*. OK?"

"Of course," Ben nodded and smiled. "Is there anything I can do for you in return?"

"Well… actually… my teenage son will be looking for work experience next year, and I think it would be good for him if he spent some time at Triangle Accountants."

"I'll speak to Roger. I'm sure it won't be a problem, and I'll let you know at the next meeting."

They both smiled and finished their drinks, and Ben left the meeting still walking on air. He gave a laugh as he realised that he might need to start counting the days now until Ludmila moved in with him. The rest of the afternoon passed slowly. He checked his email regularly for the job application form from Geoff. It was nearly 5pm when it came. Ben breathed a big sigh of relief and forwarded the email on to his own private email address.

After work Ben did not go straight home. Rather, he walked into the town centre, passed the jeweller's shop and checked on the emerald ring that Ludmila had said she liked. It was still there. He looked at it for a long time. Should he buy it now? It was quite expensive, although he knew that he could afford it.

Finally Ben decided that he had better wait until Ludmila had moved in with him. Then it could either be an engagement ring or a Christmas present for her.

Ben also passed a church. Could he also dare to think that he and Ludmila might get married there one day in the not-too-distant future? The thought of it really appealed to Ben. Would their children be christened there one day too? He shook his head, realising that he was getting carried away – but then, why shouldn't he? In the next month his life was surely going to get so much better.

When he got home he sent Ludmila a text message, which he had been planning in his head since Sunday evening:

Ludmila Tue 15 Sep 18.11

• *My dear Ludy, I hope u r well. Thank u so much 4 such an amazing & special wkend1 I can't say in words how wonderful it was & how much it meant to me that u stayed here with me on Sat night. I have some fantastic news 4 u from the biz grp. There is a job as trainee marketing assistant starting next month in Oxford and I have the job application form which I will mail 2 u now. Ludy, I can't say how much I miss u & how much I wish u were here with me now. But I know u will be coming to live with me in a month's time so I can just about wait till then. Love u loads. Talk soon. Ben xxx*

Once Ben had sent the text message he forwarded the email to her. He felt ecstatic. He leaned out of the window to look at the green but after a while realised he was chilled, as the weather was getting cold. He shut the window and made a hot drink before going to bed.

The following day at work Ben went to see Karen. He felt he still owed her a huge thank you for helping him to meet Ludmila.

"Karen, sorry if I'm sounding like a parrot, but I really wanted to thank you again for giving me the opportunity to meet

Ludmila. I am still seeing her and she is such a wonderful young lady. Dare I say it? I think she is the girl of my dreams."

"I'm very pleased for you, Ben." Karen smiled but suddenly her smile disappeared. Ben was surprised. Was something wrong? And why would Karen not be happy for him?

"Sorry, I have to go and see Mr Brydell now." Karen whisked herself away. Ben watched her go in surprise. He shrugged his shoulders. Maybe he had simply caught her at the wrong moment. By the afternoon Ben was more concerned about hearing from Ludmila. He wanted at least an acknowledgement that she had really enjoyed the previous weekend too. Also, she would need to get on with completing the job application form for the marketing assistant role. He would give her until Thursday and then he would call her.

Ben had decided to go to the cinema that evening. Of course, as with everything he did, he wished that Ludmila was there with him. He comforted himself a little with the thought that he might take her to see another film that coming weekend if he saw her. Just as he got to the cinema, there was a text message from Ludmila:

Ludmila Wed 16 Sep 19.58
• *Dear Ben. Thank u 4 text. I'm good, thanks. Thank u 2. It was wonderful wkend with u 2. I am so pleased about job as well. I will complete job form now. Call me @ wkend. Love, Ludy xx*

Ben was delighted and equally relieved. It wouldn't have borne thinking about if Ludmila had not answered at all, or if she had not said anything positive about that previous weekend. His spirits soared. Surely the coming weekend would be a repeat of the previous one and he would spend most of it with Ludmila again.

The weather took a turn for the worse on Thursday. It was raining quite heavily. Nonetheless, Ben was still a very cheerful character at work. He was dreaming about seeing Ludmila again that weekend and trying to decide where they might go. At around 10.30am Roger buzzed Ben and asked him to come to his office. This was unusual. What could it be about? Perhaps it might have something to do with the next rugby club match. He knocked and went into Roger's office.

"Take a seat, Ben." Roger's tone was grave and he was looking very serious. "Due to the ongoing recession and a significant downturn in work recently, Triangle Accountants has had no choice other than to make several members of staff redundant. Unfortunately, your role is one of those the firm cannot afford to keep."

Ben simply could not believe what he was hearing. He hung his head and then covered his face with his hands.

"But I love this job," he croaked, his throat so dry that he could hardly get the words out. "I love living and working in Oxford. I was planning to stay with Triangle Accountants for the rest of my working life and hopefully become a partner here one day."

"Ben, it has been a pleasure to have you here and we will all miss you but unfortunately there just isn't the work to justify keeping your role, and that is unlikely to change in the foreseeable future."

Roger was trying to sound sympathetic but Ben was not impressed. He blurted out,

"You know, I also have a girlfriend and she is supposed to be coming to live with me and to work in Oxford within the next month. What am I supposed to tell her now?" Ben was getting exasperated now. He then said, "And why didn't you at least warn me that my job was at risk?"

Roger looked at Ben intently for a few seconds and then turned his head away. Ben's eyes narrowed. He felt a leaping flame of anger inside. Was Roger daring to suggest that Ludmila was the reason he had lost his job? Was that also why Karen had been funny towards Ben the previous day? He opened his mouth to protest but Roger raised his hand.

"Look, Ben, what the partners have decided to do is to offer you a compromise agreement. We will pay you two months' salary tax-free and, in addition to a standard reference, I will be happy to provide a personal reference to any future employer of yours." Roger continued, "You will obviously not need to attend any further business club meetings but you are welcome to still come along to the rugby club's matches if you want to."

Ben stared at him, forcing himself to understand the words. His life had suddenly become a mess, but he did recognise that Triangle Accountants were actually offering him more money than they actually needed to. He drew a deep breath and nodded.

"You must go to a firm of solicitors to have the compromise agreement checked over and then signed. Here is a list of local firms." Roger gave Ben a list of local solicitors. It was clear that, despite trying to be civil, Roger was very keen to get the matter dealt with straight away. Ben would have to leave Triangle Accountants immediately.

"Please collect your belongings and then go and make an appointment with a solicitor. I wish you all the best for the future." He stood up, holding out his hand. It was a very strained handshake for Ben.

Outside Ben saw Sarah in tears, and Mark was shaking his head too. Sarah had also been made redundant and Mark had been put down to three days a week. Mark said he had no idea how he would be able to explain this to his wife (and with their baby, too), particularly the consequences of a reduced salary. It was of no consolation to Ben that he was not the only one being made redundant but it did make him think that maybe Ludmila was not the reason he had lost his job.

Ben collected his belongings and then left Triangle Accountants. He was still in a state of shock. He muttered goodbye to the receptionist but he certainly wasn't going to say goodbye to Karen, particularly after the previous day. Outside he had to clench his jaw very hard not to give way to his emotions. He was so shocked at his sudden redundancy that he found he was even trembling. And he also felt deeply hurt. He had always enjoyed his job at Triangle Accountants and had never dreamed that he would leave the firm, and particularly not in such a way.

The job had meant so much to Ben. It felt like a tragedy to lose it. This would surely not have happened to him in his last job in the City. Worse still, what was he going to tell Ludmila? Would she still want to come to live with him in Oxford if he didn't have a job? Where did that leave their future together? He got back to his flat quickly. The events of that morning had not sunk in but he did know that the first thing he needed to do was to go and see a solicitor about the compromise agreement. He rang a local firm of solicitors and, surprisingly, they offered him an appointment for that afternoon.

The solicitor checked through the agreement and asked Ben how much his salary was and how long he had been with Triangle Accountants. Ben was advised that he was just short of a year's service with Triangle Accountants so that he would not have had a claim for unfair dismissal in respect of his redundancy anyway. Ben frowned. He began to wonder when his departure from Triangle Accountants had been planned and by whom. Ben was advised to accept the compromise agreement in the circumstances, and Ben then signed it. The solicitor also politely asked Ben what his plans were, and whether he would be looking for similar roles locally. Of course Ben had been so flabbergasted by that morning's events, and so worried about what he would tell Ludmila, that he had completely forgotten about applying for new jobs.

Ben felt slightly better after having seen the solicitor, as at least he had been able to discuss his job situation with a neutral person. Ben then went back to his flat. There was also the question of whether he would be able to continue renting the flat and, of course, what he would tell his parents. He could easily guess who his parents would rather blame for him losing his job, and they would also be horrified at him staying in the flat if he was not working.

Despite his anguish Ben forced himself to sort things out quickly. He began by updating his CV. He was aware that it would not look good that he had spent less than a full year at Triangle Accountants but there was no way round it, and he had nothing to be ashamed of. Now he could see how fortunate he had been to have got the job at Triangle Accountants so quickly, but the way in which they had got rid of him did not feel pleasant. Next he phoned a couple of local recruitment agencies, and arranged interviews for the following week.

By the evening he had dealt with all the administrative tasks. He was so full of anger and tensions that he went to the gym to try and exercise them off. But as he returned home afterwards he agonised over what he would have to tell Ludmila.

The Friday was a strange day for Ben. He couldn't recall not having a job to go to for such a long time. He got himself a local newspaper and also checked online for any local accountancy roles but knew that he would still have to start with those recruitment agency interviews. He felt very drained after the previous day's events and had a snooze in the afternoon. Altogether it was a long, dull day with no calls or texts from Ludmila. Totally irrationally, he hoped for a call in relation to an imaginary accountancy job vacancy in Oxford that would solve everything for him. To get out for a bit Ben went food shopping, then cleaned the flat on Friday evening to save himself the bother on the Saturday.

Needless to say, Ben woke up extremely tense on the Saturday. He knew he had to call Ludmila and of course he wanted to speak to her. However, the difficulty would be what to tell her about his job. Of course, given how he had lost his job, there was no way Ben would ever go to the rugby club again. He became so worried about calling Ludmila that he was actually physically sick. Terrible as it was, he would have to delay calling her until the Sunday morning.

That night Ben did not sleep well. He was still far too troubled by his circumstances and also by what he would have to tell Ludmila, and what might well happen to her job opportunity. In the middle of the night Ben woke up suddenly. He felt very scared. It was as if there was a presence floating over him in the bedroom again. He could not see it but he could feel it. Ben did not say anything but put the pillow Ludmila had slept on over his head and kept very quiet and still until he was sure that the presence had gone.

On the Sunday morning Ben was so preoccupied about calling Ludmila that he forgot about the presence in the bedroom. He could not put it off any longer, so promptly at 10am he called her. His heart was thumping and he did feel trembly. Her phone rang and rang but there was no answer and the message Ben received was,

This person's phone is switched off. Please try again later or send a text.

He wondered whether she might be tired from working on Saturday or whether she was just having a lie-in. Nonetheless, he would try again at midday. He went out to a local cafe where he read the newspaper and made his cup of coffee last a long time. Promptly at 12pm he tried calling Ludmila. He was surprised and concerned to get the same message. He decided to send her a text instead:

Ben Smith Sun 19 Sep 12.04
• My dear Ludy, I hope u r well. I have tried to call u a couple of times this morn. How r u getting on with the job application form? I look 4ward 2 talking 2 u & it would be great 2 c u again this afternoon if poss. Love u loads, Ben xxx

He decided that he would need to tell Ludmila what had happened with his job. Nonetheless, that would have to wait until she replied. He went back to his flat and looked online for any job opportunities. Ben was surprised to see that there was an accountancy vacancy in Witney. He spent the early afternoon working out how he would apply for that job and preparing a slightly amended version of his CV to, hopefully, fit that role. He became absorbed in the task. When he had finished and submitted that job application it was nearly 4pm. He checked his mobile phone. There was still no response from Ludmila. Ben wondered whether she might be angry with him for not having called her the previous day.

In any event Ben still felt dreadful. The nightmare of losing his job was now sinking in and, worse still, the potential consequences it might well have for his relationship with Ludmila. Ben could only hope that he could find a new job quickly but that if not, she would still love him and be his Miss Right regardless. He was also very sad that he would be unlikely to see Ludmila that weekend. He decided to give her another call. He rang again at around 7pm, realising that this was really the last chance to see her that day – but again he simply got the same message from her mobile phone.

Ben certainly didn't need Ludmila being funny with him after what had just happened. He assumed that it had something to do with him not calling her yesterday.

Or maybe something serious had happened to her. Not another health scare. He could not begin to entertain such a thought. He consoled himself with the faint hope that there would be more job opportunities locally and that he would get on with applying for them during the following week. Anyway, he would surely speak to Ludmila the following day.

As it happened, Ben slept longer than usual on the Monday morning. He was woken up by his mobile phone ringing at 10am. It was the accountancy firm in Witney that he had applied to on the Sunday. They wanted to see him on the Thursday afternoon. Ben was as happy as he could be in the circumstances and immediately set about doing some preparation for that interview.

Disturbingly, there was still nothing from Ludmila. Ben was torn between concern and annoyance. If she was annoyed about Saturday Ludmila had now made her point. They needed to speak about her job application form. Ben frowned and checked his emails as well but there was still no message from her. He would try and contact her again later, but first it was more important to prepare for the recruitment agency interviews on the Tuesday and the Wednesday and the job interview on the Thursday.

Rightly or wrongly Ben suddenly felt bad about not telling his parents about him losing his job, so he telephoned them. His mother picked up the phone.

"Mum, unfortunately I have some very bad news for you. I was made redundant last week."

"Ben, that's terrible. What happened? Was it anything to do with that foreign girl you were seeing?"

"No," he replied indignantly. "Why would it have had anything to do with her? Several other people were also made redundant and one of the other accountants was put down to three days a week."

"Oh, I see. What are you going to do now, then?"

"Fortunately they have given me two months' pay free of tax so I will stay in Oxford until the twelve months is up on the flat, and I am applying for accountancy jobs locally. I already have a job interview on Thursday, so fingers crossed for that."

"Yes, indeed. We really hope that you get that job if it is suitable for you. We're devastated for you but are pleased to see that you are making a brave effort so quickly to find another job. But please do come over and see us again soon."

"Of course. Bye, Mum."

That evening Ben tried to call Ludmila again. He was shocked that the number just rang dead, which probably meant that Ludmila had not seen his text message either. Had she changed her mobile phone without telling him? He checked his emails again but there was nothing from Ludmila. Ben emailed her straight away:

From: Ben Smith
Subject: Where Are You?
Date: Monday 20 September 2009 20.13
To: Ludmila

My Dear Ludy,

I hope you are well.

I am feeling very concerned and upset not to have heard from you after I tried to call you several times over the weekend and I sent you a text message as well. I hope everything is OK for you, and if I have upset you in any way then I'm very sorry and please forgive me. I was also surprised that your mobile phone rang dead the last time I tried to call you. If you have changed your mobile phone recently then please let me have your new mobile number as soon as possible.

I have to say again how much I enjoyed that last weekend with you at my flat and I would say it was the best time of my life. I love you and I want to be with you. You are a very special person and you make me so incredibly happy.

Please also do get back to me about the job application form for the trainee marketing assistant job so that hopefully you will be able to come and live with me and work in Oxford too.

Love and kisses,

Ben xxxx

He made himself stop there. She really did need to answer him in the next day or so.

The recruitment agency interviews were straightforward. Ben explained about the job he had been doing in the City, his reasons for leaving and about his last job at Triangle Accountants and that he had been made redundant. When asked he said that he would prefer to work in Oxford but was prepared to travel up to about thirty miles if necessary, but only if there was a suitable vacancy for him. Unfortunately, neither recruitment agency had any immediate roles that Ben could be considered for but said that they would let him know as soon as they did. He had half expected such a response but it still made him feel deflated.

There was still no response from Ludmila. He didn't think he should have to keep trying to contact her if she wasn't going to respond. It was very odd that she should not have responded to him, at least in relation to the trainee job application form. It made it look as if she didn't care about that job. What might have made her change her mind? Maybe she didn't care about him or about coming to live in Oxford any more.

There was only one way to deal with this. Ben would have to go down to Bournemouth and speak to Ludmila directly, and find out what was wrong. He hadn't forgotten her health scare, and the lesson from that should have been not to let problems fester. At the weekend he would go to Bournemouth. He had his interview the next day and there was even a chance he might get the job. If so, everything would then be back to normal and he could concentrate on trying to get Ludmila the trainee marketing assistant's job.

Ben prepared thoroughly for his interview with the accountancy firm in Witney. In particular he looked at their website, checked for reviews about them and researched the local area and businesses that might be potential clients for their accountancy firm. Ben drove down to Witney and got there a good half-hour before his interview. He parked and paid for a couple of hours' parking. He found where the accountancy firm's offices were and went into a cafe, had a cup of tea and went through his notes and the internet pages for the firm that he had printed off. Ben went to the firm's offices five minutes before his interview. He waited quietly in reception and was surprised that his interview started about fifteen minutes late. He was interviewed by two partners, one male and one female. He noticed that they weren't particularly interested in his time in London: rather, they questioned him intensely on his last job and the work he had done, the clients he had worked for and the business group. The interview lasted about an hour. It was explained that the role would start in a couple of weeks' time and that they would be making a decision early the following week. The female partner showed him out after the interview, but without a smile.

He went to the gym that evening to get over the tensions of the interview. He would hope for good news but he would not hold his breath. Over the weekend he would have a look for more roles to apply for.

On the Saturday there was still nothing from Ludmila. Remembering that she would think he was at the rugby club that afternoon, Ben decided to go and see his parents. Mrs Smith hugged him and didn't ask any awkward questions or make any stinging comments. In fact, over dinner, it was Mr Smith who seemed more critical.

"I have to say that I'm extremely disappointed about you losing your job." He frowned at Ben. "I can't help but wonder whether that young lady had any part in it. I guess that once you had met her that your focus was on her more rather than on your work."

Ben felt shocked. It was true that he had taken more time off work since he had started seeing Ludmila and he had been caught out a couple of times coming in late and focusing on his mobile phone during working hours, even when the partners were talking to him. Nonetheless, he snapped back.

"I don't see what the relevance is. As I explained to Mum, a couple of other staff were made redundant too. And one of the other accountants, whose wife had recently had a baby, was put down to three days a week. I fail to see what Ludmila would have had to do with any of that."

Mr Smith shook his head.

"Also… I suppose that, coming out from the City from a relatively junior role, you weren't used to having to go out and try and get new clients and so you may have taken it for granted that you didn't need to make too much effort. I assume that you didn't bring in any new clients or contacts from your business group."

Ben opened his mouth to protest but then stopped. There was some truth in what his father was saying. He hadn't actually introduced any new clients to Triangle Accountants. Ben suddenly felt shocked as he remembered that he had refused Simon's offer of finding new clients. He felt very awkward and equally annoyed with himself.

"Anyhow, we really hope you find a new job very soon and you'll have a better idea of the dos and don'ts in your next job."

Ben nodded, although he still felt uncomfortable. He did not want to discuss losing his job any more that evening. He stayed over at his parents' house that night, realising that it would be a slightly shorter journey to Bournemouth the next day.

It was a fairly cold and rainy Sunday morning. Ben slept in quite late. He wasn't overly concerned about time, knowing that he did not have a job to go to the following day. Inevitably, finding a new job was become increasingly important to Ben as it would help him explain things to Ludmila. He checked his email but wasn't surprised to find that there was still nothing from her.

He left his parent's house towards midday and drove down to Bournemouth. His tension grew as he approached the town. Would Ludmila not want to speak to him or, worse still, would she be seeing someone else or had she got another health scare? Ben's imagination was starting to get the better of him. As he knew given Ludmila's looks and figure she could have easily have found another man if she had wanted to, but he had to assume that she had been seeing him because she had genuinely wanted to. Well, now he would ask her directly what was wrong and what he would need to do to rectify the situation. He would deal with all that first, and leave it a few days before telling her that he had lost his job. They would have to decide where they went from there regarding Ben staying in Oxford and Ludmila working there and living with him.

Ben got to Ludmila's host family's house in the early afternoon. He parked his car opposite. He had not felt this nervous for a long time. He wanted to see Ludmila so much, but for a couple of minutes he was unable to get out of the car. His heart was pounding so hard he felt giddy. He loved Ludmila madly but he knew that it would be a crisis moment for them both. Slowly and with great difficulty Ben got out, crossed the road and walked up to the host family's front door. He rang the doorbell.

It seemed an age until someone opened the door. Mrs Foster, a lady a bit older than Ben appeared.

"Can I help you?" she said, a little warily.

"Hello. Yes, is Ludy, err… I mean, Ludmila, there please?" Ben cleared his dry throat.

"And who are you?"

"I'm Ben. Ben Smith. I'm Ludmila's boyfriend."

"Boyfriend? She never mentioned anything to us about having a boyfriend."

"Oh," he croaked. His heart sank. "Well, I've been seeing her for the last few months. Is she there?"

Mrs Foster raised her eyebrows, "No. She's returned to Moldova. Didn't she tell you? Obviously not."

Ben covered his face with his hands. He was totally distraught. How could that have happened? And why on earth had he not done something sooner?

On seeing how devastated Ben looked, Mrs Foster mellowed.

"I'm really sorry, Ben. Ludmila didn't leave us her contact details for Moldova and there is probably nothing else we could do to help."

"OK. Thank you." Ben nodded politely but then turned away quickly. He walked jerkily back to his car and drove off. He was not going to hang around in Bournemouth after hearing news like that. The tears were running down his face as he drove. For a few moments he even wanted to drive into a brick wall and end his suffering but he knew that he could not put anyone else in danger. Within the space of a just over a week his world had totally come to an end. How could he have gone from being the happiest young man in the world to being a man who was now inconsolable, having lost both his job and his Miss Right?

Chapter Twenty-Six

Ben got back to Oxford without really knowing how he had managed the journey. He was in a state of total shock which then turned to utter despair. How could Ludmila vanish so abruptly when just a few days ago she had sent a text message saying that she loved him and had enjoyed their night together? He was torn between anger and helplessness. He peered at the road through the rain slashing down and thought that he could match the rain if he just gave way to his emotions. He no longer cared about the job he had been interviewed for in Witney. His world had now totally fallen apart.

Back in his flat Ben gulped down a glass of water and threw himself on his bed. How could he contemplate life now without Ludmila, whom he loved more than anyone or anything in the world? And why, oh why, had she done that to him? Who or what had caused her to go back to Moldova? Why hadn't she told him? And why, for goodness' sake, had he not gone down to Bournemouth the previous week? But it was all too late now.

He dozed for a couple of hours and woke up with a bad headache. He had a sandwich and a cup of tea and sat near the window watching the endless rain. He felt too upset to even look at the photos of Ludmila or any of her text messages. He wanted to email her again to tell her that he knew that she had gone back to Moldova. But was it certain that that was true? Should he go back and see Ludmila's host family again and ask them about her? Would they report him to the police, or might they tell him things about Ludmila that would only hurt him? But could she still be in Bournemouth somehow?

Ben thought it over and decided he would email her in a day or so when he felt a bit calmer.

Should he even go to Moldova and try and find her? What would happen if he did go there? Would he ever find Ludmila and, even if he did find her, wouldn't the pain of her not wanting to see him again or of seeing her with someone else finish him off? Ben thought.

It was long past midnight when Ben finally went to lie down again, still very much feeling as though his world was at an end. He had loved his year in Oxford and Ludmila becoming part of his life had made his time there complete. In his mind they were going be a happy couple and spend the rest of their lives together. Staring blankly up at the ceiling in the dark with tears trickling down the sides of his face, he struggled with some desperate thoughts. But, somehow, he would have to pull himself together as best he could. He dashed his arm across his face and decided he was strong enough to carry on. Life and business did not make exceptions for anyone, as he had discovered so painfully to his cost in the past ten days.

It was nearly midday on Monday when Ben was woken by his mobile phone ringing. It was a polite call from the firm in Witney to say that although they had very much enjoyed meeting him and had considered his application very carefully, they had decided to go with another applicant who had slightly more experience and stronger local connections. Ben let his mobile phone drop to the floor afterwards. So there was something in what his father had said about the reasons for him losing his job. But without Ludmila Ben still no longer wanted to stay in Oxford. It would feel like a ghost town to him now.

He got up slowly and went out just for a newspaper but came straight back. He had no energy or enthusiasm to do anything. By the afternoon Ben started having angry thoughts towards Ludmila and also towards Karen. In particular he thought along these lines:

Had Karen known beforehand that Ben would be made redundant?

Did that explain her funny behaviour just before he lost his job? And if Karen had known in advance that he was going to lose his job, had she told Ludmila or informed her friend in Bournemouth so that Ludmila also knew? If Ludmila had known that Ben was going to lose his job, did that explain why she only wanted to spend one passionate night with him and then forget their relationship afterwards or was that all she had ever wanted from Ben right from the start? And at what point had Ludmila planned her return to Moldova?

The other issue which now increasingly bothered Ben was whether his relationship with Ludmila had contributed to him losing his job. Looking back, he accepted that he had made a few faux pas. However, he had worked diligently and there had never been any complaints about his work. He had got through his appraisal easily enough. He always went willingly both to the business group's meetings and to the rugby club's home matches. Yet, when he started seeing Ludmila, he had concentrated more on her than on his work. Before meeting her he had never been late to work in his life. Hell, he had hardly even taken any time off for holidays. Yet maybe the partners at Triangle Accountants had not been keen on Ludmila and their frowns might have been warning signs that he had mistakenly ignored.

Ben walked moodily up and down in his flat as he pondered it all. He stared out of the window without seeing anything. But then he reminded himself that Ludmila had had nothing to do with Sarah being made redundant or with Mark being put down to three days a week. He sighed and threw himself back on the sofa.

Give up, he told himself. *You'll never know the answer to any of those questions.*

Now he became preoccupied with sending Ludmila one last email. It pained him beyond belief but it had to be done to try and at least put his mind at rest. He spent the rest of the afternoon considering what to write. The pain he felt while writing was indescribable, and he had to wipe his eyes several times. He eventually managed to write the email:

From: Ben Smith
Subject: I Am Devastated Without You.
Date: Sunday 26 September 2009 17.03
To: Ludmila

Dear Ludy,

It was with great shock and sadness that I found out you had gone back to Moldova! I can't begin to describe how devastated I feel that you, the girl I love and the most important thing in my life, would leave me like this without even letting me know or at least telling me the reason why you were leaving.

The time I spent with you was the best time of my life. I loved every second of it. I never believed that anyone like you existed before I met you or that anyone could ever make me feel so happy.

Now I simply feel totally rotten and miserable. I can't be happy without you. If there is anything at all that I can do or say that would make you come back and be with me, then please tell me and I will do or say whatever it is that you want me to. I love you more than life itself.

Please, please, please come back to me. I hold your pillow every night wishing it was you.

With all my love,

Ben xxxx

After sending that email, Ben simply gave up any effort to keep up a normal routine and he started to neglect himself. He didn't bother with the gym or trying to look for a new job. He would stay up late at night and then get up late in the morning. He was a constant slave to his mobile phone, although he knew in his heart of hearts that Ludmila was not going to answer him. Worst of all, he would wake up crying in the night thinking about Ludmila. The break-ups with his two previous girlfriends paled into total insignificance in comparison. He had never imagined that he could feel such endless pain!

Ben spent his days either watching television in his flat or reading in the library. Depending on the weather, sometimes he wandered around Oxford. When he walked through the parks or by the river he did not now look at the young couples or the young ladies with any sort of anger or resentment. He was in too much despair over Ludmila. He really didn't know how to face life any more. However, he did speak to his parents and told them there were no suitable accountancy jobs in or around Oxford and that he would be moving back home shortly. Fortunately they were very supportive, and suggested he should look for jobs near Winchester and also apply for temporary work in the City. None of that appealed, although Ben knew that he could not put his life on hold on the almost-impossible chance that Ludmila might somehow come back.

One morning his mobile phone bleeped. His heart gave a massive thud, stopped, then started pounding. Ben raced to pick up his mobile phone. It was a text message from Simon:

Simon Wed 21 Oct 11.18
• *Hi Ben. Hope u r well. Had a fab hol but glad 2 be back now. Will pop round 2 c u this eve. Cheers. Simon*

Ben had not tidied his flat for a couple of weeks and could not be bothered to do so for Simon. He felt envious. Simon had it all: no worries about losing his job as he was self-employed and he was loaded, as well as having a devoted fiancée. Now Ben wondered that if he could have swapped places with Simon, would Ludmila have stayed with him?

The one thing he had in good supply in the flat was beer.

That evening the bell rang. When Ben opened the door Simon's broad smile turned to shock.

"My God, Ben, what on earth has happened? You look absolutely dreadful."

"Thanks," growled Ben, looking somewhat offended. "I lost my job and Ludmila went back to Moldova without even telling me or saying goodbye."

"Oh, no." Simon came in. He cast a look around the flat and then he focused on Ben. At length he shook his head and said firmly,

"Ben, I can see what a terrible effect all this is having on you but you must pull yourself together. I'll tell you what. I'll treat you to a curry tomorrow evening. But before then tidy this place up, have a proper wash and shave and get yourself a haircut too." He moved to the door and opened it to leave.

"I'll see you tomorrow evening at the same time. OK?"

They shook hands and Simon left. Ben scowled at his reflection in the bathroom mirror. Simon was right. Neglecting himself was only going to hurt one person and that was himself.

The next day Ben got up early. He tidied his flat and did several loads of washing before jumping in the shower and shaving off his beard of several weeks. Ben then went out for a haircut before having a snack lunch. He checked online for job vacancies but noticed that the only suitable accountancy jobs he could apply for were in the City. He was looking forward to catching up with Simon who might also be able to offer him some words of comfort and wisdom.

Ben got to the restaurant promptly for 7.30pm. Simon was already there. He smiled as they shook hands.

"See, you look better already," he said.

Ben smiled and nodded, knowing that he might look a bit brighter on the outside, but inside he was still in great pain about Ludmila and it was really only the thought that he needed to find a new job fairly soon that was keeping him sane at the moment. They had dinner and Simon gave a short account of his holiday. After dinner they bought drinks at the bar then found a quiet table in the corner.

"OK, Ben, you had better tell me now what happened with your job and with Ludmila. I can see that you are very distressed about it all. I don't know if I can help in any way but I will, of course, if I can."

"Thanks," said Ben appreciatively. It was a minor relief to be able to talk to someone other than his parents about the tragic recent events. "Well… " Ben choked, struggling to hide the hurt.

"It was after you had gone on holiday. I spent a wonderful day in Wales with Ludmila and we became closer. The following weekend she spent the night with me in my flat and we talked about the future and her coming to live with me and work in Oxford. I expect that you remember that I told you in confidence about the job opportunity for Ludmila through Geoff at the business group to work in Oxford in marketing, which is what she wanted. I told her about it and I even got as far as emailing Ludmila a copy of the job application form, but I never heard from her again.

"That week I was made redundant at work. I didn't want to tell Ludmila straight away but when I tried to call her there was no answer and she didn't respond to any of my texts or emails. So I went down to Bournemouth the following weekend and, to my absolute horror, her host family told me that she'd already gone back to Moldova. They also said they didn't even know that she had a boyfriend. I can't begin to tell you how devastated I felt and still feel as though my whole world has been ripped apart all at the same time."

Simon shook his head.

"Ben, that is dreadful. I am devastated for you. But, if I may, let me ask first what is happening now for you."

"Not much. I've only had one interview locally and that didn't work out. I'll have to leave my flat shortly and go back and live with my parents and probably start again with some temporary work. This is the last thing I would ever have wanted to happen when I came to live and work in Oxford last year."

Simon nodded. "I do appreciate it's very hard for you when you compare yourself with my situation. I am very lucky to be self-employed as well as having a lovely fiancée."

Ben felt a little awkward but he was grateful Simon was willing to help. He knew his friend could offer a much more realistic perspective on Ludmila than his parents could. After hesitating for a moment, he asked,

"Simon, based on what I have told you, what do you make of Ludmila and her departure?"

"It's very hard to say as I didn't know her at all and I've never had a girlfriend or known any women from that part of the world either."

Ben then interrupted.

"I do accept now, looking back, that I'd got into a rather lazy lifestyle in the City. It wasn't difficult going out for drinks with colleagues and friends and then talking to girls in groups. You didn't really see what they're like individually and, as you can guess, most of the pretty ones were taken anyway."

Simon nodded and smiled. Ben continued,

"It was always a torture at weekends. I would have a walk on Sundays and would notice the happy young couples with their small children. I was sure they had been through the pubbing and clubbing lifestyle but were probably secretly glad to be away from it. I then realised that that was what I wanted too and that it was never going to happen in the City, so that's why I left. Also I needed to stop living with my parents.

"It was a huge change living in Oxford and I felt isolated at times without large groups of colleagues or friends. By the spring I went and tried things such as speed dating and lonely hearts-type adverts, as it was clear that I wasn't going to meet any young ladies by chance. I was very shocked by the unpleasantness of the young ladies I had first dates with. They seemed to be snarling at me, anxious to find fault with me as well and, equally, to get away from me as soon as possible. I'd never seen any of that in the City. I did despair of ever being able to meet any young ladies I could consider having a long-term relationship with. Of course, reaching thirty last year was a shock too. Time was starting to catch up with me and I didn't know quite what to do.

"When I met Ludmila she really was a breath of fresh air… a beautiful, slim young lady who was so different from girls here. She made me feel good about myself and didn't seek to put me down. She was firm and abrupt but there was never any undercurrent of unpleasantness about her. I didn't ask about whether she'd had boyfriends previously or what the customs were in Moldova. I didn't feel jealous, either, as I knew she could have easily have found another young man if she wanted to.

"I fell in love with Ludmila quite quickly. I saw that things would have to be done her way and that she wasn't one for endless phone calls or text messages or for meeting up all the time. I did miss her terribly when I wasn't seeing her. She could be extremely frustrating at times and I was very conscious that most people in this country would have found our relationship bizarre (to say the least), and I did have serious doubts as to how close we would ever become. Worst of all… after the one time when we did become intimate I never saw her again. I am totally devastated now. I've lost the most important person in my life. She's irreplaceable. It feels like a vase smashing into a million pieces or having all the lights in the world going out and being left in total darkness and despair. I still agonise over many painful and unanswered questions. Please, Simon, what do you make of all this?"

Ben put his head in his hands briefly, but it was a relief to be able to pour his heart out to someone who would hopefully understand his situation and possibly be able to offer him some helpful advice.

"Well… " Simon, smiled and then sighed. "Where do I begin? And what could I say that would be of any benefit to you?" He paused and thought for a few moments. "As you know, even as good friends, it is a basic courtesy not to pry into other peoples' private lives too much but this is obviously not something you don't feel you could talk to your father about, so I'll try and help as best I can. We've had some laughs on our nights out, even involving some females, but that's all it was. Of course, I would be ferocious where Natalie is concerned. However, as you know, we men never say it but we never really take anything seriously on lads' nights out."

"That's partly why I left the City," said Ben raising his eyebrows.

"It's funny, but things don't really change over the years and life on the whole does tend to follow a certain pattern. You grow up, get yourself an education, start a career, get married, have children and then the pattern starts all over again for them.

"Stereotypically, any girl who is vaguely attractive usually gets snapped up in her twenties and it's never really been any different. You notice how quickly men get their wives pregnant after they get married. It's always been the most effective means of keeping other men away."

"Oh, my God." Ben gasped loudly to himself, covering his mouth with his hand and looking away. He had never thought about the possibility of Ludmila being pregnant. Simon patted him on the shoulder.

"There, there, Ben. It is a great credit to you that such a thought would never have entered your head where Ludmila was concerned. I doubt that Roger and the other partners would have been very pleased with you or that you would have lasted much longer at Triangle Accountants if it had.

"To continue, life gets harder in your thirties if you're single." Simon paused for a moment. He drank some of his beer before carrying on.

"I'm thirty-six and Natalie is thirty-one, so I will be looking to get married and then start a family within the next couple of years.

"As far as you are concerned, Ben, I think you did get left behind by working in the City and by living at home. It's easy to be critical now but perhaps you should have had a couple more serious relationships before you met Ludmila, and then she might not have been so important to you. I agree that moving to Oxford after the City would have been a major culture shock for you, and you would have found yourself isolated. Apart from hanging around the nightclubs regularly, there probably wouldn't have been many opportunities for you to meet girls locally. It was obviously never going to happen for you at Triangle Accountants."

They both laughed. Simon continued.

"I'm not sure those blind dates were necessarily the right thing to do. I'm surprised by the extent of the hostility of those young ladies you describe. Maybe they just didn't like you or you quite simply didn't fit what they were looking for in a young man if they were indeed genuinely single. You have to accept that not all young ladies will appreciate your good looks or your kind manner. Equally, perhaps you should have tried those events for longer and not given up so quickly.

"It's a female thing that if they feel uncomfortable or threatened then they will be unpleasant instinctively. Maintaining a polite, dignified silence isn't in their nature. But there was no point in them pretending to be interested in you if they weren't. I can only guess that they might have taken more of an interest in you if you'd been richer or run your own business or had been better established locally. Don't forget that while those young ladies might have been single they probably weren't short of men propositioning them, so they could discard any young man that didn't fit their requirements very easily. Otherwise, I would say that it's a good idea not to be put off so

243

quickly by their initial hostility. It does take some effort to see their nicer side. We young men have all been through the stage of fancying girls we thought could be nice to any other man except us. It certainly wasn't just you, Ben. Sadly, very few men can ever expect women to like them for no reason – at least, not initially. Also, for example, if you tell any girl that that there's a party, disco or some other social event with a large crowd they'll go running to it. But getting them to spend any time with you on their own? Now that certainly does take some effort."

"You know," Ben interrupted almost absent-mindedly, "I walked around for over a year both here and at home. I watched young couples. It made me sad, resentful and angry. It felt as though those girls could make the effort for every other young man but never for me. A year ago I would never have believed how difficult it would be to find a single young lady in Oxford."

"I trust you've been listening to what I just said," answered Simon quite abruptly. Ben nodded.

"Good." Simon shot him a severe look and went on. "I can understand how Ludmila would have appeared to be a breath of fresh air for you. Yes, she was beautiful, and I don't think that that many girls here look as good as her and the few that do would probably already be engaged or married by her age. Again, I don't know that part of the world but as you said, Ludmila was different and obviously from a stricter and more conservative, family-orientated culture."

Ben half opened his mouth. He had suddenly thought again of Ludmila's very naughty but equally exciting behaviour when they were on the beach in Aberystwyth.

Simon continued.

"She was not quite your generation but I can easily see how she would have appeared to have been a prize catch for you at her young age and with her looks. However, it does seem odd that she never talked about herself or her family and never wanted you to see her friends here."

"We only talked about our supposed future together when she stayed with me." Ben propped his head on his hand.

"The obvious point I should make here, Ben, is that Ludmila was in an earlier phase of her life from you. You'll never know what brought her to England other than, I suppose, the usual better life and money idea or perhaps what exactly she was trying to escape from back home. I know you certainly did everything you possibly could to help her, even going as far as virtually finding her a job in Oxford. I don't think that anybody could ever have been any kinder to her than you were, but I am sure it must have overawed her at the same time.

"Ironically, it probably suited her better being an au pair girl and studying English. She could cope with that even if she found it dull. Let's not forget that she was probably experiencing a lot more freedom here than in Moldova. Of course, it would have been very different if she had grown up in England or had gone to university here and then stayed in England. I think that, even unintentionally, you may have expected far too much from her in a very short space of time. Perhaps she should have had a full-time job for a couple of years first, then that might have helped."

"Who knows? She might well have got snapped up in the meantime." Ben tried to laugh, but found himself choking while trying to control the sudden rush of anguish.

"Simon, I must ask you a question which has troubled me more and more recently, and that is whether Ludmila cost me my job with Triangle Accountants."

Simon raised his eyebrows.

"That's a very tough question indeed, and most probably there is no satisfactory answer." Simon paused and thought for a moment. He then continued, "At a guess, I would say that she was not one of the main reasons that you were made redundant as other people were made redundant too, but quite possibly she didn't help matters either."

"How do you mean?" asked Ben sadly but with interest.

"I mean if Roger and the other partners felt that your focus was away from work, particularly when times were getting bad and that you would rather go off with Ludmila than stay late, you might have got into their bad books."

"But I always worked hard, did my best and completed tasks and nobody ever complained about my work. I also joined the business group and went to the rugby club's home matches, just as Roger had asked me to." Ben had forgotten the few times he had come in late to work and had been caught on his mobile phone at that point.

"Ben, it's a completely different ball game outside the City. You don't really have the protection of large clients with plenty of work and other tasks to carry out for them. It's very much a case of sink or swim in the provinces. You also told me things were fine at work when I asked you, but I realise I should have asked you far more often about how you doing in getting new clients for Triangle Accountants. I would assume that the partners might well have thought you were content to reap the rewards with their existing clients. It's easy to say it now, but you should either have trained with a similar sort of firm of accountants in the provinces – or perhaps you should have waited a few more years, by which time you could have joined Triangle Accountants with more money, a client following and possibly a family. I am sure they would have looked after you much better then."

Ben really sat up at that point.

"That actually reminds me… You know at the business group there were quite a few members with daughters in their mid to late twenties who were single – and, although I would never have suggested it out of politeness, none of them ever hinted that they would have liked to have introduced me to their daughters."

"Hmm… that's true, but probably for the same reasons as at Triangle Accountants. You were probably a bit too inexperienced in the ways of the world for them. You were also new to Oxford, and you were quite simply not rich or well-connected enough at that stage. Notice the pattern?"

"I see it." Ben was feeling very exasperated, but was following what Simon was saying. He suddenly remembered the reasons why he had not got the job in Witney.

"So if Ludmila had come from a very rich family or I was seeing someone or had a fiancée who was working in business locally and who was well-connected, then we might not have been sitting here now and having this conversation."

Simon nodded somewhat awkwardly but did not respond.

"Finally, Simon, I have to ask whether you think Ludmila knew that I was going to lose my job. You know about my former secretary having a friend who was Ludmila's host family's neighbour."

Simon puffed out his cheeks.

"It's quite likely that your former secretary knew you were going to be made redundant, but I don't know that she would have gone as far to tell Ludmila or get her friend to tell Ludmila that you would be losing your job. That does sound a bit far-fetched to me. However, on the other hand, if Ludmila had known that you were going to lose your job and that was in fact the only reason she left you then it would be totally unforgivable."

"My former secretary did become somewhat awkward around me just before I was made redundant."

"That would suggest that she knew that it was going to happen. But whether she actually did tell Ludmila or her friend about your redundancy you'll never know. I must say, Ben, that I don't think you'd have been happy staying in Oxford if Ludmila was working full-time here and you were unemployed. Your male ego would not have been able to take it and Ludmila might possibly have been on the lookout for a new prospective young man."

Ben groaned loudly. He really did not need to be reminded of his worst nightmare of Ludmila being with any other man although deep down he knew that it might well have already happened, particularly if she had gone back to Moldova.

"Sorry to keep on, Simon, but do you think I should go and see her host family again and try and find out more about her?"

"No. No. No." said Simon emphatically. "Her host family probably did tell you as much as they knew. Either you might get into trouble for harassing them or, although probably unlikely, you might even hear things from them that you wouldn't want to hear about Ludmila. The same would apply to their neighbour. You know the old proverb: *Let sleeping dogs lie*, which is what you'll have to do here."

"I had pretty much ruled out going to Moldova. I wouldn't know where to start or even what might happen to me there." Ben knew he sounded mournful.

"Exactly. Remember, some people don't want to be found and where females are concerned, once they have done something wrong they try and forget it and put it behind them as soon as possible. They never like to be reminded of their wrongdoings. That may well be in part why Ludmila would not contact you now. As I don't know Moldova at all I won't try and judge the country but I hardly think that you would be well received by her family or anyone else, even in the extremely unlikely event that you did actually manage to find her." He shifted in his seat and smiled kindly.

"Look, Ben, as painful as it is, you must accept that you'll probably never know what was going on with her. Ludmila might have had another boyfriend either in Moldova, here in England or maybe even somewhere else. Alternatively, perhaps she was trying to escape or delay an arranged marriage back home. So whether she was stringing you along or whether you in fact got more from her than you should have done is anyone's guess. However, she probably was very fond of you in her own way but circumstances meant that she couldn't stay here with you, or else she chose to go back to Moldova. The timing of her leaving could not have been any worse for you. I know this is absolutely the last thing you would want to hear but I would say that it is extremely unlikely that you will ever hear from Ludmila again wherever she is now. For your own sake, you must let her go."

Ben put his head in his hands. How could he even begin to contemplate such a thing when Ludmila had told him that she loved him and that he was her king? Simon was right, but it was nonetheless so incredibly painful to hear. Simon was still speaking.

"Do remember your parents. I can understand why they would certainly have not been pleased about Ludmila, particularly after the way she left you. It is at times like these that you should realise just how important families are."

Ben nodded. He decided that he would make more of an effort with his parents from now on.

"OK. And finally… as for the future… it would be fantastic if you could stay in Oxford, although I can see that it's highly unlikely at the moment. You need to find yourself another job quickly now, and once you've settled into it you should build up a group of colleagues and friends. Go out with them regularly and, hopefully, get to know some girls that way. If it doesn't happen after a while then do try things like speed dating again. Of course, do try and get over Ludmila first, as rebound relationships are never fair either way. It may take you a while but at the same time don't leave getting to know any other girls too long. And another thing… you'll need to move to wherever you're working as no girl will want you while you're living at home.

"Remember, there have always been far fewer women than men in the world and most of them can still pick and choose their men. So as I said, you'll need to make a really big effort if you want to impress them and win them over. Look at it like this: imagine you are walking past a group of young women all talking to each other. One of them will notice you and might just be interested in getting to know you better. Focus on that particular girl. Know what I mean?"

Ben nodded and smiled, albeit somewhat ruefully.

"I hope I'll be like you one day with a great business behind me and a fiancée," he said.

"Natalie is wonderful, but don't think that I don't have the occasional happy memories of a couple of girls I used to know before her. One day there should be someone else in your life who is more special and Ludmila will then just be a happy memory for you. I should add that it was also a great shame that your relationship with her could not have run its course as you'll never know what might have happened." Ben sighed again.

"Also, Ben, try not to be so judgemental about young women here. I'm sorry to have to rub it in but I know for a fact that they don't all disappear when their partners have serious problems or lose their jobs."

Ben instinctively hit the table with his fist. He looked away for a few seconds and then started intently at Simon and finally managed to nod his head. It had got very late and they realised they had to go home. As Ben would be leaving Oxford the following week and Simon was going away on business they would not be able to meet up again for a while. They shook hands and hugged. Ben said,

"Simon, you've been a great friend this past year, and particularly at this very difficult time for me. I'm really going to miss our drinks evenings but I hope to catch up with you again soon. Stay in touch and I'll let you know when I get a new job. At the very least let's meet up again before Christmas."

"All the best, Ben. Chin up and I sincerely hope everything works out for you soon. I'll definitely see you before again before Christmas. Look after yourself in the meantime."

Ben was sad to see Simon go. He now appreciated just what a good friend Simon was, especially as Ben had had nothing to offer Simon business-wise. It had been a very constructive evening for him. Simon had made him look at his relationship with Ludmila in a difficult but realistic way and had also forced him to accept some painful truths.

However, Ben suddenly realised that he had not mentioned Ludmila's cancer scare to Simon. Would that have changed Simon's view of what had happened and the advice Simon might have given him? Was that also another possible reason why Ludmila had left? Rightly or wrongly, Ben felt that he owed Ludmila that much not to mention her health scare to anyone ever, regardless of whether or not it had been genuine.

Nonetheless, Ben accepted that he would now have to let Ludmila go. There was no point in speculating about whether she still had any fond thoughts about him, even if he had been her first serious boyfriend as such. She was quite simply not coming back. He felt slightly better as he went home. Of course he couldn't even try and pretend to be happy, but at least he had now started to face up to things properly. Ben determined to act on Simon's advice when he found a new job somewhere else.

Chapter Twenty-Seven

However, the moment Ben arrived back at his flat and had closed the door behind him he broke down again. He simply could not bear to think about life without Ludmila! Further, his worst nightmare that she might well be with someone else still haunted him. And what if she was pregnant as well? What would she do then, and where would she go for help? When he had finally managed to calm himself down Ben reluctantly accepted that he could not contact Ludmila again nor try to find her, even if she was indeed pregnant. That night he woke up frequently, overcome by a feeling of total helplessness and frustration at not being able to do anything about his lost love.

After getting through that low point Ben did make an effort to improve. His parents agreed to come and help him move out of his flat. He arranged a time for the estate agents to come and inspect the flat just before he left. He finished at the local gym and arranged a session at his old gym in Winchester for the following week.

On his last day in Oxford Ben had a final walk around the town. Despite recent events, he did feel sad about leaving. It had been a great year until the previous two months. Thinking over what Simon and his father had told him, Ben began to appreciate why things had not worked out for him in Oxford. He avoided going past the rugby club and made his way to the river. That was where he had felt so lonely and awkward watching all the young couples, and then had felt so happy and complete when Ludmila had been there with him. He no longer felt anything as he passed the young couples: rather, he despaired, as no other girl could ever replace Ludmila. On his way back to his flat Ben passed the jewellers where she had pointed out the emerald ring she liked. The ring was still there. He wondered for a moment if he could read anything positive into that but he then simply shrugged his shoulders and walked on.

The following day Ben moved out of his flat. His parents came over early and filled up their car with some of his belongings to take back to Winchester for him. While waiting for the estate agents he looked around and had to swallow a lump in his throat. He was leaving behind a hugely (if not the most) important chapter in his life. He kept the pillow case that Ludmila had slept on, having bought another identical one to leave in its place. From now on it would be his most prized possession of her along with her photos and texts. He loaded his car with his remaining belongings. He managed to retain his composure in front of the estate agent. But after signing the relevant paperwork and handing over the keys he shuddered, and his heart sank as he walked out and heard the door to the flat close behind him.

Goodbye, darling Ludy, he thought. He closed his eyes, stood still and breathed in for a moment. But alas, there was no magical reunion with Ludmila. Ben then walked quickly to his car. He drove off and left Oxford without looking back.

It proved to be a fairly awkward and quiet first week back for Ben with his parents. They sensed a deep sadness in him, but assumed that it was more to do with him having lost his job in Oxford rather than because of Ludmila. He started going back to his old gym and old pub and slowly got used to being back in Winchester. He spent a lot of time looking for a new job. His parents continued to be very supportive and there no hints about him leaving home this time round. They had understood that it was important for Ben to find the right job and not to rush into a job that would result in him being kicked out again in the same way as he had been in Oxford.

Ben was still heartbroken about Ludmila but he did find it slightly easier being at home and having people to talk to, although he did not mention her again to his parents. It was hardest when he was on his own. Out of habit he would check his emails several times a day, even though he still did not expect any messages from her. Ben had decided that he would prefer not to hear from Ludmila if all she was going to say was that she did not love him, that she regretted the night they spent together or, worse still, that she had another boyfriend or was now engaged or perhaps even married. Ben also wondered if Ludmila might have thought that he would have found someone else by now, if indeed she ever did think about him. He knew, of course, that there was nothing stopping him going out and looking for a new girlfriend as such except that no other girl could ever matter to him now. Ben also wondered how Ludmila might have tried to explain being pregnant to her family, if she was pregnant, and how they would have reacted. But he still somehow doubted that she was.

By December, Ben had made numerous job applications and had had a couple of interviews at recruitment agencies in the City. One morning he received a call from a local agency, saying they had a vacancy near Swindon. Ben said "Yes" without a second thought, and he was pleasantly surprised to hear a couple of days later that the accountancy firm concerned wanted to see him. Ben's parents were pleased too, though they did understandably urge caution. He prepared thoroughly for that interview, looking the firm up online and checking on updated websites for specific interview questions as well as researching the region.

As the interview was at 11am Ben drove down very early on the morning of his interview with the firm near Swindon. However, he thought a lot about his time in Oxford, about what Simon had told him, how he would approach this job if he got it and the important mistakes he would need to avoid in a new job. As it turned out, two partners interviewed Ben. He noticed that they were late starting the interview, and one of the partners seemed to pull a face at him. The interview turned out to be quite short. They were not particularly interested in Ben's time in the City but again, were far more concerned about his job in Oxford, the work he had done and the clients he had worked for. He observed that they were not pleased when he said that he did not have a client following and that they made a lot out of him having been made redundant.

"So you were made redundant after less than a year at Triangle Accountants. That does not look good," said Mr Squires.

"It was an unfortunate but inevitable consequence of the recession. Everything had been fine up to that point," answered Ben.

"Really?"

"Yes. I have a good reference from Triangle Accountants if needed."

Mr Squires said no more about Ben's redundancy but Ben felt that he was still trying to read negative things into it. Mr Squires frowned at him for the rest of the interview. As Ben drove back home he knew he hadn't enjoyed the experience at all and it would be very unlikely to go any further. He telephoned the agency and told his parents about the interview as well. His father was understandably concerned about how short the interview had been, and commented that he thought that that firm probably just wanted his client list and then might have got rid of him after a couple of months.

About a week later Ben got a text message from Simon:

Simon Wed 10 Dec 11.45

• *Hi Ben. I hope u r well & that things r better 4 u now. Have u found a new job yet? I'm delighted 2 let u know that Natalie & I have set a date 4 our wedding next year. Wld be great to catch up with u again next Wed eve in Oxford if u r around then. Cheers, Simon.*

Ben texted Simon back later that day:

Ben Smith Wed 10 Dec 14.58
• *Hi Simon. Great 2 hear from u again & many congrats 2 u & Natalie. I'm feeling a bit better now but still looking 4 a new job. Wld be great 2 c u again next Wed. Ben.*

Ben was by now learning to manage his grief about Ludmila. She was still in his thoughts within seconds of him waking up each day – and it was only when he was asleep that he could forget about her, if he wasn't already dreaming about her.

The following Tuesday Ben received a call from another recruitment agency. There was a large firm of accountants based in the City which had several temporary vacancies for accountants for up to six months. He said "Yes" and the recruitment agency called him back later that day to say that the firm wanted to see him, and could he go up the following afternoon? He discussed the job opportunity with his parents. They all agreed that a temporary role was not ideal and Ben did not really want to work in the City again. However, the pay was good and he could start looking for a permanent job once he had completed a couple of months in that job if he got it. By now Ben realised he had been too quick to judge the City. He also reminded himself that if he stayed in his previous job he would most likely never have been made redundant but, then again, he would never have met Ludmila!

The job interview was at 4pm. The firm was running late. It was a very lengthy interview but Ben performed well. The interviewers were far more interested in what he had been doing in his job in the City than in his job in Oxford. It also helped that it was a temporary role. It was made clear to him that there might be an opportunity to extend the role afterwards but that it should not be assumed any job offer now would automatically lead to a permanent position there. Afterwards Ben noticed that the interview had lasted for over an hour and a half. He telephoned the agency straight away and they asked him to come to their offices. He would not now be able to go and see Simon that evening.

Ben had to wait for a further hour at the agency's offices. It was worth it, however, when one of the consultants came to see him and said he had been offered one of the vacancies and that there had also been a glowing reference from Triangle Accountants. Roger had kept to his word. Ben's heart lightened. In fact, he was almost happy for the first time in a couple of months. He then signed some of the paperwork relating to his new job.

Ben realised the irony of almost being happy to go back to work in the City. With Simon's words still ringing in his ears, Ben recognised that he could build on this job opportunity to find a full-time role. He was grateful that he did not have to bring clients with him and he assumed that, barring any mishaps, he should be able to see the job through for the full six months.

As soon as he left the agency, Ben called Simon.

"I do apologise. I can't make it this evening. But it's for a good reason."

"It had better be good." Simon sounded very disappointed.

"I've just been offered a job in the City, initially for six months."

"Ben, that's splendid news. In that case, I'll forgive you for this evening. I'll be sending you a wedding invitation soon. We've decided on the date for early next year."

"Congrats again. I'll look forward to that. Thanks, Simon."

"I hope you're feeling better now. Have a great Christmas and we'll catch up again soon."

Christmas was now approaching. It would be good to see his sister and her family again. Ben didn't feel particularly nervous about his new job. It would be easier for him to live at home for the time being, while the job and the commuting would help take his mind off Ludmila a little.

However, when Ben's sister and husband and their children arrived on Christmas Eve, Ben suddenly felt as though Ludmila should have been there too. He would have been introducing her to his sister as his fiancée. Ludmila would have laughed and played with his nephew and niece. As had become tradition, Ben's nephew and niece had an early dinner and then went off to bed. They would be up before dawn on Christmas day.

During the grown-ups' dinner, Helen asked Ben how he was getting on.

"Unfortunately, I was made redundant from my job in Oxford which I was totally gutted about, as I loved it there. It's been very difficult to find another job. However, I have a six-month contract with an accountancy firm back in the City starting in January. I hope it'll enable me to get another permanent job."

"And what about the young lady you were seeing?"

Ben looked a bit surprised and awkward at that question.

"Oh… nothing. I'm not seeing her any more," he said, quite defensively. Helen looked a bit taken aback. There was a short pause and she then changed the subject. Just as everyone was going to bed, she knocked on Ben's door.

"Ben, are you OK? I'm sorry if I upset you."

"That's OK. I know you were only politely enquiring. Actually, it's more complicated." Ben then explained briefly what had happened. He concluded, "You see, just as our relationship was becoming serious she left me."

"Was she really that special?" asked Helen, looking unconvinced.

He showed Helen a couple of photos of Ludmila. Helen gasped.

"Wow. She's stunning, and you look so happy together. Ben, I'm really sorry. I understand now why you're so distressed."

"She was the best thing that could ever have happened to me." Ben knew he sounded helpless. "I don't think Mum and Dad have any idea."

Helen nodded and patted Ben on the shoulder.

"Well, I really hope things work out for you next year."

Although Ben enjoyed the family and festive atmosphere, that Christmas had very little meaning for him. Talking to Helen about Ludmila had simply reminded him again of just how much he still missed her. On Christmas morning he did his best to appear cheerful, and to see that his nephew and niece had a good time playing with their Christmas presents and building snowmen with them outside.

New Year approached. Ben did start to have a couple of butterflies about his new job, but more about making sure it worked out properly rather than being afraid of actually starting in a new firm. He bought himself a new suit and briefcase for his new job. By now he almost knew by heart what Simon had told him the last time they had met up. Although Ben would probably be teased a little about living at home at his age, he hoped he could make some friends out of his colleagues in his new job. He would try and get to know some young ladies properly too although he would take things slowly and try not to wear his heart on his sleeve again, either.

One thing, however, was constantly on Ben's mind. He needed to somehow say goodbye to Ludmila. He had finished with Oxford and would have been too upset to go back there anyway, so he decided to go to Bournemouth one last time and make a gesture of saying farewell to her memory. On New Year's Eve Ben told his parents he was going to catch up with an old friend, but that he would be back in time for their celebratory dinner.

Ben reached Bournemouth in the late morning. He couldn't bear to go anywhere near Ludmila's host family's house. He therefore parked in the town centre. He then walked to the train station and went directly to the spot where he had first met her. It was a freezing cold day and it was also raining hard. Remembering Ludmila checking his pockets he tried very hard to smile, but he simply couldn't bring himself to smile. He remembered how he had been in awe of her great beauty and all the attention they had received from other people. Afterwards Ben walked towards the beach and along the seafront. He closed his eyes and tried to imagine life as though Ludmila was still there holding his hand and laughing and joking with him in the summer sun. But all Ben felt was the howling wind and rain on him. He could not have been more alone.

At last Ben found a flower shop and bought a red rose. It was now time to perform a ritual and say goodbye to Ludmila. Holding the flower, he walked to the very end of the pier. He stared out at the sea and the roaring waves. Ben was about to throw the rose into the sea when all of a sudden it felt as if his whole life was flashing before him. He saw Ludmila with him, making and sharing love. He saw them getting married, having children, smiling as their children did well at school and university and then going on to successful careers... and at them becoming grandparents. He could not now say goodbye. Although it had been a few months since Ludmila had gone, Ben still felt as though it was only yesterday. He stared out at the sea again and without thinking, he shouted out loud,

"I love you, Ludy."

There was no response, and a couple of people passing on the pier gave him a funny stare. Ben could not have cared less. This was a private moment. He knew that his personal tragedy would never concern the world at large and that he was hardly the first person to ever suffer a broken heart, particularly as more and more personal relationships, whether casual or serious, began and ended all the time. Further, life in general with its wars, natural disasters, terrorist acts, murders, accidents and illnesses brought tragedy to many people. In such a context his personal tragedy was very minor.

However, since meeting Ludmila, Ben had come to realise that the family was the most important thing in life and that Ludmila, in having been his prospective Miss Right had been the key to his future happiness, which he had hoped would have included marrying her and starting a family one day (had she not left him). He reflected – unrequited love and remaining single was one thing: it was quite something else to have had someone so special come into his life and make him feel fulfilled and his future seem secure, and for that person to then depart so suddenly and without any explanation and to be left afterwards with such an unfillable void. So of course, Ben's personal tragedy did matter.

Did Ben wish that he had not met Ludmila?

Never, he thought. Despite their bizarre relationship, which had finally looked as though it was going to work out fine for him and all the pain and anguish that she had caused and would continue to cause by having left him, Ludmila was irreplaceable. This was the biggest compliment that he could pay her, as no other young lady would ever matter to him again.

Tomorrow would be 2010. Ben did not want to think about that, either. Since meeting Ludmila it was as though she had been a part of everything he did, even when she wasn't there. Now the thought of a new year in which Ludmila would have no involvement at all was extremely unpalatable to him. Life would inevitably move on but for Ben it had stopped after the last time he had seen Ludmila. Surely nobody else's anguish could compare to this. He also realised that she had been his best friend and his companion as well. There would be nobody now he could laugh and cry with while sharing all of life's experiences.

Although it still troubled Ben that Ludmila might be pregnant he did not fear for her health otherwise and in his heart he knew that she was somewhere in the world, although he would probably never find out where she was. Instinctively Ben got his mobile phone out and although he had not intended to contact Ludmila again, he now felt compelled to email her one last time.

From: Ben Smith
Subject: Farewell.
Date: Thursday 31 December 2009 13.09
To: Ludmila

My dear Ludy,

I hope you are well and are having a nice Christmas.

I am writing to you this one last time to tell you how much I still miss you but that I really hope that you are happy wherever you are.

I will gladly tell you again and again that meeting you was the best thing that could ever have happened to me and that the time we spent together was the best of my life. I loved you then and I love you now. I can never be happy without you but I accept that it is far more important that you should be happy with your life.

Please understand that I am not angry with you but I am still very sad that you left me and did not even tell me why.

Remember that I am always thinking of you, Beautiful. I really hope and pray that I will see you again one day. I am waiting here for you all the time with open arms. As long as I am breathing I will always love you. But if I don't see you again, I can only hope that one day I will find you in my dreams and that we can then be reunited in love eternally.

With all my love now and forever,

Ben xxxxx

He sent the email. The tears were streaming down his cheeks. His heart was irretrievably broken. He finally threw the rose into the sea. It floated for a couple of seconds before sinking under the leaping waves. Ben shrugged his shoulders. That summed up life for him. He clenched his hands on the rail. The wind was still howling and the rain pouring down. It was time to go. The summer with Ludmila was over and it had changed his life forever. It would surely have been the romance of the century and Ludmila should have been there too, with her head on Ben's shoulder and wearing the emerald ring.

Ben covered his eyes for a moment as he did not want to think about the sadness and the empty space in his heart. But it was time to face the world again and try his best to cope. Who could tell? One day Ben might achieve great things and he might even become rich and famous as well, but what would it matter to him without the person he loved more than anyone or anything in the entire world? He stared out at the roaring waves a final time with his head in his hands. Ben sighed deeply and braced himself to return home.

Suddenly, a voice behind him said,

"Ben?"